Shoes, Ships and Cadavers
Tales from North Londonshire

Shoes, Ships and Cadavers
Tales from North Londonshire

Edited by Ian Whates and Ian Watson

NewCon Press,
England

First edition, published in the UK October 2010
by NewCon Press

NCP 033 (hardback)
NCP 034 (softback)

10 9 8 7 6 5 4 3 2 1

ISBN: 978-1-907069-16-1 (hardback)
978-1-907069-18-5 (softback)

Cover layout by Andy Bigwood
Front cover photograph of Lucy Galding's 'Discovery' by Ian Whates

Text layout by Storm Constantine

Printed in the UK by MPG Biddles of King's Lynn

Contents

Introduction

Alan Moore

Now, see, this is what I'm talking about.

Globalisation doesn't seem to have worked out particularly well for anybody except Rupert Murdoch, and increasingly we come to understand that the whole world, at least for us, is right where we are standing now, here in these boarded-up and fraying neighbourhoods, these vanishing communities and liquefying towns. Faced with a tapestry that seems to be unravelling it might be in our interest to adjust our focus, paying less attention to the aesthetics of the overall design and more to each endangered individual stitch. Localisation, that's your only man.

And if the places where we live seem flat and dead, seem to be voids of meaning or vitality, then it is up to art to do what it has always done and fill those empty spaces with imagination, with significance. When all of the material streets and landmarks have been pulverised and brushed away only the fictions and the dreamtime are left standing, so that when we think about Victorian London we're almost inevitably thinking of a Dickens yarn. Think of contemporary Sheperton, and once the Ealing film associations are exhausted we are left with J.G. Ballard's crystallised or flooded dreamscapes and his haunted airmen. All the narratives we live in, be they economic, personal, historical, political or social, are upon examination only different genres, different categories of fiction. If we are unwilling to be written into some rapacious city banker or anonymous town planner's lifeless continuity, we'd better be prepared to generate more satisfying and fulfilling new mythologies, romances and hair-raising pulp adventures of our own; create a less restricted and more fertile mental space that's rich in possibilities and not so draining and corrosive to inhabit.

In commencing such a project, you could do a lot worse than choosing Northampton as your starting point. It's difficult to call to mind another British town that is comparable in size... Northampton is the largest town in Europe... and yet which is such a featureless and empty blank space in the consciousness of both the wider public and a goodly number of its own inhabitants: the place seldom receives a mention on the TV weather map, even on those occasions when the news is regional. It's also difficult to think of a location with a richer soil of legend, where the coal seam of imagination has been gradually compressed to diamond by the forces bearing in upon it from all sides, pressures of doctrine and geography or else the unrelenting crush between a massive past and equally intimidating future.

Centre of the land, at least according to the angel (one of several hanging out in Marefair prior to the Norman Conquest) who directed a lone pilgrim from Jerusalem to halfway down the gradient of Horseshoe Street, just opposite the snooker parlour. King John kicking off Crusades from his imposing castle at the top of Andrew's Road or Cromwell's regicidal morning canter down Black Lion Hill and out across the drawbridge he'd had built over the Nene to Naseby. Both of England's two greatest internal conflicts were concluded here, War of the Roses and the English Civil War. Here kings were captured, queens beheaded and princesses buried. This was Offa's main retreat, deep in the heart of Mercia back in the times of Charlemagne, and it was in Northampton that Hitler's invasion plans for England were concluded. Saints and radar and the western world's first parliament; a haven for politico-religious dissidents of every screwball stripe from Lollards and Moravians to Ranters, Levellers and Swedenborgians; a perfect social pit-canary and barometer, the exact point at which the cash runs out, with the North-South divide a dotted line down Gold Street's centre; a crossroads of history settled since the Neolithic on the limestone spine of the Jurassic Way, one of the country's earliest navigable paths if not its very first; the warzone Washington and Franklin's families high-tailed it out of to create America; all this crammed into just a few square miles of turf along with John Clare, Dryden, mammoth bones, witch panics, Lucia Joyce, a mentally unbalanced and inebriate Sir Malcolm Arnold kept as virtual pub prisoner, rolling out the barrel on the old Joanna every night for the abusive locals...all of this and yet the town remains invisible, much like the singularity which we suspect is lurking at the centre of our galaxy and holding all those hundred billion suns together.

It is these distinctive native energies that have been harnessed so efficiently in this present anthology, the black and smouldering fuel that this book and the town itself are running on. A first collection from the startlingly good Northampton SF Writers Group, I read it in a single sitting, something that I can't remember managing with an anthology for a considerable while. These stories have been harvested from the authentic steam of ghosts and sinister charisma that hangs over the town's weathered paving-slabs, and along with the obvious technical accomplishment of the contributors what most impresses here is the diversity of new and interesting voices that are conjured from the landscape, the array of variant (and yet somehow compatible) Northamptons with which we're presented, each one with an atmosphere that's recognisably indigenous.

Beginning from an admirably wide-angled definition of the term 'science fiction', as had noted predecessors such as Moorcock's excellent *New Worlds* or the eclectic and compelling *Interzone*, the writers represented in *Shoes, Ships & Cadavers: Tales from North Londonshire* have crafted visions of the town that are distinct and separate, covering a generous and sweeping arc of this tiny and yet deceptively expansive area of spacetime. Andy

West's *Mano Mart* identifies what seem to me to be two of the place's most consistent themes, violence and language, and reverberate with the not-unfamiliar sense that there are elements embedded in this area's past that are possibly best left undisturbed. *Arthur the Witch* by Donna Scott, a stylishly-told glimpse into the mindset of an earlier century by an incisive modern eye, navigates similarly murderous and occult reaches of the local spectrum, giving a meaty humanity to the burned-flesh barbecue pall of witch lore that still persists across the county.

Ian Watson, who has been for decades one of science fiction's most arresting and original performers, has extrapolated from Northampton's past into a credible and haunting future in his lyric and characteristically remarkable *A Walk of Solace with my Dead Baby*, with its brightly coloured Pinyin banners scrolling down the white stone flanks of Bradlaugh's truculent, accusatory statue and the moving sense of pharmaceutically and technologically-adjusted loss that's at its broken heart. Mark West's *What We Sometimes Do, Without Thinking* convincingly occupies a present day that nonetheless, as with so much of this town's current circumstances, turns out to be predicated on the unresolved narrative tangles of the past, wringing a story that is almost M.R. James-like from the modern villages and roads and railway bridges held in geostationary orbit between here and Kettering.

Hanging Around by Neil K. Bond arrives eventually in present-day Northampton after a few hundred years of enforced idleness by way of another local mainstay, the pub ghost. Back when I was growing up in the Spring Boroughs area, a half square mile which had at one point boasted more than eighty pubs, approximately half of those establishments were crawling with dead Cluniac friars from the St. Andrew's Priory that had stood in the district several hundred years before. Meanwhile, the former Black Lion in St. Giles Street, now the Wig & Pen, was hailed as the most haunted spot in England by both early 20th century ghost-busters such as Elliott O'Donnell and the one surviving landlord of the place who still remains a close personal friend. In Neil Bond's tale we are affectingly served up with a distinctly Northamptonian eternity, a theme which is picked up, albeit in a different sense, in Nigel Edwards' piece *The Tower*. Here we have a spirited attempt to re-imagine and therefore reclaim at least a small part of the alienating architecture that has been imposed upon the town, namely the Express Lifts tower hulking over Jimmy's End, which has been granted listed building status on the grounds that it would now be practically impossible to pull it down. Edwards' story offers us a more redemptive and much gentler interpretation of the structure, which we will encounter in a more oppressive light during *The Last Economy* by Paul Melhuish.

Melhuish's work, perhaps the most dystopian in the anthology, depicts a worryingly credible posterity where this town has itself become a kind of interzone, squeezed to a horrid smear between the two implacably encroaching masses of the Birmingham and London conurbations and yet still with the same looming and redundant tower presiding over the doomed landscape, an acknowledgement that it will very likely still be standing, irremovable, in any science fiction future that we care to contemplate. In its role as Northampton's lighthouse, a resigned ironic joke that puts it in the company of Wigan's pier, the tower features as an off-stage and unmentioned presence in *The Old Man of Northampton and the Sea* by Sarah Pinborough, one of the wistful marine evocations, like the Carlsberg's brewery's alleged Viking longboat stylings, that this furthest inland point is prone to. Much-missed local troubadour Tom Hall once ventured the opinion that Northampton's cobbled alleys and back-entries were the landlocked town's phantom canals and it is this implicit yearning for the coastal breakers, an impulse which once propelled half of the populace to Yarmouth for the factory fortnight, which Pinborough's atmospheric tale identifies and speaks to. As with the Express Lifts lighthouse and the Carlsberg

11

longboat, here the ocean dominates the story with its absence, eerie as discovering wet strands of kelp caught in the swing doors of the Grosvenor Centre.

Susan Sinclair's touching and uplifting *Lifeline*, while ostensibly returning to the theme of the pub spectre, treads a careful path between the supernatural and the plausibly scientific, and picks up on one of the more usually unmentioned strands of the town's fabric, this being its biker population. This community has been a staple feature of Northampton life since they were known as Ton-Up Boys, and Sinclair's story is a sympathetic nod towards that slowly disappearing and already ghostly subculture. Sombre in its tone and placed entirely in the present day, it stands in contrast to the funniest future dystopia contained in the collection, with this being Tim C. Taylor's *I Won the Earth Evacuation Lottery*. Delivered with an expert sense of timing and considerable panache, Taylor advances the gloomily probable idea that when this planet's number is eventually up, whether through ecological collapse or through the intervention of the story's casually apocalyptic Engineers, then mankind will most probably respond with the intelligence, resolve and dignity we witness in the less presentable *Big Brother* inmates. In his portrait of the panicking and frantic human herd crowding contemporary local landmarks like the Fishmarket or Roadmender, Taylor's entirely modern opus simultaneously evokes the best of British science fiction past, akin to Wells or Wyndham in its juxtaposing of unknowable and hostile forces with the poignant, clueless viewpoint of the ordinary English person on the ordinary English street.

Completing the anthology...at least in the last-minute, incomplete and therefore thoroughly Northampton-friendly version I was sent... we leave the splendid Ian Whates to somehow tie this marvellously disparate curio cabinet up in a neat conceptual bow with his *These Boots Weren't Made for Walking*. Here, in a light-hearted fantasy, Whates underlines the locale's status as a nexus, as a shifting and phantasmal junction of realities and fictions, as a haunted intersection of disputed past and multivalent future, as a crossroads culture so unfixed and liminal that it can readily accommodate all of the wildly different vistas and interpretations that are to be found within this excellent and expectation-raising volume. In *Ships, Shoes & Cadavers* we see a ray of hope for this town and the countless others like it, places that are circling the fiscal drain in grubby suds of plasterboarded high-street businesses, charity shops and nail bars: only if somebody cares enough to actually imagine meaningful alternate histories or a more energetic reading of the present will our past or our contemporary condition be, to us, empowering and nourishing. And only if somebody cares enough to conjure or hypothesise a future is there any chance of us actually getting one. Read and enjoy the many fine examples in this book, then, in whichever overlooked and disenfranchised hamlet you are currently contained, go out and write a future of your own.

I don't expect to read a book this year that is more personally satisfying or a greater cause for optimism than the one which you are holding. Passionately recommended.

Alan Moore
Northampton,
September, 2010

A Walk of Solace With My Dead Baby

Ian Watson

Dr Zhang easily slips into a parking space opposite the statue of Charles Bradlaugh close to RadioTV Northampton, due to a black van with a red star on its side conveniently pulling out just as we were approaching. Solicitously Dr Zhang hurries round to open the door of the Beijing Brilliance for me, so that I can step out easily with my dead baby.

From the back of the car emerge Mr Wu and my grief counsellor Jim Stewart who both quickly pretend an interest in the window of an IG shop, while keeping an eye on our reflections. Maybe I should try immersive games again; I just didn't like the way my time was gobbled. Wu and Jim are both wearing screenspecs and fly-on-the-shoulder video cameras. SightShare is so popular that hardly anyone will pay attention unless my escorts seem to be zooming in on me especially. I'm not too sure of Wu's role; an orderly, yes, and in this case a cameraman, but I think he's a bodyguard too, just in case. I've seen him at the clinic practising the slow dance of Tai Chi which, if you speed it up, becomes unarmed combat.

A brand new red banner, Chinese characters in white, hangs down the tall pedestal upon which Bradlaugh stands.

"What does that say?" I ask Dr Zhang. I need a pause before setting out on my walk.

"Miss Sullivan, it says Honour to the first atheist Member of British Parliament."

But of course. As schoolchildren hereabouts learn, Charles Bradlaugh was elected by the voters of Northampton in the late 19th century then promptly expelled from the House of Commons for refusing to swear allegiance on the Bible. For the next six years he was re-elected, expelled, re-elected. Northampton people often went against the grain. And Bradlaugh's lover at one time was Annie Besant, pioneer of birth control and socialism, which way back then was very progressive and transgressive of her.

"So it's symbolic that I start from here..." Doubtless the van driver had been keeping the space for us. To have arranged for a police car, or for road cones, would have been blatant. Ever since the financial rescue of Europe by Chinese wealth, our new co-prosperity advisors and partners have done their best to wear velvet gloves.

"This Northampton has been denied honourable status of city many times."

My pioneering walk might make a difference?

More to the point, because of its apparent nonconformity and free-thinking – at least in their view – the Chinese had decided that Northampton was the most appropriate British town to host the social experiment which began in China the previous year. In which I am helping.

Before we set out from the clinic, Jim Stewart gave me 40 milligrams of propranolol, nano-targeted at the soft almond in my head that bothers about events.

This mild dose of beta blocker shouldn't overly zap my perceptions of coping with anguish but should lessen anxiety due to the walk itself.

The proximity of the RadioTV Northampton building isn't because I shall head there for an interview after my first walk; that would be premature and unsubtle. RadioTV Northampton just happens to be there on the corner.

"Well now, Miss Sullivan, I stay twenty or thirty metres behind you. As also Dr Stewart and Mr Wu. In case of problem. Though in different parts of street, not together. Go where you wish. Follow your feelings."

So I set off at a stroll, my stabilised dead baby in a sling across my chest like a soft pearly doll. Rachel, I was planning to call her. She is still Rachel to me, although different now. She was only a few weeks premature. A few gold curls, like my own, are on her crown. My centre of gravity has shifted since her stillbirth; I mustn't stumble.

To reach the arch towards the top of Abington Street, celebrating Francis Crick and DNA, only takes me three or four minutes. Planted in the middle of the pedestrianised main street, two great bars of steel belly out and bend to cross over, becoming two symbolic naked human bodies, male and female, soaring upward – just as we have soared upward from being fish in ancient oceans towards knowledge of what makes us tick. Crick went to school in Northampton. Crick rhymes with tick. The problem with poems I've written is often that rhymes seem compelling at the time, but later on read like banal doggerel. Will I ever write immortal verse? Maybe I'll have to settle for a different, footnote-to-history kind of fame: the first walker along a British street with a dead offspring.

Alternatively this tribute to DNA reminds me of the giant silvered jawbones of a whale balanced on end. Discs set into the paving illuminate the archway at night. Naturally I walk through the archway because that will please Zhang and Jim.

A chubby black woman pushing her dozing corn-rowed daughter in a buggy notices me and my burden and stares for a moment. Perhaps she saw the TV documentary a few months ago, or the stills taken from it that were splashed in newspapers under misleading headlines such as *The Living Dead* as if my still baby is some kind of zombie. I did see the documentary, and Zhang and Jim showed a similar film to me again in the clinic.

A mother chimp puts down her baby so as to be able to break open a nut. The baby chimp lolls limply on the ground. Then the mother hoists its body again, slinging it over her back like a floppy satchel, and proceeds onward, on feet and knuckles. Visibly the baby is a corpse.

The voiceover says soothingly, "After an infant dies, a period of continuing contact is valuable to help the mother chimp adjust herself psychologically to the loss she has suffered. If the weather is wet, the corpse might fall apart within a few days. But during the dry season a corpse can become semi-mummified, and a mother may carry her dead child for as long as two months. Chimpanzees and human beings share almost ninety-nine per cent of their DNA in common. We are apes in very many respects, with common ancestors. May what consoles a chimp also console a human being? The Chinese people, due to their advances in science, are finding out in the most practical way…"

I clearly remember the footage of a young Chinese woman carrying a dead baby through politely clapping crowds, her expression serene.

"The injected nanotech," Zhang told me, "allows Two Ways, two options."

How Chinese. The Six Wisdoms, the Five Goals, the Four Paths… and the Two Ways of Solace.

"In truth, programmed nanos are able to fossilise dead ones, but result too heavy. Or are able to mummify permanently – however, this will perpetuate situation of regret. So Two Ways remain. Either nanos gradually diminish dead body by conversion to odourless gases released harmlessly into atmosphere, retaining appearance while shrinking till finally disappears. Or else retain size while reducing mass until lost baby is like empty cocoon which finally you crumple or fold."

"Could I fill it with helium and let it float away up into the sky?"

Jim darted me a glance of caution. Did he think I was being flippant? However, Zhang beamed.

"Ha! Balloon baby! However, openings in body leak helium immediately. And if sealed, pressure will burst."

Had the Chinese experimented with this possibility, in view of the supposed Christian heaven in the sky? To see the chrysalis of one's dead offspring floating heavenward like a soul might be beautiful.

But then the balloon baby would come back down to earth somewhere else, maybe hundreds of miles away. One could always attach a tag with name and address. Might be depressing if the soul was retrieved from a sewage farm.

I must curb my imagination. From the sympathetic interview in hospital only a couple of hours after I'd lost my child, plainly they sought someone intelligent to be a British pioneer. Had they interviewed a dysfunctional teenage un-mother before they hit upon me? Or a more socially 'stable' woman with a supportive husband?

That would imply a rather high rate of neonatal mortality in our very own Northampton General Hospital! Although maybe Zhang & Co were in touch with all hospitals, public and private, for miles around.

Anyway, after an hour they had returned to my bedside, and I'd signed their consent form and was soon on my way by ambulance to the clinic, along with little Rachel in a chiller box so that she could be nanofied.

Bed and board at the clinic, but no fee. I couldn't appear to have been bribed. That might look bad later on.

I chose the way of reduction rather than the chrysalis option. Rachel had swelled from embryo through all the stages of foetus until baby. Over the weeks she would return once more to the size of an embryo before disappearing from the world.

I would also lose some of the unwanted extra pounds I'd put on. I might be doing a fair bit of walking.

I decide to go into Costa Coffee on the corner with Fish Street for a skinny latte. Windows run along two sides, so Zhang and Wu will easily be able to watch me while loitering in one street or other, perhaps smoking. Many Chinese still smoke. Or else they can play with their webphones.

Jim himself comes in, a couple of customers behind me. Rachel high upon my chest, I'm fumbling in my jeans pocket for a recent RMB fiver which looks like any green five pound note of the past twenty years apart from the discreet Chinese characters at the bottom, which most Brits can't read as *renminbi*; nothing so blatant as a translation, no "people's currency" to offend the eye. So far I can only read about fifty characters.

Renminbi pounds and renminbi euros are unacceptable in the USA, but who wants to go there? We can go everywhere in Europe, as well as Africa and Asia if we're rich enough. I'd like to see the glories of Beijing and Shanghai. Maybe I'll be invited later on as a reward.

"Is that what I think it is?" demands a shaven-headed bloke who's waiting for his order. "If that isn't a doll, then it's one of those nano-corpses! So they're finally here, are they? I don't want to breathe bits of your baby into me!"

"You don't breathe bits of baby. Harmless gases, that's all. A lot of it's oxygen. The nanos convert the, um." I don't want to be anatomical about Rachel.

"Gas *with nanos* getting into me! What if they start taking me apart while I'm alive?"

"That can't happen. Nanos deactivate outside the body. Normally there's always dust in the air. If the sun was shining through the window you'd see motes and motes. From clothes, from skin, from everything."

"You think I want to know this? You think I want to drink a coffee anywhere near you? Are you crazy? How much are the Chinks paying you?"

"Nothing. They're paying me nothing."

"She's lost her baby," says the manager woman, chief barista or whatever. "I saw about this on TV." She sounds halfway sympathetic.

"She hasn't fucking *lost* her baby! She's pushing it in our faces!"

My little Rachel.

"I'm sorry this is upsetting you," I say, "but don't you think I'm upset too?"

The bloke's coffee is ready, loaded with cream and sprinkled chocolate. Angrily he seizes it and heads off, threatening, "Don't you sit anywhere near me."

"People will get used to this in time," I assure the manager woman. "People get used to most things. In a few years a new widow may be pushing her dead husband around in a wheelchair while he diminishes." Or else a strapping lad may be carrying his dead mother piggyback after she diminishes somewhat. But I don't say this. This hasn't happened as yet in China, although surely it will, given their respect for ancestors.

"Dead people don't drink coffees," asserts the manager woman as though a vision has assailed her, of Costa Coffee quarter-occupied by nanofied corpses.

"Neither do babies drink coffee, but you don't stop them from coming in here."

"Maybe you should sit over there, by the toilet."

I think I see the subconscious connection in her mind: disposal of waste. Propranolol keeps me quite calm. Jim has witnessed all of this casually, although I can tell he's alert. The two chubby adolescent girls queueing in front of him seem embarrassed, pretending nothing unusual is happening. Both of them stare at their phones in mirror mode as though inspecting themselves for pimples.

I suppose it's convenient to Zhang and Jim that I don't have a partner or a husband who might have accompanied me on this outing like a watchdog, hovering – as it were – by my side protectively. Roddy ran off soon after he learned I was pregnant.

Roddy the rod who impregnated me. But I decided to have my baby. And now I am unhaving her. Rachel looks much more like me than like Roddy, at least potentially so, her potential now paused forever and being rewound, unwound.

What is the correct name for a mother with a dead baby? You have widower and widow for a husband or wife who lost a loved one – maybe not a *loved* one, exactly, after years spent together, but someone you were accustomed to anyway; or maybe you were lucky in your relationship. That's different from a relationship with a baby born dead. A dead toddler who already started to babble and prattle would be in a different category. We need new words. Might I find them? Then my poems will become unique.

As I leave Costa, a long-haired gingery giant comes striding slowly down the middle of the street, aided by a huge knobbly walking stick. Of course I recognise him. It's the sage of Northampton, indeed the complete parsley rosemary and thyme. Sage and fantastical chronicler amongst his rainbow of achievements. Northampton's watchman, as it were, still impressive with the passage of years. Looking half-sage, half-tramp. Mage-tramp. He's said to be busy with a vast opus called *Xanadu*, although whether this relates to the new Chinese hegemony is anyone's guess. Zhang actually turns aside from his surveillance of me to capture images just as the sage or mage halts briefly to stare across searchingly at me and Rachel reclining in her sling. I think he understands.

At that moment a freckly young couple pass him, cooing at a living bonneted baby in a sling that the fellow wears on his chest, and I almost lose it as a sob tries to break free, to rack me. But the mage-tramp raises his stick to salute or bless me, revealing the carved snake hidden before by his grip. Then he strides onward slowly.

I cross to look in the window of Waterstone's, and reflect – in more than one sense. Book of the Week is a lavish abridged edition of *The Water Margin* boasting animated 3-D illustrations.

One of the Four Great Chinese Classics. Which reminds me of the Two Ways of Solace. Personally I don't much like books from which horses gallop out at you, powered by infalling light, but the Chinese are going far. On the Moon already, despite one disastrous loss. They'll go all the way. Asteroids, moons of Jupiter and Saturn. The Great March Forward. No, I'm confusing two things: the Long March of Mao under horrendous circumstances, and his Great Leap Forward much later which set China back years. Whatever the ups and downs, this is the Chinese century.

I have my own Little March to continue, onward towards the Market Square. I shan't do any leaping. Yet in my own way mine is a leap towards a brave new world where we shall grieve like the chimps, remaining physically bonded.

The Market Square may be one of the largest in the country, but stupid developers did their best to uglify it. What was once a Victorian arcade is now a wretched stark walkway leading to the bus station, and only a few old buildings survive unmauled. At least the market stalls themselves are lively, especially one called Tiger Dragon. Quite a few of the more elderly members of Chinese community are crowding around, while a youth dressed as a scarlet and gold dragon plays a wailing flute. Discarded LottoChina tickets litter the paving.

As I approach, an old man glances at me impatiently but when he spies Rachel he beams, and babbles to others, and they open a path for me to the front. Signs in English and Chinese (though I can only read one of the characters): *Real Tiger Bones! Tiger Bone Wine!*

"You want tiger bone wine?" asks the wrinkle-faced stallholder, Mao cap on his head. "Will not restore nano-baby, lady!"

So he too knows by sight what a nano-baby is. He may have seen them with their slightly pearly sheen in magazines from China, or else on the Chinese satellite channels. As an apothecary, or whatever, he'll have an interest in such things.

Then he leans across his display of vacuum-wrapped bones

and bottles and bags of herbs, to hiss, "Or you want *sell?*"

"How could I sell her! What use would she be to you! How can these be *real* tiger bones!"

The dragon youth looms behind me. "They're printed by a fabricator, built up in layers. Stored amplified tiger DNA provides the pattern for bone cells. So they're real. It's the coming thing! Another year or two, replicators will be able to print tiger penis for these old guys to soak in alcohol for new virility. More important, later the machine'll print a lost finger for you if you had an accident – a hand, a whole arm! After the tests with animals."

"Will your machines be able to print a living baby?"

"That would be forbidden. One-child policy, except in Zones of Excellence." The youth sounds quite clued up.

"Would Zones of Excellence include future asteroid colonies? Colonists might be too busy to be pregnant. Also, the gravity would be tiny."

Gravity, gravid, heavy with child...

My centre of gravity has altered now that Rachel is outside me.

"We don't know effect of minimal gravity on pregnancy," says the dragon-youth. "So will you buy some tiger bone wine? Great health tonic."

To drink the pulverized bones of what was never a tiger but which were nevertheless printed authentically, although without flesh. A skeleton tiger, a kind of ghost tiger.

To drink the ghost of a tiger in wine... is almost the start of a poem.

"How much for a bottle?"

That's very expensive. I only have pocket money at the moment.

An old Chinese woman flourishes a fistful of Renminbi-Pounds. Surely it was illegal for the stallholder to offer on impulse to buy Rachel. Crazy too, since she will fade away. But Chinese are very commercially canny. Maybe Rachel could act as a temporary charm. As she diminishes, so might a tumour inside the final purchaser shrink where radiotherapy and drugs failed, and surgery wasn't possible.

"Girl baby," observes the stallholder as money and wine bottle are exchanged.

And the dragon-youth tells me, "Tiger nose suspended over marriage bed begets a boy."

I am in a world I do not understand. Not yet. Perhaps I'll understand it by a poem. Shall I explain this to Zhang and Jim? Is their therapy working already?

Meanwhile there's a little physical problem to deal with. My breasts feel tender and damp. But this market's the perfect place to cope with the problem, so off to a fruit and veg stall I go to buy a cabbage. Over by the Moon on the Square the usual four or five alcoholics are debating, doubtless incoherently.

"That one, please." And I point.

For a moment I think that the weather-beaten stallholder is offering the cabbage to me to put in my sling along with Rachel, but no, he's letting me inspect it more closely in order to let himself see my baby from closer quarters because she must look subtly wrong, although he doesn't know why.

"She's dead," I say brightly. "The placenta failed." Jim advised me to be upfront if people ask questions. There's nothing to hide.

"Whatever you say, love." Into a khaki-coloured paper bag pops the cabbage. The chap hadn't actually asked a question, yet his look implied one. A problem with computers creating digital faces for films in the past, so I've heard, was called *the uncanny valley*. Something which looks very close to lifelike, yet isn't exactly so, can seem creepy to people. Disconcerting, even horrific to some. My Rachel may seem uncanny too – far from horrific because she's real, or *was* entirely real before being nanofied, but perhaps slightly unsettling, at least on first acquaintance. As she diminishes in size, this subconscious effect should also diminish, if indeed it bothers strangers seeing her for the first time.

Is my sling an uncanny valley wherein Rachel reclines?

Now to solve the problem. I head into the Grosvenor Centre and walk along past the stairs then the shops till I can use the escalator to reach the upper floor. Jim advised me to avoid tiring myself unnecessarily, and he isn't far behind. Takes it out of you giving birth; you can say that again, and I'm only a week away from the event, non-event. *Event*, whatever transpired! Pretty significant event in my life! Thus I arrive at the toilets, and the mother-and-baby changing room. Down goes the shelf. On to it, Rachel in her sling; but it's me who needs changing. Off with my top and the snugtight bra. The cabbage leaves within are soft and soggy. Discard in the bin. Strip fresh leaves from the cabbage I bought; crush their veins lightly, lay them in the cups. Next I express milk from my nipples on to toilet tissue.

How can I express the inexpressible?

Drugs to suppress milk are very strong. Zhang and Jim didn't want my feelings to be interfered with. Bruised cabbage relieves engorgement. Waste not want not; I'll keep the rest of the cabbage. Once my tits are recabbaged, I resume Rachel.

Zhang, Jim, and Wu are loitering nearby as I emerge. I trust they realized what I was doing, which wasn't pretending to change my baby's nappy. They couldn't have failed to see me buy the cabbage.

Back down I go by escalator to the lower level, where I'm within thirty metres or so of the Grosvenor Centre's rear doors, leading me out into fresh air just across from the same Costa where I stopped not too long ago. Shall I have another latte? Do I dare to eat an almond croissant? I'm alluding to Eliot's "Love Song of J. Alfred Prufrock" which invokes Lazarus come back from the dead. Rachel is a sort of dead Lazarus who comes to the streets of Northampton, who non-sees these streets for the first time ever through little glassy eyes which aren't glass. The Incredible Shrinking Rachel: has she diminished a little yet? Has she diminished my grief a bit?

I almost expect to see the ginger magus walking backwards up the street in a rewind of what happened earlier. But no: time moves onward, contrary to the destiny of Rachel. In a few weeks time when she finally expires, might she cause in the emptiness within me a pang of pleasure reminiscent of when she was first created, an orgasm of departure, a bright star imploding inside me? I shall find the words. Dr Zhang and Dr Jim may be dazzled.

And really this is probably long enough for my first walk with dead Rachel. So, instead of a latte or green tea, I direct my steps gently uphill – a very gentle slope – towards the DNA archway where I'll pause a while before heading onward to the Beijing Brilliance. Scarlet banners hang down the tiled dividers of the four tiers of windows on the Art Deco façade of what used to be a Co-Op building. They're decorated in gold with the clever inquisitive rat, the fun-loving though self-centered monkey, and the energetic charismatic dragon, three animals all compatible with each other.

At the DNA archway I'm waylaid by RadioTV Northampton in the persons of a bearded anoraked cameraman and a slim Brit-Asian interviewer woman dressed in pinstripe jacket and skirt and jet-black boots that are almost fetish. What's her name, again? I've seen her enough times on screen. Aha, Sally Sharma.

"Excuse us, Miz…?"

"Sullivan," I tell her. "Juliet Sullivan."

Since apparently she didn't know my name till now, the tip-off must have come from someone who saw me and Rachel during our walk and promptly phoned in, perhaps passing some of his SightShare on to RadioTV Northampton hoping for a small fee. Rather than this being an ambush tip from Dr Zhang; he's looking wary. Jim and Wu are closing in protectively, although that bulks up an audience of curious bystanders already attracted by my being accosted on camera.

"Well, Juliet, it seems you may be the first woman in Britain to carry a dead child with you around the streets, Chinese style."

To *carry* a child is ambiguous... That's what I mean about needing new words. The cameraman closes in upon Rachel in her sling, but I don't avert her from the lens.

"You're quite right, Sally."

"Wow, this is breaking news. Were you coming to the station to talk to us?"

"Not quite today. This is my first outing."

Outing suggests a gay person revealing their sexual orientation. Now it also implies a mother revealing her dead baby to the world.

"I'm privileged, Juliet! And full of sympathy, of course. Can you tell me how you were chosen?"

"To honour Northampton," I say. "Rather than somewhere else in Britain. As for me, my placenta failed."

"I'm so sorry about that. Can you tell me: *How do you feel?*"

I summon up the words.

"Breasts don't know
    "That a baby's born dead.
    "So the cabbage leaves are wet.
    "Dinking the ghost of a tiger in wine
    "Can't restore Rachel to me now."

I can see Sally Sharma is nonplussed, but I press on.

"Soon any son may carry
    "His dead mum piggyback
    "Till she floats up into the sky.
    "Whereas Rachel will reduce
    "In her uncanny valley
    "Slung from my neck
    "Until she vanishes.
    "No need for anyone to beware.
    "There's always dust in the air!"

28

That last bit should please Zhang.

A couple of the alcos, on their swaying way to somewhere, cheer and clap so I sketch a little bow. Rachel inevitably bows too. Alcos are different from ordinary drunks; they having more staying power even if their brains are half-rotted.

Above my head the silvery male and female soar upward in opposite directions. As I set off again from my impromptu historic interview I'm sure that the rat and the monkey and the dragon are following me, even if Zhang and Wu and Jim can't see them.

Lifeline

Susan Sinclair

Anne flipped her collar up and headed down Bridge Street. A south-easterly wind from Delapre Park blew icy rain down her neck. Her sodden fringe glittered with the glare from every passing car that sprayed her coat with oily water and splashed her jeans above two inch heels.

This outing on a bleak October night was intended to brighten her day, but had turned into a twilight endurance mission with missed buses and inclement weather.

At the corner she glimpsed the welcoming glow of pub lights. The noisy trickle gave way to the low murmur of conversation as she pushed through the door. She was expecting, however, the loud drone of a crowd, or, better still, the deafening beat of live music.

She stood dripping over a barstool as a barmaid, with almost adolescent curves and far too much makeup on her thin face, laughed with several regulars. They were older male bikers, grey-haired and heavily bearded. The woman attended to one of the few younger men that came across, but still failed to notice Anne.

As Anne was finally handed a refreshing vodka and lemonade, she took a quick sip and struggled to keep the barmaid's attention.

"Is the *Skeleton Krew Rebellion* starting late?" she enquired.

"The *Skeleton Krew Rebellion* was on last night," said the barmaid, "and tonight's band cancelled. The list of gigs is over

31

there."

Turning, Anne saw a chalk board by an empty stage where the band should have been.

The conspiracy against her seemingly complete, she slipped back from the counter and wandered towards the stage, knowing that this belated attention to detail would not make any difference. Childcare was arranged for tonight. She took another sip, too much, too fast, spilling most of the drink down her chin. Stumbling forward, she almost banged into a man slouched in the corner beside the board.

He looked startled

"Sorry," Anne choked.

His dark eyes grew wide.

"I said sorry," Anne reiterated defensively.

"Good God," the man said, "you can see me."

There was a momentary silence in which Anne stared at the man, and the man stared back. A young man, who almost brushed the low ceiling as he stood slowly upright. His hair was dark and tied back in a ponytail. His solid jaw line softened by a neat beard. He wore a shapeless white shirt with sleeves turned back above tanned arms. Green and red dragons swirled in combat down his muscular forearm. Beneath the tattoo, a sharp red and grey motif livened up his sleeveless leather jacket. Details on the jacket were shadowed, but they could be skulls or American symbols that suggested this lad was part of the biker crowd.

"Come again," Anne said, sure she had misheard.

"You can see, *and* hear me." The man smiled. "I've been here since the May bank holiday. Two weeks, and I've not managed to get served yet. The large lass at the bar could see me at first, I think. She gave me some very strange looks before totally ignoring me."

Anne took another quick sip, and began to move away. Attention from a young man was flattering at her age, but drunks could be unpredictable.

The man moved smoothly to intercept.

Not a drunk, then: worse; the pub nutter.

"Have you any idea how lonely it is," he continued, "with no one to talk to, and people trying to walk through you? If you're worried people might stare because you're talking to yourself, then we can go over here."

She was reluctant to follow. She looked around for pub security, or at least some burly biker annoyed by the noisy entertainment.

Everyone was deep in their own discussions. No one even noticed her there, cheeks suddenly dried by flushed humiliation.

They might not be able to see him but she couldn't *stop* seeing him, no matter how much she willed him to disappear. Conceding defeat, she sat down in a dingy alcove, and stared silently into her drink.

He took a seat opposite.

"Do you see ghosts?" he asked.

Anne shook her head.

"Good." He seemed relieved, "that gives me one less theory to work on. Of course, this could be your first time."

Anne digested this information slowly. He had clearly thought long and hard about things, but she felt she should be shocked, or shivering, or something. She was not cold enough now to be shivering, and she just felt helplessly harassed. She took another sip.

"How did you get here... two weeks ago in... May?" she said quietly.

"I was following a girl."

"Who?"

"Her name was Eleanor, I think."

"Your girlfriend?"

"I don't know. She seemed to have a prior engagement – off to meet some handsome soldier I could just see in the distance. She was angry at me and told me to go home."

Harassing his ex maybe? He seemed the type.

33

"Why didn't you go home?"

"I couldn't remember where home was. It's a big house, I think, with a big garden in a small village. A place where you can hear the sea and see white cliffs."

Not Northampton then.

"What's your name?" Anne asked.

"The only names other than Eleanor that come to my mind are Davey, Duke, William and King Billy."

"The King Billy would be the name of this pub," Anne pointed out, and took another sip.

"That leaves Davey, Duke or William," the young man said.

"Or how about King Willy," Anne giggled suddenly. This was absurd.

The man pouted. "Not Willy, you can have Davey, William or Duke."

"I choose Duke, Duke."

His shapely mouth curved up at one corner, revealing a dimple just visible above the beard.

"I can see you're a cheap date, flirting after just one drink."

"Flirting?" She was certainly tempted. One drink and he was not bad looking for an invisible man. "Was I flirting, Duke?"

From this point on the evening became much more relaxed, if a little disjointed. There was nothing to stop Anne flirting with an invisible stranger in a quiet corner. They had much in common. They had wandered into the King Billy for the same reason, to listen to live music. He could still hear the strum of a rock ballad, and the sexy squeal of an electric guitar. Her vivid imagination did not quite extend to this, but she could appreciate his enthusiasm. She bought another drink and one for him just in case. He did not attempt to drink any. She drank for both of them and then ordered another two.

Duke decided to escort her home.

"Under the circumstances," he told her, "this is the gentlemanly thing to do."

She bought two tickets from a bemused bus driver and

flirted with Duke on the top deck. Teenagers in the seats behind moved downstairs.

After waving goodbye to the babysitter she invited him in for coffee. She forgot to put the kettle on, and apologised. He smiled. When she fell over a chair and playfully rebuked him for failing to catch her, he lost his smile. When she was attacked by smothering bedclothes, his handsome face hung above her, and his smile returned with a tantalising invitation.

Anne woke amid bedclothes in disarray, and with the father of all hangovers. She took some time to sort out her thoughts. Recollection of the previous night was somewhat bitty, like a badly edited B movie. Once she had her thoughts in some semblance of order she turned on the light and searched the room with a worried frown.

The limited space was cold and reassuringly empty. The small living room was equally empty, as was the tiny kitchen: the bathroom had to be small for her to get in through the door.

She gazed long and hard at her reflection in the bathroom cabinet. Summer office-grey skin had turned seamlessly to winter-grey, showing every drawn line. She self-consciously tucked a strand of greying hair back beneath the brown. Had she really spent all night talking to herself?

"Are you finished in there, Mum?"

Anne exited the bathroom, coming face to face with her leggy young daughter. Kelly was her youngest child, and only a small hop away from womanhood. A reminder of what she herself must once have been, when her husband had called her a pretty young thing. Unfortunately Anne was no longer a pretty young thing. Kelly, a late addition to an already fledged family, had been the end of Anne's marriage.

Anne had not seen much of her ex since. He, his latest young girlfriend, and what little money he had not spent on this latest bit of totty, had moved to Australia. Anne had struggled valiantly with the mortgage until redundancy this year. Unable to get a decent replacement job and still in negative equity, she had lost their home. Belongings had to be given to charity and the dog re-homed when she and Kelly were reduced to emergency council housing, then tenancy of a second floor flat on a rough town estate. Life was very stressful at the moment.

Kelly tilted her head, the cheeky grin on her face revealing the full sparkle of new braces, a cheap purple gem for every tooth.

"Did you enjoy yourself last night, Mum? Can I go out with you next time?"

Anne drew breath before returning the smile.

"No, it would cost too much in Coke, which your orthodontist says is bad for your teeth, and it's embarrassing for a child to have to steer her drunken mother home from the pub. Now, don't you have school this morning?"

Anne was relieved that the day appeared to be progressing in a normal fashion; mislaid school kit and gloves, burnt toast, doorstop sandwiches that were stuffed into Chinese takeaway containers, that wouldn't stuff into overfilled school bags, and spilled out on the back seat of Anne's old banger.

Kelly re-stuffed her bag at the school gate, and gave her mum a peck on the cheek.

Anne tutted. "Go on, you'll be late."

Kelly's new school was grey and impersonal. Life was stressful here too, although Kelly put on a brave face. She took a few quick steps and then turned back.

"Will Duke be there when I get home, only I forgot to say goodbye?"

Anne felt she had been hit by a cannon ball. Her jaw dropped.

"It's all right," Kelly shrugged. "He's nice."

Back at the flat, Anne pushed open Kelly's bedroom door, and then checked every room twice. No one could have avoided her, but she could not rid herself of the feeling that Duke was there. If he had been part of her imagination, then how could Kelly have seen him?

You can't see me now?

The voice, if it was a voice, was disappointed and remote.

She threw her head back against the door she had closed behind her.

"No," she said to the empty room.

What had Duke said about the barmaid being able to see him, and then not see him? Perhaps this had happened with her, and would happen with Kelly too.

Anne felt a surge of hope and relief for the thought, and then a guilty sadness. They would be leaving Duke alone again.

"Do you want some music?" she said brightly.

She lifted a Jethro Tull CD and hoped Duke liked folksy poetic lyrics with his rock music.

Over the next three weeks Kelly kept up a constant dialogue with their invisible lodger.

Anne was at a loss. She had introduced this imaginary companion, so how could she rebuke her daughter for talking to him. To do so would be hypocrisy and an acknowledgement of a problem she felt inadequate to deal with for many reasons and on many levels. She had no one to talk to. Her friends were already worried about her in a pitying ineffectual way while getting on with their own uneventful lives; her elderly parents had retired to the Lake District; her youngest son was at college in Exeter while his older brother hiked down to see their father in Australia; and her GP was the latest name in an ever changing line up at her local health centre. Anyway, perhaps her daughter needed an imaginary companion when she had so few real friends at her new school.

In the fourth week things seemed to come to a head. Kelly began to call Duke, quietly to get his attention at first, then more impatiently. Her calls quickly became urgent with frustration and concern. She was becoming stressed, and Anne knew she had to say something.

"One of the mums at the school gate says you've begun to make friends in the netball team, Kelly," she said. "It's quite usual to stop seeing invisible companions when we no longer need them."

"Then why don't you still see Duke?" Kelly asked reasonably. "You needed a friend too. Anyway, it's not that I don't see him. He can't see me. He seems to be... lost. And he's really upset. There must be something we can do."

Anne was always amazed how children could believe their parents were invulnerable to stress, had never-ending supplies of money, and could solve anything. Anne had failed to live up to expectation in at least two of these categories recently and was feeling increasingly inadequate as a parent.

"We'll think of something," she replied weakly.

Friends in the netball team proved not to be such a blessing when Kelly confided in one of them. Her Mum's invisible boyfriend became the talk of the team, then the class. Sensible girls no longer befriended her, and she became a target for bullies.

Anne did not notice at first. She was so grateful that the in-house one-sided conversations had ceased that she failed to realise her daughter was far quieter than normal. Eventually there was a call from the school. Kelly had attacked one of her tormentors.

Anne collected her. There were bruises and blood where Kelly had torn her lip on the braces. One of her nails was ripped back and there was a deep cut above her brow where she had banged heads with her adversary.

"You should see the other girl," Kelly muttered as they sat in casualty.

"I'm hoping we won't see her in here," Anne said. "I'm sure we'll see enough of her and her parents when we go to your school disciplinary meeting."

But Kelly was not listening. Her eyes were wide. She tugged

excitedly on Anne's arm.

"Mum, that's Duke. He's here."

Anne rubbed the side of her face uneasily.

"Shush, darling," she whispered, "this is a hospital. Sick people won't want to hear you yelling."

People in the waiting room were beginning to turn towards them, and toward the empty corridor Kelly was pointing down.

"Let's follow him," Kelly said.

Anne had no idea when Kelly would be seen by the doctor, so the idea of escape from a now curious waiting room held some appeal.

"Yes, let's."

Anne would have stopped Kelly once they were beyond sight of the waiting room, but her daughter was already well ahead. She seemed to know her way in the maze of long corridors and echoing stairs. By the time Anne caught up, Kelly was outside a closed door peering through one of the windows onto the ward.

"He's in there," she said.

Excitement was causing her to bounce up and down, and Anne could not help laughing as she grabbed hold of her arm.

"All right, calm down. Where is he exactly?"

"On that chair."

"Which chair?"

There were several very empty chairs by sleeping patients.

"That blue one at this end."

Anne was about to turn away and have words with Kelly, but something caught her attention. In the bed beside the chair was a sleeping man surrounded by complex machinery. A sensor was strapped to an arm that lay across the sheet. There was a tattoo on the arm.

"Green and black dragons...?" she said in wonder.

"Yes, fascinating, isn't it, but you can't stand around in this corridor unless you are a close friend or relation."

Anne almost jumped out of her skin, and turned to find a

young nurse standing behind them. She stammered an apology.

The nurse nodded acceptance. She looked very professional in a clean uniform and neatly collected auburn hair, but she had a kindly face. Anne became brave.

"I had a friend once who had a tattoo like that. His name was…," she put on a forgetful expression. "Duke?"

The nurse smiled politely, but was otherwise unimpressed.

"No… Davey, Will? He lived somewhere on the coast."

The nurse raised a brow. "Suffolk?" she queried.

Anne had never seen any white cliff in Suffolk.

"Dorset, or thereabouts," Anne guessed. "We were at a rock concert on the south coast."

The nurse drew breath and relented. "His name is David Williams. *The Duke* was apparently the name of his bike, although I guess he may have picked up that nickname because of the bike."

"Big… manly thing, a bike," Anne said vaguely.

The young nurse sighed in exasperation. "A dangerous thing, a bike. Judging by his injuries I imagine *The Duke* was a write-off."

Kelly tugged at the nurse's sleeve.

"Does he get many visitors? Can we visit him?"

"Not many visitors," the nurse said sadly. "I think a few of his biking friends came at first, but he's been in a coma for a year. There are visiting hours, and it's not as if he will notice, but you'd better tell the duty nurse that you are more than a passing acquaintance."

Kelly had finally been seen and neatly butterfly-stitched by a doctor, and now, much against Anne's better judgement, they stood with other visitors in the corridor outside the ward where Davey lay in a coma.

"We're not going to get away with this," Anne hissed. "We'd be lying if we said we were his friends."

"You lied earlier," Kelly argued, then smiled winningly at the older nurse who was walking towards them.

"We've come to see my mum's boyfriend, Davey Williams," she said.

The nurse frowned. "Would this be the first time you've visited?"

Anne could feel her underlying disapproval. The age gap, probably, as well as the fact that she had not visited before. She felt obliged to make some suitable excuse.

"Davey and I had a silly tiff last year. I was drunk.... Anyway, I assumed he wasn't talking to me. Man-pride, you know... I didn't hear about the accident until recently."

The nurse nodded and went about her business. Breaching ward security with shades of the truth was much easier than Anne had imagined. She still felt guilty as they walked over to Davey's bed.

This David was far older than the Davey Anne had met, probably several years older than her, in his late forties. The ponytail was gone and his receding hairline was flecked with grey. Lined pale skin was sunken around his cheeks. Paler areas round his jaw suggested a large beard had been shaved off, probably by the hospital.

On the sinewy arm the dragon tattoo was darkening, losing definition and colour. Rough, wel- used hands with long fingers lay limp against thin thighs beneath the blankets. Deep lacerations on his bony shoulders had been left unbandaged and already healing to white scars.

He was wearing a set of ear plugs, and there was the low buzz of sound. She assumed they were trying to rouse him with a melody. There was no visible response. The laughing eyes that still haunted Anne's dreams remained closed.

Anne was both saddened by his plight, and relieved. She could not be entirely mad to have imagined a man that really existed, and Kelly did not seem disappointed by this older incarnation.

41

The nurse was still around and might expect some signs of affection, so Anne sat down in the chair, picked up Davey's hand and held his fingers gently. She promised him a rock CD to replace the classical one when they came again.

"Well, the rock CD seems to be working." The older nurse had begun to approve of Anne and Kelly's belated vigil. "We think he may be coming around."

"Oh," Anne said, uncertain what else to say.

It was Christmas, and she had just put a new CD wrapped up in snowflake paper on the bedside table. Anne had brought Kelly's present too, as she was staying at her grandparents over the holiday. Kelly's present was large and soft, a dark blue fluffy dressing gown wrapped in galloping reindeer. Anne had not told Kelly that Davey might never need it, she had not the heart to, and perhaps, after all, he would.

"He may not remember everything at once," the nurse warned.

So, should she be alarmed if he did not remember her, or alarmed if he did?

Holding Davey's hand and stroking the coarse hairs on his wrist, Anne waited on into the early hours; worrying about Davey's reaction when he woke; worrying about the agency job she had recently started, and might not get to in the morning. She was too worried to sleep easily, but must have dozed.

A glow on white under dim night-lights was the first thing she was aware of. Then the starched clean hospital sheets smooth against her cheek and the background hum of a working hospital with which she had become familiar. Lastly, she became aware that the hand she was clasping for comfort had tightened around hers. She looked up, startled, into the dark eyes of her dreams.

"Hi," croaked Davey.

There was a faint baffled frown on his craggy face.

Anne felt guilty, like a child caught picking flowers by the

42

elderly gardener.

"Hi," she whispered.

Her nerve was failing and she would have fled at this point, but the hand around hers was surprisingly strong for a sick man.

"You're…?" He thought for a moment. "Anne?"

By early summer, Anne was becoming used to slipping her finger into Davey's palm and feeling the reassuring response of his strong hand around hers.

Slowly rebuilding his strength, and re-growing his ponytail and beard, he was the solid reliable type.

They were in the Kingsthorpe Cemetery, standing on a quiet hillock of grass staring down at a plain black headstone. Other graves around had been brightened with plastic flowers, flags and windmills, but this was the first time Davey had been back.

He laid a small bunch of fresh flowers beneath a gold inscription that still echoed his thoughts, Eleanor May Williams, loving and loved mother. Eleanor had been born sixty-six years ago in Northampton and had fallen in love with a soldier while studying in Oxford. They had intended to wed when he returned from tour, only he had not returned. Eleanor had moved away with her bastard son David to get away from lingering prejudices, but she had wanted to be buried in Northampton.

Heading homewards in the early hours of the morning after the funeral, Davey had reached the Queen Eleanor roundabout at speed on *The Duke*. He had probably been understandably distracted, and may have missed the change in traffic lights. Or perhaps the tired lorry driver had not seen him in the twilight and chanced an otherwise empty road. Investigations into the accident were held in Davey's prolonged absence.

There was nowhere in this life scenario for Davey and Anne to have occurred, but he never said anything. He remembered her as younger, but he remembered Kelly too, and that would not logically fit. Nor did a council flat in a city he had only ever visited once since infancy. This did not stop him being discharged to Anne's flat as soon as humanly possible. Anne's single bed became a double mattress on the floor, and not as uncomfortable as that might sound.

Maybe Davey put the many inconsistencies down to lapses in memory. The hospital had warned him there might be lingering disorientation. He hung on relentlessly to the illusion that Anne had created, forestalling any attempts she made to enlighten him. Anne had no excuses to make if she had been able to think of anywhere to start.

Having inherited his mother's large coastal house, Davey's time was spent calling up old clients to get his bike repair business back on track. He just assumed that his girlfriend, Anne, and her daughter were going home with him. He could see no reason why they would want to stay in a Northampton council flat, and Anne had to admit he had a point there. Discussion consisted of him proudly showing Anne pictures of his bikes and prized Gibson guitar. He told Kelly how close the sea was, and the best places to walk a dog. Kelly was over the moon. They would take the train.

As they made their way back through the trees towards the main gate, Anne walked slowly by his side in the dappled sunlight. He was still struggling on the crutches, but she knew better than to highlight his weakness with a suggestion that he should sit down for a moment on one of the memorial benches.

"We still have time to go for a drink before leaving," Anne said.

"Where, The King Billy?"

There was an edge to his voice.

"Well," Anne said uneasily, "we could go down to the King Billy when we get off the bus, and then take a taxi down to the station..." Her voice trailed off and she held her breath.

"Did it really happen like that?" he asked at last. "It can't have, but I don't see any other way it could have."

"I know what you mean," Anne said, "but I do have a theory."

"I'm intrigued. I don't even have that, and I've been trying to work it out for weeks."

"When you were in hospital," Anne said, "one of the nurses let slip that they'd had you on a new drug they were trialling. The intention was to keep your brain active and encourage recovery. I think the drug did more than that. What do you remember?"

He shuffled awkwardly, turned toward her and balanced his arms across his crutches.

"I remember the dark despair that afternoon, grief for my mother, but also for all those frustrated years. As a young man I tried to create the family I'd missed out on. Perhaps my expectations were too high, my wife moved away with my sons and I lost contact. When Mum became ill there was no chance to try again, she was the only family I had and needed me. Her death was inevitable and a relief in many ways, but my life was suddenly very empty. Then there was a big bang, a young girl called Eleanor, a beautiful woman, Anne, and her daughter, Kelly. Dreamlike *and* very real, as most dreams are when you're in them, I suppose. It was like I had known you always. Except that I couldn't touch all the sweet things I saw." He ran his fingers gently across Anne's cheek. "You think I was having an out-of-body experience?"

Anne nodded. "You saw people as they saw themselves. People talk to each other unaware of how old they have become. Inside, none of us are a day over twenty. The anorexic barmaid still saw herself as fat even when she had become painfully thin. Why I saw you when others couldn't, I don't know."

"Then the trial ended and they took you off the drug."

Davey frowned. "As the dream began to fade, I tried desperately to hang on to it. I didn't want to come back to a miserable pain-filled reality. I thought I was losing the fight. Then I heard the music..."

He leaned towards her, a battle-scarred old warrior trying to find a meaning to life.

"Do you think we should mention these curious side

effects?" Anne said.

"Who'd believe us?"

Reassured, Anne became lost in the handsome dark eyes, the moment...

"Hey!" Kelly's voice brought them back to reality. "No time for snogging, we've got a train to catch."

These Boots Weren't Made for Walking

Ian Whates

Terry Wainwright was just a spit away from his thirtieth birthday. Young enough to still have ambitions but old enough to worry that life was somehow passing him by

He was a journalist, but had never yet progressed beyond the local rags. A few years ago he'd decided to go freelance. This was a big step, and one he'd taken only after a lot of soul searching, a careful weighing up of the available options... and the redundancy notice he'd received the previous day.

This particular day of all days, he was wondering why the hell anyone would ever want to become a journalist. He was exhausted. Not in the 'what a fantastic night of partying, isn't life incredible' sort of way, but more in the 'I spent last night in a police cell and didn't sleep a wink; life stinks' fashion.

He'd been released late morning and was now wandering around the town centre in a bit of a daze, trying to get his head together. He stared up at Lucy Galding's steel sculpture 'Discovery' which rises above Abington Street. The eight metres high monument was erected to commemorate Francis Crick, co-discoverer of the structure of DNA, whom Northampton claims as one of its own by accident of birth and schooling. Two vast steel strands curve elegantly past each other in suggestion of DNA's double helical nature, each supporting a magnificent depiction of humanity thrusting towards the sky; a celebration of life, of joy and freedom. All of which struck Terry as ironic comment given recent events.

Costa Coffee beckoned and he was soon slumped over a latte at one of the tables outside, battling to come to terms with his frustration and disappointment. His gaze drifted to Waterstone's bookshop diagonally opposite and for a moment he almost smiled, recalling how a few years ago he and Billy Corbitt had gone in there pretending to be visiting authors – names chosen randomly after a quick glance at the shelves – and had then each apocryphally autographed a small stack of books while the beaming assistant added 'Signed' stickers to the covers.

The memory provided no more than transient distraction and he soon returned to staring into his coffee feeling sorry for himself. The problem was that nothing ever *happened* in Northampton. No, that wasn't true. Things did sometimes happen – he'd see them on the news or read about them in articles written by *other* journalists. They simply never happened to him.

Then, when finally something exciting did crop up in his life, something so huge he knew it would catapult him straight into the nationals, he buggered it up; which was how he ended up being interrogated by the police the previous evening and spending the night in the nick.

Abington being one of the town's central shopping streets, people were wandering past him all the time, but he didn't see them. They were wallpaper – a fact of life but not one requiring his attention – until somebody spoke to him.

"Terry? What are you doing here?"

He looked up, to see, "Billy!" His fellow fake author. Serendipity or what?

"You look like shit."

"Thanks. That's what a night in a police cell does for you."

"In a what...? Oh, I see, research for something I suppose."

"I wish."

"Look, can't stop now but I'm glad I bumped into you. I've got a little present, something you'll love... It's at home I mean, not here. Do you fancy meeting up later, after work. I'll bring it along. Six thirty at the Bear?"

"Yes, sure," Terry said without thinking.

"Great, must dash. See you at six-thirty and you can tell me all about 'the cell'."

Only after his friend had disappeared back into the wallpaper did Terry stop to wonder whether he was really up to going out tonight, even with Billy.

The coffee had revived him a little. Enough to realise that he was hungry. He'd missed out on a meal the previous evening and hadn't really eaten in the past 24 hours. He needed food. Correction: he needed a curry.

With a firm purpose in mind for the first time that day, he headed down Fish Street.

One thing he loved about Northampton was the sense of history. You didn't have to look hard to find it, no further than the street names much of the time. Fish Street, for example, where the fish market used to stand, and now he was about to cross the Ridings, where a riding school had been. He glanced wistfully at the Fish Inn to his left. Why hadn't he suggested to Billy they meet there? Better choice of beers, for one thing. Oh well.

Coming towards him was a man who looked so in keeping with the company he'd associated with of late that he almost stumbled to a halt. Black leather jacket, tight jeans and the cocky, exaggerated swagger of someone who wants to impress: 'I walk this way because my thigh muscles are so well developed I couldn't possibly walk any other.' He was talking into a mobile phone with an earnestness that suggested the person on the other end wasn't taking him as seriously as he would have liked. At the same time he flicked up the lid of a cigarette packet – a green box, not a brand Terry recognised – preparatory to having a smoke. It must have been his last one, because after manoeuvring

49

a slender white tube between finger and thumb he tossed the packet to the ground.

Even in his current dejected state Terry was appalled. Had the man no social conscience? There were rubbish bins aplenty in the pedestrianised Abington Street ahead. Was it really too much to ask him to clutch the empty pack until then? Terry was so incensed he nearly took the man to task. The only thing stopping him was the nagging suspicion that perhaps the fellow's thigh muscles really *were* that impressive and he might have biceps to match.

The moment passed as had the man, and Terry contented himself with merely feeling superior.

Into St Giles Street and he turned right, heading for Bridge Street, where he knew there was a decent Indian. In the process he crossed the top of Guildhall Street, home to both the Derngate Theatre and the Northampton Museum and Art Gallery. The latter was one of his favourite places in the whole city, because it housed the most fantastic collection of shoes – purportedly the world's biggest.

Those privileged few who even knew about the collection tended to enthuse about the giant pair of boots on stilts, famously worn by the Pinball Wizard himself – Elton John – in the rock opera *Tommy*, but Terry had always preferred a far more modest example of footwear. Namely, a pair of men's grey and black George Boots, as made by Jeffrey West in 1998 – Terry knew all this by heart. Exquisite red lining, black laces across the front, but, most impressive of all, the entire boot was covered in a digitally printed Warhol-esque series of images showing the glowering face of Pete Murphy, former frontman of the Goth-rock band Bauhaus. Murphy, who had recently cropped up in the latest teen-magnet vampire movie *The Twilight Saga: Eclipse*, was another Northampton native and had always been one of Terry's heroes. These boots were the coolest things he'd ever seen. He'd once even contemplated breaking into the museum and stealing them, but hadn't. Of course he hadn't. He was never involved in anything *that* exciting. Until recently.

He refused to dwell on that now, though. A curry beckoned.

Little happened during the rest of the day – no surprise there – and he arrived at the Bear that evening with his mood only marginally improved. He'd nearly rung Billy to cancel several times but that would only have led to a protracted battle of wills, as his friend tried to convince him to change his mind. He didn't have the energy for that. Easier to just turn up for a quick drink and cry off early.

No sign of Billy when he walked in, so he slouched up to the bar to buy a drink. Good Lord, the place was getting adventurous. Two hand pumps were in operation and beside the ubiquitous IPA was a beer from a brewer he'd never heard of. So many micro-breweries popping up all over the place these days; a good thing, of course, but it made it impossible for a bloke to keep track.

The lad behind the bar looked too young to be there (what was it people said about policemen looking too young being a sign of getting old? Did the same hold true for bar staff?). Gaunt, painfully thin, his body draped in a faded black T-shirt... and was it really possible to attach *that* many rings to a single ear?

The apparition stared at him with a blank expression which, while not openly hostile, still fell a long way short of welcoming.

Terry decided to attempt communication in any case. "I'll have a pint of..." He glanced down at the hand pumps, his eyes falling on the second, whose badge boasted a gesticulating wizard, complete with robe and a flowing mane of white hair. "Gandalf's Revenge," he declared, while wondering whether the brewers paid any royalties to the Tolkien Estate.

After the appropriate monies had passed hands he headed over to a corner table, nursing his drink. The beer looked disconcertingly dark. He took a tentative sip, and grimaced. At least he now knew who Gandalf was seeking revenge on: the drinker.

"It really must have been a bad day," said a familiar voice.

"Billy! Sorry, I didn't see you there," which was quite an achievement, considering his friend was sitting at the next table.

"Yeah, you did seem a bit preoccupied. Not surprising after you've had a run in with that alien behind the bar."

"You won't *believe* what a weird few days it's been. Anyway, he's not an alien, the kid behind the bar I mean – just a different generation."

The other shrugged. "Same difference. We were never like that when we were teenagers, were we?"

"Worse, probably."

Terry moved tables, to sit opposite his friend. "So, do you want to hear how I ended up in the nick or not?"

"Course I do?"

"Well..."

Terry and Billy were both so engrossed in the ensuing conversation and neither spared a glance as the pub door opened. Had they done so, they would have seen a tall, slender girl enter. She wore a faded black T-shirt above artfully slashed jeans and with her straight, black hair and pale features, cut a striking, darkly fey figure. Had they been looking, they would certainly have noted the reaction of the barman, which was one of joy.

There was a marked resemblance between the pair and any observer would have been forgiven for thinking them related. In actual fact they weren't. It was just that their species boasts far less genetic diversity than our own.

She crossed to the bar, her smile mirroring the barman's. They clasped hands and, as they did so, the flesh of their respective digits seemed to ripple, to flow together like viscous liquid. In an instant the outline of entwined fingers had shifted and blurred, the skin fusing so that they were joined by a shared appendage. The melding lasted just a few seconds, but in that brief space an entire conversation had taken place, without a single word being spoken.

"You came!"

"Did you doubt me?"

"No, of course not," he assured her, *"but this place... You have no idea what it's been like living here. They're primitives, utter primitives."*

"Hush. You won't have to worry about it for much longer." She emanated comforting waves of reassurance.

"You brought the crystals?" The elation which welled up and spread from him was overpowering. *"Thank you, thank you so much. I can finally escape from this barbaric backwater."*

The link faded, their fingers once more gaining definition and separating. She handed across a small cloth pouch, the sort of thing in which a jeweller might carry loose gemstones, but the crystals it contained were far more precious than any diamond.

"So you were involved in that drugs thing that's been all over the news!" Billy exclaimed, clearly impressed.

"Yes," Terry replied wearily. "Three months I've been working on this bloody story."

"And you never said a thing? All the evenings we've sat and jawed over a pint or three and you never mentioned it once!"

"How could I? Biggest drugs bust the Midlands has ever seen. Biggest story I've ever had a sniff at. Wasted. Three months of my life, of sweat and toil, mixing with thugs and killers and risking discovery at any time... all for nothing." Terry sighed and took another sip from the black brew in front of him. He drank from habit, not because the taste was growing on him in any way. "Nothing ever happens around here, you know? I mean, I'm a journalist – I *need* things to write about for goodness sake. I finally get a lead on a huge story, my big break, and it all blows up in my face. How was I supposed to know that another journalist had infiltrated them, was working on *my* story?" His rant ran down for the moment into hyper-ventilation and a glare.

"But you can still salvage something from this, can't you? I mean, you were there after all," Billy said.

"Oh yes, sure. You saw the papers this morning – plastered

over every front page: 'My Life with the Drug Barons'. What do you reckon I should call my story: 'I Was There Too'?"

"You'll sell it somewhere," Billy said, without a hint of conviction.

Kings, geniuses, eccentrics, balloon festivals and even the whole of parliament crop up in Northampton's rich and colourful history, which might be what attracted the Xar. Northampton is a town accustomed to the unusual, and the Xar certainly qualify. Tiny winged beings that resemble beetles and are about the size of a small pinhead, the Xar are a parasitic race who burrow unnoticed into a host, working their way to the Brain. Here they settle, gaining nutrients from the cerebral fluids and stimulus from their ability to siphon off sensory input. As they grow more established and more accustomed to their host, they are able to influence its actions without the carrier ever being aware.

The Xar is not a perfect parasite and after a while its presence kills the host, who subsequently displays all the symptoms of having suffered a fatal brain aneurysm.

Fortunately the Xar are not numerous; only one has ever visited Earth, where it has been for the last ten years. It came to Northampton and had worked its way through three hosts. The third of these, a self-confident male with a penchant for leather jackets and cigarettes, had proven surprisingly strong-willed, refusing to stop smoking; though the Xar had at least persuaded him to swap to menthol cigarettes. The alien liked the green packaging. This man had eventually broken, as they all did, and now lay dead in a nearby alley – if the body hadn't already been discovered – while the Xar was in the Bear, sizing up its fourth terrestrial host.

"Damn it, why can't something *happen* around here?" Terry exploded, slamming down his glass and inadvertently crushing a small bug that was about to bestow upon him a slow and lingering death.

"Are you really enjoying that?" Billy wondered, eyeing Terry's glass and its treacly contents with obvious suspicion.

"No, not really."

"Let me get you a pint of something drinkable."

"Thanks." Force of habit made him take one final quaff of the medicinally flavoured beer before passing it across.

Billy was already standing and on his way to the bar, so he failed to see his friend's eyes glaze over in a fixed, blank-faced stare that the barman would have been proud of.

Instantly, Terry was somewhere else. In contrast to the familiar dinginess of the Bear he was suddenly engulfed in brightness. Everything was gleaming white and sparkling. For a terrifying split-second his mind froze, unable to assimilate the abrupt change in surroundings and refusing to register anything meaningful. Then, mercifully, perception began to adjust and he was able to discern recognisable features – walls, a desk or worktop... and a wild-eyed man with flowing grey hair and white lab coat. The stranger looked disconcertingly familiar. In fact, replace the lab coat with robes and he looked a lot like the wizard on the badge of a certain beer.

"Are you supposed to be Gandalf?" Terry blurted.

"What? Oh, you mean the beer badge. I had a lot of fun posing for that – dressing up and everything. No, not even a wizard I'm afraid; just a scientist."

A scientist? Images from the *Back to the Future* movies flashed through his mind.

"So why Gandalf?"

"Well, it was that or Merlin... and Gandalf seemed more in vogue at the time."

"Look, forget all that," Terry said, abruptly remembering to feel indignant. "What's going on and where the hell am I?"

"Yes, I suppose you are owed an explanation." The other sighed. "But time is short, so this will have to be brief. You're familiar with the concept of other realities?"

"Well..."

"Come on, come on. I presume your world went through the usual progression – string theory, super gravity, membrane theory?"

"That does sound vaguely familiar," admitted Terry.

"*Vaguely*? Dear, dear me, what on Earth do they teach you on your Earth?"

Not enough, it would seem.

The man shook his head. "You'll just have to accept that other realities *do* exist; in infinite numbers come to that, and you are currently in one: mine to be precise. The reason you're here is simple. We are facing something of a problem. In our world, the human race has managed to come up with a most ingenious way of killing itself off – a nano-virus: microscopic self-replicating robots, not much bigger than a natural virus, and they're out of control.

"They infect an individual, breaking down the normal cellular structure and using the components to create countless duplicates of themselves. The body then dies, releasing the nano-virus spores, allowing them to move on and infect more victims. Our whole world's resources have been dedicated to stopping them, but to no avail.

"Finally our computers identified a compound so toxic, so corrosive, that it can literally melt the nanospores as soon as they enter a body, destroying them completely."

"And this compound is...?" Terry prompted, growing increasingly concerned about the way all this was headed.

"Your blood."

"What?"

"Oh, not your blood in its usual state, just at this specific time... at least, so we assume. Have you eaten anything today?"

"Ehm...yes, a curry," he then admitted. "Chicken vindaloo."

"That's it! A unique dish of noxious fire unknown in any other reality we've encountered, containing ingredients and spices found in very few and unfortunately not in our own. When combined with certain other elements, which we included in the recipe of Gandalf's Revenge, it produces the required compound, which will have filtered into your bloodstream by now."

"So you're telling me that this corrosive toxin, so deadly that it smears nanobots in an instant, is flowing through my veins?"

"Precisely! That's the whole reason we created Gandalf's Revenge and placed it on your world, knowing that before long someone who had eaten a vindaloo would drink the beer, or vice versa, and so create the compound, at which point, they would be drawn here. It just happened to be you."

"Lucky old me."

"How much beer did you drink, by the way?"

"About half a pint, I think."

"My goodness, then we really *don't* have much time." As he spoke, transparent bands materialised, wrapping around Terry's arms, legs, neck and body, holding him motionless. Even as he thought to struggle a hypodermic was pressed to his arm and he watched in fascination as the syringe behind it proceeded to fill with blood. His blood.

"This will give us enough. From this single sample we can isolate the compound, which will then act as a template, enabling us to synthesise a serum and save our people. You have the undying gratitude of an entire world. Statues will be erected in your honour, though you will never know it, of course. After all you've done, we could never allow you to be considered mad in your own world, so you will remember none of this *on your return...*" The last words became faint as the scene faded.

"But I want to remember. I'm a journalist! I *must* remember," Terry tried to call out. Too late.

Suddenly he was back in the Bear, staring into the too-close face of a concerned Billy.

"Are you all right, mate? You blanked out for a minute there."

"Yes, yes, I'm fine." There was something hovering at the edge of his thoughts, something important, which he had to remember. Before him sat a full pint of beer. That was right –

Billy had gone to the bar and then... but still the thought eluded him.

"What's that on your arm? Looks like an insect bite."

"Mm? Probably." He glanced at the puncture wound and for a moment he almost had it, but the thought slipped away and continued to tantalise, just out of reach.

"So this girl you hooked up with," Billy persisted, still eager to hear more of his friend's recent adventure, "turns out she was a cop?"

"Caz? Yes." If only Billy would shut up and let him think.

"And you didn't suspect?" Clearly he had no intention of shutting up.

"Had no idea." Whatever the thought had been, it was gone. With a sigh, Terry turned his attention back to the conversation. "Makes you wonder if there really was a drug racket at all. Sometimes I think we were just a bunch of reporters and cops running around and creating the whole damned thing between us."

Talking about it was helping. Whoever said something about a problem shared being halved or whatever, knew a thing or two. Terry felt some of the tension and gloom slip away as he unburdened himself.

"This Caz, did you...?" The words tailed off as Billy let his eyebrows do the talking.

"No; wish I had though. She was really fit and there was something about her; an edginess, a sense of the exotic... She was exciting, intriguing..." For a writer, he was finding it embarrassingly difficult to express himself.

"Maybe you'll see her again when this is all over."

He shook his head. "No chance. Even the police are being really cagey about who she is and which department she works for. Some hush-hush unit; that was my impression. Caz probably wasn't even her real name. No, I'll never see her again."

Unknown to Terry, there was a good reason why the police were so vague about the lady in question: they had no idea who she was either. One of their own, certainly. Spook, was the general consensus; MI-something-or-other. Once all the loose ends were in hand, she promptly vanished.

Kazaquah-7 Che had already left the earth's surface and was preparing to leave orbit permanently. Terry would have been in for another shock had he ever succeeded in his more amorous designs; Kazaquah-7 Che was male. Members of his race just happened to bear a close physiological resemblance to slim and willowy human females.

This latest mission had proven highly satisfying. Not only had he managed to smash the entire distribution network, rounding up everyone that mattered, he had also traced the off-world supply chain all the way back to its source and, in doing so, prevented an entire world from falling prey to the most invidious and addictively lethal narcotic this section of the galaxy had ever seen. To cap it all, he had succeeded in convincing the local authorities that this was just another sizable but routine drugs bust. Of course, with all the rivalry and tight-lipped secrecy that existed between different security and law enforcement departments, establishing his credentials with the police had been the easiest part of all. Yes, an excellent result in every sense.

He had even enjoyed the female alias. Teasing that over-sexed journalist had been the most fun he'd had on a job in years.

Kazaquah-7 Che issued the appropriate command and his ship leapt to life. The engines flared, boosting him homeward, leaving behind a brief-lived arc of ionised particles as the drive grazed the Earth's atmosphere. Aware of this, the detective smiled. One final deception: somebody below would probably mistake it for a shooting star.

"Anyway," Terry said. "I'm absolutely knackered. Think I'll head off while I still can. Thanks for this, Billy, it really has helped."

"Pleasure, mate. Oh, before you go, I got you this." He

produced a flimsy plastic bag – one of those non-biodegradable things churned out by the supermarkets that are slowly strangling the planet.

"What is it?"

"Well, you know that shoe collection at the museum you're always going on about?"

"Yes."

"Seems they're having to downsize the collection, due to funding cutbacks. They've had to get rid of a load of shoes. Rather than just sling them out, they sold 'em off."

"You're kidding."

"No, seriously. This sort of thing's happening all over; Warwick Castle even had to sell off some of their swords to help with running costs, so I guess this is just Northampton's equivalent. I know how much you love that collection, so I got you these." He held the bag out to Terry.

Could it be… *would* it be…? Terry took the bag with suddenly trembling hands. This day, the worst of his entire life, might be on the brink of turning into the very best. He peered inside.

No, of course it wasn't. No Pete Murphy, no red lining, not even any leather, just a pair of trainers; white with blue flashes.

"I know they're not much," Billy was saying, "which is probably why they were so cheap, but you've gone on about that fucking shoe collection so much…"

"Thanks," Terry said "I… I don't know what to say." Nor did he.

Terry was almost home, having refused Billy's offer of a lift. He gazed up into the cloudless night sky, focusing on what appeared to be a shooting star. "Why can't I get a break, just once?" he murmured at the heavens.

The star disappeared.

Having stepped inside and locked out the rest of the world, he made himself a coffee – he defied the caffeine to keep him awake *this* night – turned on a single table lamp and sat in the gloom, spurning the TV. The trainers rested on the seat beside him, still in their bag. What was he supposed to do, wear them? He bet they didn't even fit. Only one way to find out. He took them out and wriggled his feet into them. Actually, they were really quite comfortable. He stood up and flexed his toes. Yes, not bad at all.

"Where would you like to go?" said a voice out of nowhere.

Terry jumped and looked around. "What?"

"Where would you like to go?" the calm, androgynous voice repeated. It seemed to be coming from the vicinity of his feet. He stared down at the trainers and said, "Is that you?" not caring how absurd he sounded.

"I am a Klevtch bi-polar transport module. Please state your desired destination."

Terry laughed. "Billy, this is fucking amazing! What is it, a tiny mike stuck on to the shoe somewhere?"

"Please state your destination."

No wonder Billy had given him the trainers – always the practical joker, though this was something else. "All right," he said, deciding to play along, "where can you take me?"

"Anywhere you wish."

"*Anywhere?*"

"Absolutely anywhere you command. All you have to do is speak aloud the name of the desired destination."

"Sounds great… and how fast can you go?"

"Travel is instantaneous."

"Wow! Anywhere *and* instantaneous? It doesn't get much better than that. Well then, let me see…" Where should he ask for? Tropical island, bank vault, a Parisian brothel? Terry was enjoying himself now, something he really hadn't expected to do today. He wondered how long Billy intended to keep this up. "Before we go, one question," he said on impulse. "How exactly did a… Kevitch…?"

"Klevtch," the shoes corrected.

"Klevtch binary transport module get into a Northampton museum's shoe collection?"

"Bi-polar," the trainers corrected again. "This system was abandoned, still configured for Terran camouflage mode, following the assassination of my former owner..."

Before the shoe could say anymore there came a loud knocking at the door.

"Mr Wainwright? It's the police. My name's Detective Sergeant Jacks."

Terry's fragile good mood evaporated. "Oh Hell!" he said.

DS Jacks could have done without this. Normally he'd have left it to the day shift, but the higher-ups were clamouring for results on this narcotics bust, preferably yesterday. So he'd been told to bring the so-called journalist back in. Quite why the dayshift had let him go in the first place was anyone's guess. At this rate the man would be suing them for harassment.

Mind you, he could understand why they wanted to talk to this Wainwright fellow again. He'd read the man's statement and didn't believe a word of it. Nobody could be *that* stupid.

Jacks didn't break in, of course he didn't. The door was open. Unfortunately the flat was also empty. Which was odd, because the DS could have sworn that he'd heard a man's voice seconds before he broke... ehm, *went* in.

Terry Wainwright was never seen again. All that greeted DS Jacks inside the flat was the faintest whiff of brimstone.

Mano Mart

Andy West

My mind wandered.

Even judged by our own aspirations, we are but half-men. I forget who said that now. Nietzsche, perhaps. I read it second hand in a book about cultural evolution, where the quote was deployed to emphasise that men are not the free agents they believe themselves to be. Apparently we donate half or more of our consciousness to rampant cultural machines. I used to think one who could reclaim that half would be an immensely powerful thinker. Now I know better.

"I was subject number five. Don't ID me."

"Okay okay. I said I wouldn't. But you know what really happened, right?"

We had to raise our voices above the roar of traffic; a multi-coloured river of speeding metal connected the nearby Northampton ring-road to the town centre down the hill.

I resisted the temptation to say 'yes' and gazed at the Eleanor cross. The ancient monument rose against a background of majestic trees on the other side of the torrent of cars. Of course the actual cross at the top was missing; knocked off during a battle in 1460.

"I didn't say I witnessed everything directly. You mentioned three thousand pounds?"

"If I get detailed descriptions. Dates and times. The others are too frightened, and someone in authority is covering up."

We were both sweating. With the heat of the afternoon sun on us and the fumes and noise from this damned traffic, it'd be hard to think back to moonlight and chill winter. The location was my choice though. I'd forbidden the reporter to record me; the din was insurance that would rob my voice of much character.

"Okay."

Justin's lips briefly compressed. He opened his laptop, placing it between us on the bench. I liked his name, it reminded me of 'justice'. I notice word similarities all the time nowadays, it's become an obsession.

We thought we'd taken our own justice, blood justice, but I was still alone and still out of work; most of us were.

"So, it's a matter of public record that Professor Merrill came here to do research on this language, errm... proto-Sapiens. Yet why did he pick Northampton?"

"Most places he took data from were exotic. Syria, southern Iraq, East Africa, Rome, India, China, you know, cradle of civilisation type locations. Or from 'roots' kind of populations, Aboriginals and American Indians and such. But only able to afford just one data-point for the whole UK, apparently Northampton was his best bet."

Justin's brows rose. "But nothing ever happens here."

"No, not now. It's a backwater and that's helpful. It means the noisy confusion of modern overlays are easier to strip out. Like if most of this traffic disappeared, we'd be able to hear each other better. He picked old families too, people long rooted hereabouts."

Justin frowned. "I'm not technical. Do you understand enough of the late Professor's work to clue me up?"

"Well I'm no linguist either. But I picked up quite a bit during the sessions and I've done a lot of research since. Nothing better to do, you see."

Justin nodded and typed more words than I spoke. No doubt he was noting my unkempt appearance, those haunted eyes that stared back every morning from my bathroom mirror. 'Shabby layabout on benefits, possibly on drugs.' Once I was a top-notch systems analyst.

"It's speculated that there was once a *single* language, from which all other languages evolved as Homo Sapiens Sapiens, that's us modern humans by the way, spread across the globe from an origin in East Africa."

"Ah… hence this language was named *proto-Sapiens*."

"Yep. Or *proto-World* is another name. Now back in the eighties and nineties a lot of work was done to discover this language…"

"Hang on! How the heck can you do that? No one's spoken it for what… ten thousand years?"

"Probably over a hundred thousand. You compare all known languages phonetically, then you find common roots that lead backwards. By lining those up with known population distributions and migrations, from other sources of course, you end up with a tree whose branches get less and less further back in time. Right back where modern man emerged, you get the single trunk of proto-Sapiens."

Justin's face was a map of scepticism.

"All this from phonetics? Like they use to teach kids at school?"

I could see he'd need examples. Simple examples. Not just for him, but for his readers.

"Phonetics is very powerful. I could teach you Northamptonian in just days using phonetics."

"Okay, you're pulling my plonker now. There's no such language as Northamptonian."

I smiled at fond memories. "There's even subdivisions of it. I knew people who joked about the differences in speech between Far Cotton and Jimmy's End." The areas were only streets apart; streets my lover grew up in. "And then there's the extra tenses of Kingsthorpe, *I've been and am and gone and done it.*"

Justin's brow rippled. "Does that still mean you *did it?* Or something else?"

"I think it means you emphatically did it, or maybe you regret having done it." I pulled out pen and paper, and scribbled two words. "Say this."

"Brain ace."

"Congratulations. You just said *brown house* in Northamptonian."

He looked impressed.

"Okay, so phonetics is powerful. But how far back did they get? Can the experts speak proto-Sapiens? That'd be pretty cool."

The fond memories turned bitter. My lover had abandoned me. I couldn't blame her.

Often these days I perceive ancient habits lingering in the streets, like the stale malty odour from the Carlsberg brewery which fills the sleepy hollow that is Northampton. I see the routes of shepherds who drove their flocks into market, still preserved in modern roads. I hear echoes of plainsong from stone churches founded by Saxons. I sense industrious activity behind the walls of converted redbrick factories where shoes were once made. I guess it's a blend of knowledge and hallucination. I fancy even now I can see the colourful court of Edward I kneeling between those trees, praying for the soul of Eleanor of Castille. The king escorted his beloved wife's body from Harby near Lincoln to Westminster Abbey, resting overnight at twelve locations. As a dedication to her memory, he caused a grand monument topped by a cross to be raised at each place. The final one was at Charing Cross in London, but that spot is inside the railway station somewhere now, recalled only by a plaque on the outside.

"So can they speak it?" Justin's gaze was puzzled and expectant.

"They didn't get that far. They got a couple of dozen words, plus additional roots that contained unresolved vowels, along with some structure. So *woman* is *kuna*, *child* is *mako*, *finger* or *one* is *tik*, water is *akwa*."

Justin seemed disappointed. "Pretty basic. And how come they don't sound at all like the modern equivalents? Except maybe I'd make the link of *aqua* for water."

"Yep. Basic. Hence the frustration of many linguists including our late and unlamented Professor Merrill, and the beginning of a very dangerous path. But the words *do* make sense, even to amateurs, if you have the background data. You see, language evolved through many parallel paths and often criss-crossed itself over the millennia."

"I guess I'll need one detailed example then. A simple one!"

"Right. We'll take dog, which is *kuan* in proto-Sapiens. *Kuan* evolved through proto-Indo-European *kwon* to Phrygian *can* and then Latin *canis*, and so into English *canine*. See, you do recognise that! Simultaneously it branched to Greek *kuon*, then eventually to English *hound* and German *hund*. Early Germanic languages often migrated 'k' sounds to 'h' sounds. There are many other routes, such as proto-Uralic *kuina* for *wolf* to Mongolian *qani* for *wild dog* and old Turkish *qanchiq* for *bitch*. The Far East ended up with shortened versions like the Chinese *kou* and Korean *ka*. The original pronunciation is known quite well because the pronunciation of every surrounding language is known quite well too."

"Okay. Got that." Justin glanced at his watch. "We'll need to move on from this technical stuff to the jui... the action events that'll engage readers. But how come *none* of those words sound like *dog?*"

The juicy bits. Blood and gore. I remembered that the gore was black in moonlight.

"Well, that's a part of the modern confusion problem I mentioned earlier. You can't always recognise the real roots immediately. You have to strip everything back real carefully. *Dog* is from Old English *dogge* from Anglo-Saxon *docga*, and is probably the word for a particular *breed* of large and powerful canine. In early English, *dogge* came to be applied generically. It eventually displaced *hound* and pushed that word into specialised meanings, so a 'hunting dog', or greyhound, bloodhound etc. But once you know what you're looking for you can often make the connections, for instance going back to *kuna*, that turns out to be the root for *queen*, and also our word *ten* stems from *tik*."

"I see. That makes sense. So as part of his world research on this lingo, Prof Merrill sets up shop in Northampton. But what did he hope to achieve? And how?"

"Ultimately he wanted to blow away the mists of uncertainty surrounding proto-Sapiens. It's the how that caused trouble. You see, progress had stalled after the early years. It seemed the detailed language was just too elusive for phonetic backtracking to capture, even when allied to DNA analysis of historic populations and also archaeological evidence, like hieroglyphs, or pictograms with known linguistic associations from later times. And doubts arose. The competing hypothesis of language multi-genesis gained a lot of ground. Academic stakes were high and eminent linguists supporting the proto-Sapiens theory got pretty damn worried. What they needed was a new approach, a big breakthrough, and Professor Merrill promised to deliver."

"Ah. So he's committed to a pre-judged result. A significant result too, and he needs it quickly. So maybe he's tempted to take shortcuts." A huge truck thundered by, its steel joints clanking and screaming, causing Justin to pause for a couple of seconds. "But what shortcuts could possibly be dangerous? After all, this is just scholarly drilling for words, not real-world drilling, like for oil."

"That's the perfect analogy, in fact. He did drill. He drilled into people's heads using deep hypnosis."

Understanding dawned across Justin's features. "So *that's* how all the weird stuff came in!" He tapped frantically on his laptop.

Weird. A mild word for such fundamental madness, like a hippy-trip that'll soon go away. But it never does.

I still go to Danes Camp. It's even better there after the sacrifice; that calm circle, the whispering leaves, a strong sense of brooding history. I imagine the angel flying there, and I get some relief.

"So is ancient language stored in people's heads then?"

"No. No it's not like that at all, though detractors frequently claimed Merrill was chasing junk science of that sort. No. Before his interest in proto-Sapiens the Professor uncovered a map of pathways in the language centre of the brain that were semi-hardwired, a kind of 'default setting' if you like. He realised that he could explore these pathways using test sounds played to subjects under a very deep form of hypnosis. By comparing responses from many subjects around the world, who were all racially identified via genetic tests, he sought to open up a whole new front into the study of proto-Sapiens. His theory was that the default map must surely be aligned to language pre-cursors and to the subset of sounds and structure necessary for *all* language. Hence the map would also help him navigate to proto-Sapiens, the root tongue that was once the *only* expression of the brain's language centre."

"Ah. So he didn't expect his subjects to suddenly spout proto-Sapiens. He expected to go away for a year or so, compare all the results and run a whole bunch of statistics, then declare the field wide open for progress, showing a new pearl or two of proto-Sapiens for proof. After which everyone would be happy for another dozen years and maybe he'd get a Nobel Prize."

"Exactly." Justin had clearly done pieces on scientists before. He was not unfamiliar with their narrow motives.

"And he ignored the risks to get to his prize."

"Right again." And had an arrogant unconcern for consequences regarding pronouncements or process, which sadly occurred much too often.

I slipped a suppressant into my mouth and wondered whether Justin had the money on him. I could swallow without water; a trick easily acquired when you take as many pills as I do.

"So how many subjects were there, and how long did the research go on for?"

"Over two hundred volunteered, but we were whittled down to about thirty after DNA testing. You see, Northampton's a nowhere kind of place now, but the parliament was held here in 1131 and the town almost became the capital of England. For millennia prior to that this area was a hub of great events. Various races fought their way here, settling down and leaving echoes in the current population. The name of the town comes from *Hamm Tun*, the Anglo-Saxons called it their *home town* after they recaptured the place from the Vikings. The front line between a reduced England and the Viking Danelaw ran right past here, along what's now the A5. Of course centuries before those kingdoms it was the Romans who built the original road. They first settled where the Northampton suburb of Duston now stands and spread south, but before even that the Iron Age Celts had an important centre here which…"

"All right, all right. Enough with the history, I can grab that off the Internet. Get back to Merrill's research programme."

But the history sucked at me. I found it difficult to disengage and return to the real world. The thought of three thousand pounds helped.

"Well, the professor wanted the purest racial threads he could get that lead back into those old populations. I think to better avoid the confusions of modern intermingling, but I also heard him mention that any potential differences between the threads would be very informative too. Point is he could get them all in the one place; Northampton is perfect. Anyhow I ended up in the Scandinavian bin. My family's been in south Northants at least four generations on both sides, we're English through and through, but maybe we're really descended from those rampaging guys who came in long-ships. I guess that's why I've got blue eyes. There were also bins for Celtic and Latin and Anglo-Saxon."

"What about Normans? They invaded us too, William the conqueror and all that."

"I thought you didn't want history. *Normans* just means

70

northmen. They were originally Vikings who bullied the king of France into giving them a chunk of his country. They learned French and gave themselves fancy names, bred with the locals some. Then 150 years later invaded England. So mainly Scandinavian origin I guess, though the French component was already multi-flavoured by then."

Justin smirked. No doubt he was thinking about French women and breeding, especially breeding with foreigners. Good job I was heavily suppressed or I'd be thinking about it a lot more than Justin.

"It took a few weeks to sort the bins out. Then the hypnosis sessions started. I think Merrill must've had trouble at some of his other locations because the whole operation was hush-hush from the start. We were told we wouldn't get our money if we ever talked about what went on. And the recession was biting, you see. I'd not had an IT contract in months. The professor's assistants spouted about 'academic integrity' and 'unbiased input' and the need to avoid sensationalism, but it was only much later that we thought to question the need for secrecy."

"I'll get the paper to sniff out what they can about Merrill's work abroad. We've got a number of representatives and contacts in Iraq and the Middle East. It'll make a nice change for them from religious bigotry and suicide bombs. How long did the sessions go on for?"

"A long time. Once a week for almost six months."

"And when did the weird stuff start? I heard about midnight blood ceremonies and orgies and people foaming at the mouth and…"

I waved my hand to cut him off. "There was none of that. At least not until… you know."

"Ah. I guess we'll get to that later then."

"I started to feel strange after only a few weeks though, jumpy, emotional. It was harder to concentrate on anything complex. My libido went up, but my temper rose with it; I was angry much more frequently. I didn't connect these symptoms to

71

the hypnosis. A girl at work had been trying to catch my eye. I started to flirt back, more than flirt, and I thought the anger was with myself for being so weak. Then a few of the others said they were often tired and squabbled at home. The professor said we'd be fine once the sessions were complete, and he doubled our money."

"Whoa, hang on. Let me catch up."

He wasn't just writing my words, he was writing my mood. Perhaps anger was starting to leak past the pills. Perhaps it showed in my eyes. I thought of Danes Camp again, where we'd left the angel. It's misnamed in fact, the place is actually an Iron Age fort and also has pre-historic roots; just a mile away there's a Neolithic camp too. But local tradition has it that the fort was reused by the Danish branch of the Vikings as a front-line post against the English. Northampton was certainly a military centre for them, they fortified the town in the early tenth century.

Despite the warmth I shivered, remembering a frigid night, blood and a Viking rite… The chant started in my mind… *Kama ksi, ksi uto kati-mano, chuna shym, mano mart…*

"Okay, carry on."

With an effort I switched my concentration back to the narrative.

"After five months there was the incident with subject 23. I now know she's Lisa by the way, from the Anglo-Saxon bin. She was found in the early morning at the bottom of that monument there, clinging to the stone, drenched from the night's rain and muttering strange words. She'd almost frozen to death. Later on she said she was praying for Eleanor. Well her husband had left her the week before and everyone figured it was mainly due to that, a breakdown or something. It seems unbelievable now, but we carried on with the programme."

Justin fished a garish can out of his bag and offered it to me. I shook my head. Although I was thirsty in this heat I didn't want those vile chemicals on my tongue. I've rediscovered the joys of water, though the chlorinated stuff from the tap is no good.

Justin drank deeply, then tried to stifle a large belch.

"Looking back, I remember that Merrill seemed excited. I now think that he viewed the incident as a sign of success, a sign that he was breaking through our cultural layers to reach something primitive beneath. And we subjects failed to realise that we'd got the causation backwards regarding Lisa. Her husband hadn't been able to cope with her strange behaviour for months, that's why he walked out."

"Something primitive beneath?" echoed Justin.

"No one knows what the professor did. I'm not even sure *he* knew. But somehow he weakened the social norms that modern people adhere to. Cultural imperatives from earlier times can suddenly ambush us, take hold of us. As occasionally can primitive instincts from earlier still, from perhaps before there was *any* culture. We might just be embarrassing, but we can be violent or strange, very frightening to normal people. Some of us started to hallucinate. In my case I also became obsessed with history. I'm not sure whether my intellect is trying to feed the hunger of my new instincts or trying to cure itself somehow, maybe neither. Sometimes we utter curious sounds and foreign words too, perhaps echoes of the stuff played to us under hypnosis."

"The one language? Proto-Sapiens?"

"Sometimes, I guess. But we'd all read up on proto-Sapiens by now, even though we weren't supposed to as that might contaminate the programme. So it's probably regurgitation."

"Maybe." Justin's eyes glittered. I had a feeling that the *maybe* would disappear from his story.

"About eight or nine days after the Lisa incident, subject 16, a male, was arrested for attempted rape and subject 7, a farmer, was found drinking blood neat from the slit throat of a lamb."

Justin ignored the sweat trickling down his brow as his fingers danced over the keyboard. No doubt he was embellishing already. I waited for him to catch up.

"So that's when you reported Merrill to the authorities?"

"Yeah. We all met up and needless to say we pulled out of the programme. We realised at last that he'd damaged us all and we demanded an investigation, and some kind of cure or compensation. I never did get another contract and I couldn't have held one down if I had. I just can't concentrate anymore. But our attitude then was just another naïvety. We hadn't grasped that our condition would worsen, or that a cure was impossible."

"So when did you decide to errm... I mean..."

"No one *decided* as such. Weeks went by. Prof Merrill was asked a few questions but nothing seemed to come from that. Meanwhile we felt ourselves slipping into madness. Then we heard that Merrill was off back to the States – he's a U.S. citizen. We were frightened he'd get off scot-free, no prosecution, and no compensation for us. We all met up, well, all but the two who were now in prison.

"Fury seemed to mushroom out of nowhere. Yet it wasn't confused or self-conflicting. Everyone knew just what to do, like bees if you disturb their nest. I don't remember much after that, it's a kind of haze."

"The official position is that professor Merrill died of exposure at Danes Camp, under suspicious circumstances."

I laughed. Ugly joy coursed through me. I stopped when Justin's alarm became obvious. No doubt he'd picked up the demented triumph in my tone.

"*Exposure?* Well that's a colossal understatement if ever I heard one."

"Really?" A subtle 'do tell more' tone.

"We all know what happened. *But I'm not saying I was there. We weren't all there.*"

"Right. Of course."

"Danes Camp is an ancient encirclement, inside the park just ten minutes walk back there." I twisted my head over my right shoulder, then paused to gather memories. "That night was cold, deep cold, with a clear sky and a jaundiced moon near full." The land's memories emerged as mist from the dark ditch dug two thousand years before, drifting through the ring of trees surrounding the eerie space.

The chant ran through my head once more, I couldn't get rid of it. No one pre-arranged the words, they just seemed to grow out of darkness and fury: *Kama ksi, ksi uto kati-mano, chuna shym, mano mart...* Muscled arms and bouncing breasts, suits and shirts and skirts torn open or torn off: *Kama ksi, ksi uto kati-mano, chuna shym, mano mart...* Flying tresses and frenzied chant, faster now: *Kama ksi, ksi uto kati-mano, chuna shym, mano mart...* Breath pluming, the flashing arcs of knives in the moonlight.

"Hey!"

Someone was shaking my arm. I was breathing heavily.

"What does it mean?"

Justin's intent face appeared through my confusion. His nose for a story had overcome his apprehension. I must have spoken aloud. His gaze demanded.

"Everyone was smeared with ochre mud," I recalled. Blood of the Earth, *shym-tika*.

"What were you saying, what does it mean?"

I looked out at the passing vehicles, let them drag me back to the modern world.

"*Kama ksi* means *hold knife*, implying also *in the hand.* Then *ksi uto kati-mano* means *knife uncovers bone of man*, or better, *man's bone.* *Chuna shym* is *smell blood.* And *mano mart*, well... that's *man...*"

"Right, right" encouraged Justin. "*Mano*, man. *Mart?*"

"Think French *mort* or Arabic *mawt*. Dead. Via Indo-Aryan *marta*," I added superfluously.

Justin breathed deep and looked down. "Okay. So it wasn't exposure then. Or suicide, there's a rumour of him hung from a tree. But stabbing, a revenge killing, a crime of passion."

"Oh, from a tree. Yes, that too. And exposure, well, *ultimate* exposure."

Justin looked annoyed.

"Hey, are you messing me about?"

I shook my head. "Have you heard of the *blood eagle?*"

Now Justin shook his head.

"Viking execution method. Hold the condemned face down on the ground, then slit the skin down his back to expose the spine. With a chisel, delicately but swiftly detach all his ribs from the backbone. Then pull on each half of the ribcage until it splays like wings out of his back. Subject 17 was a butcher, and in haste we'd all snatched up weapons of every kind."

Justin paled and his mouth sagged open.

"The Vikings pulled out the lungs too, but once they're separated from the diaphragm there's only tens of seconds before suffocation, worse to leave them in place. Despite the loss of pressure, very shallow and swift breathing delays death a couple of minutes more." Naked flames revealed lungs still fluttering with tenuous life. Lisa had brought along some scented torches, she wouldn't be needing them for urban barbecues any more. "Then hang him high, from bound hands above his head, on a long rope thrown over a branch." Merrill swung in a wide circle, a dark angel flying with his new wings, wings that were black with gore under the moon.

Justin croaked, then found his voice. "Man. Fuck. That's extreme. I see what you mean by ultimate exposure." His fingers slowly started up again.

"The professor was tortured for minutes. We're tortured for the rest of our lives. And it was Merrill himself who released the primitive fury that killed him."

"So how come nobody found him? I mean, not one of the public."

"Someone did. A jogger. There'd been a severe frost some time before dawn. Merrill was transformed into a real angel, his wings gleaming white in the early morning sun. But the jogger was a police guy from the main HQ that's just across the ring-road over there." Trees obscured the view, but I pointed anyway. "He takes a run around the park every morning after his night shift. That's how they kept it quiet. I saw the photos when they interviewed me."

"But they haven't arrested any of you?"

"They don't know which of us was there and they don't want a fuss. Perhaps primitive justice suits them too. Anyhow, while charges are held off we've participated in the silence, which means we get no help either. But it doesn't really matter, there *is* no help, except pills." And the sweet sustenance of revenge, of recalling the angel flying. "They know that one day we'll all be inside institutions anyhow. Some sooner, some later. Did you bring my money?"

Justin fished a fat envelope from an inside pocket. "One thousand now, one thousand when I've written it up and plugged in more detail, which you *must* supply when I call, and one thousand on publication."

I must have looked desperate.

"Don't worry, I'll fast-track this story, and it's bound to get published. My editor loves blood, and she can't resist a high level cover-up either."

I watched Justin dwindle down the hill. No free parking spaces anywhere near this bench. No doubt he was looking forward to air conditioning in the civilised environment of his car.

I long to worship… something. But all the recent gods and their priests, benign or banal or terrifying, including God and the Pope, Communism and Karl Marx, Gaia and Gore, the cult of empty celebrities or the cargo of improbable pronouncements that so overwhelm real science, they're all far too new. And people rarely question these cultural machines to which they so willingly donate their minds, the utter lack of truth behind them. My gods are far simpler, truly basic and therefore real. I long for the metallic smell of blood, its name, *shym*, appears often like a whisper inside my head. I scent women, *kunae*, and long to unleash my lust. Yet maybe I do have a priest: revenge.

We are half-men, but what is the other half? For most of us it is the careless cultural machines. For me, it is the beast.

What We Sometimes Do, Without Thinking

Mark West

I got the email on Tuesday, telling me that Eva had committed suicide. It came from Lynn, a well-meaning busybody who'd created a Facebook group for my school year. She remembered that Eva and I'd something going for a while and decided to pass on her condolences to me. The news made me reel, not because Eva particularly meant anything to me anymore, but because it was shocking that someone my age had died and by her own hand. Lynn didn't have any more details, thankfully, but promised to keep me updated.

I wanted to email her back, to assure her that an update wouldn't be necessary, but I didn't.

In 1983, I was fourteen years old, I lived with my Mum in a little terraced house and I'd just started a school where I knew no one. I'd never really drunk before, I'd only kissed four girls and I was desperate to feel a bit of tit. I liked to think I was fairly worldly but I knew I wasn't - I loved "Star Wars" and Blondie, DangerMouse and American detective shows and had just discovered the benefits of hair gel. I liked my Sta-Prest trousers, I virtually lived in my Harrington jacket and I thought my skinny red leather tie was the dogs bollocks.

We'd moved to Kettering when Mum discovered Dad's inability to keep his knob out of someone other than his wife, leaving my childhood home and

79

friends back in Rothwell. I hit my new school just after the Easter break and stood out badly that first day, my uniform so pristine that it immediately marked me out as a newcomer, even if my vacant staring at the timetable didn't. I wanted to cry and only two things stopped me – one was that if I did, I'd get beaten up and two, I'd cried so much recently I doubted I'd ever be able to shed a tear again.

Neil Dawson was the first kid who spoke to me. I was trying to figure out how the rooms were numbered and he took one look at me and my sharp uniform and said, "New?"

Thankfully, he was in my form and made me sit next to him, which wasn't difficult as it appeared nobody normally sat there. As the day wore on and I tried my hardest to look like I belonged, I realised that Neil didn't quite. At first glance, his uniform was spot on – trousers, white shirt, tie, blazer – but it was all slightly off somehow, as if the colour grading was out by a fraction or his stuff was the tiniest amount too small for him. His bookbag was the same, a tired old army surplus rucksack that he'd covered with names of bands that I only vaguely recognised – AC/DC, The Cramps, all manner of stuff.

We walked out of school together.

"So what made you move to Kettering then?"

"My Mum," I said and realised that it would kill the conversation to tell him the story. "Well, my Mum and Dad."

"Where did you come from?"

"Rothwell." We walked in silence for a while. "So what is there to do around here?"

"The usual, I suppose," he said, "youth club, park, school clubs. I like to go train chasing."

"What's that?"

"It's great, it's a new thing I've invented." He grinned broadly, as if insanely proud of himself.

"Is it like trainspotting?"

"No. Listen, you've got a bike, yeah?"

"Of course." What a stupid question, what kind of Joey did he think I was?

"Do you know the railway bridge at the end of the Headlands?"

I shook my head. I'd explored my new neighbourhood a little, but I didn't really want to get to know the place, I just wanted to be back in Rowell. "I haven't got any further than the fire station."

"Near enough, keep going from there and you can't miss it. Meet me there at six, on your bike and I'll take you train chasing."

We reached Hawthorn road. "I'm this way," I said.

"Somebody has to be," he said and laughed. "See you at six."

The first thing Mum asked me when I got in was whether I'd got on all right. I told her I had and that I thought I'd made a new friend. She seemed really pleased, even though I saw the tears in her eyes as she went "upstairs to sort some stuff out".

When I got home, I felt winded and unready to face the evening. Becca was already in, pottering around upstairs.

"Hey," I called.

"Hi, Adam, how was your day?"

How was it? All I could come up with was, "I've had better." Becca knew about Eva, we'd talked openly of our pasts - though I'd kept a little secret back - but I didn't know how she'd react to my reaction. The news had really taken its toll and, though I never once felt close to tears, I was shaken enough that I didn't feel steady.

Becca came downstairs, pulling her hair back into a loose ponytail. She was wearing shorts and an old t-shirt of mine that was much too large for her, so that Mr Lazy appeared to be the same size as her torso. Her feet were bare. She looked beautiful. "So what happened then?"

"I got an email, from the woman who set up the Facebook site. It seems my friend Eva has killed herself."

"Really? How awful."

"I know; I don't quite know what to say. I mean, it's been probably twenty years since I last spoke to her face-to-face and even through Facebook, it was only a couple of messages to bring each other up to speed with our lives."

"It's terrible," Becca agreed and I could see from the look

81

on her face that she didn't quite remember who Eva was. I decided that was for the best and went upstairs to get changed.

I was at the bridge - past the fire station and Bishop Stopford School - a little before six. Bishops Drive branched off the Headlands to the left and to the right was a footpath that seemed to disappear into a tunnel of trees. The bridge was ahead, with signs warning me about cars, since the road led directly to the golf course. There was nothing on the road now. I rested my racer against the abutment and walked onto the bridge, which looked old but well kept. It was made with dark blue brick, as solid as you like, and the walls on either side were metal plates, with rivets half the size of my hand. At the far end of the bridge, on the west abutment, was a splash of graffiti – 'Look Behind You!' Directly across from it were a ravaged looking tree and some bushes. I leaned against the west wall, looking at the rails and waited.

Neil arrived a few minutes later, as I heard the distinct sound of a train engine approaching. He dropped his bike next to mine and ran onto the bridge.

"It's the 6.05!" he yelled as the rails seemed to sing under the pressure and the engine sound increased. We crossed to the other side and watched as an Intercity 125 came into view. Neil waved until the driver sounded his two-tones and then the train was under us and away.

"Leaves St Pancras at five," he said, "I like to watch it come in. When I leave school, I want to work in London, doing something exciting that I can't do around here."

"That's more plans than me," I said and looked at him, trying to figure out if he was taking the piss or not. My only plan for when I left school was to pass my driving test so that I could drive by my Dad's house and flick my Vees at him. I had no career plan - for fuck's sake, until last year, I still wanted to be a private detective.

"So, let's go train chasing. It's dead simple, come on."

He led me off the bridge and up to the narrow alleyway I'd spotted earlier. Following a gravely path, it led us to an overflow car park at the train station. Another Intercity 125 was idling on the nearest platform.

"We go through the side-gate," Neil said, "but don't let the guard catch you, because then you'll have to buy a platform ticket and they're 20p. I'll

check the timetable and as soon as that train starts to move, we take off."
"Where?"
"Back to the bridge. We race up the alley, get on the bridge and try to get a two-tone off the driver. That means we've won, you see?"
It all clicked into place. "So that's why you call it train chasing?"
He pursed his lips. "Wasn't that obvious?"
I laughed, which made him smile and I stood with my bike whilst he sneaked onto the platform to check the timetable.

I'd always assumed that Eva hadn't tortured herself about the tragedy as much as I did, but I know it still really affected her. She got out of Kettering as quickly as she could, married almost immediately and had a couple of kids, fell into a life she didn't like and ended up a divorcee before she was thirty.

I got all of that from our Facebook catch-up. We never once talked about Neil Dawson.

As stupid as it probably sounds, that first train chase was one of the most exciting things that had ever happened to me.
Neil came running off the platform, grabbed his bike and seemed to turn it even as he was getting on. He opened his mouth but the train started to move and I knew what he'd planned to say. Instead, I quickly turned my bike and we took off across the car park, even as the train noisily eased itself into activity.
Up the slight hill, into the alley, ducking to avoid low branches. The train moving now, the wheels creaking and squealing. The horn sounds once, quickly, as if the driver can see what we're doing. Neil is pedalling fast, off his saddle now, leaning over the handlebars. I stand on my pedals too, my hands finding the lower curves of the handlebars, fingers nowhere near the brake levers. The train is gaining speed and I can see it in flashes through the bushes where the growth is thinnest. The alley is on a slight incline, but I don't feel it, keeping up with Neil easily, though it's been a long time since I've ridden this fast.
"Come on," he yells over his shoulder, "we've got him."
I pump the pedals, giving them everything I've got. I risk a sideways

83

glance at the train and it seems to be behind us, but I know that we haven't got long – two kids on a pair of Raleighs are no match for a modern train.

I see the end of the alley, the square of light that heralds the Headlands. We're really moving now, tyres whistling over the gritty path. We burst out of the alley and bank right and I hope the tarmac isn't greasy. It isn't, and the tyres grip and then we're on the bridge. I hear the clatter as Neil's Grifter hits the ground and, though I'm more careful getting off the racer, I'm not too far behind him.

Neil stands above the line, waving his arm high and wide. When I reach him and start waving too, the train is about a hundred yards away. The driver sees us and nods his head as if in acknowledgement of our success. He waves and Neil yells "Sound the horn", though it's obvious the driver can't hear us.

But the horn does sound, a hearty two-tone that makes me jump and then Neil and I are laughing and suddenly gasping for breath, leaning on the bridge.

"That's what train chasing is," he says.

"That was fucking brilliant."

Neil & I were best mates through that summer of 1983. We train chased and went on bike rides, went to see "Return Of The Jedi" with great excitement at the Ohio cinema on Russell Street and I convinced him to go and see "Octopussy" with me, even though he wasn't a Bond fan.

I thought we'd be friends forever but we moved forms in September and once school had started, Neil and I saw less and less of each other until we only really spoke when we passed in the corridors. I sometimes went to the bridge on the Headlands, hoping to see him there, but I never did.

I went into work on Wednesday feeling odd and dislocated, touched by grief but not quite close enough for it to be completely effective. The morning went by in a haze, making vague entries in spreadsheets and checking on Facebook. Eva's death was getting a lot of attention. I decided to go into town for lunch.

I drove to the Grosvenor centre without thinking and

wasted valuable time going up, trying to find a space. I got one, finally, one level off the roof, facing towards the bus station. I ignored the lifts and went down the dingy concrete staircase, picked up a sandwich and bottle of Coke from Boots and went out into the market place to eat.

The market was noisy and vibrant, full of people lunching, and the pigeons were enjoying a bounty of pickings. I leaned against the wall, watching one of the painted lions and the attention it drew from small children, until I'd finished my sandwich and realised it was time to go back to the office.

As I passed the lifts, one opened and released its cargo of impatient office workers. No-one else was waiting, so I got in and enjoyed a solo ride up to floor five. The doors opened on to an empty foyer. I walked out onto the car park level and saw the man immediately.

He was standing on the wall, not far from my car, looking out over the roadway towards the bus garage.

My stomach rolled as if I was on a vicious fairground ride and I took a couple of deep breaths, completely unsure of what to do next. I reached into the inside pocket of my suit coat and felt the reassuring line of my mobile. Should I ring someone? Who?

The man on the wall and I were the only ones on this level. I didn't think it was a good idea to leave him and go to find someone because, by then, he'd either have got down and I'd look like an idiot or he'd be a smear on the road and people'd be calling me a bastard for leaving him alone.

"You all right, mate?" I called out and, even as the words left my lips, I realised they were stupid. They were also loud and it occurred to me that I couldn't hear anything else now, just the beat of my pulse. I knew I should have heard the road, perhaps a plane, perhaps a train, but there was nothing.

The man didn't move, didn't jump, didn't turn to acknowledge me.

I took a step closer, instinctively holding my arms out in a calming gesture that was completely useless. "Excuse me, are you okay?"

The person shifted slightly and I could see that he wasn't a man at all – a kid, maybe in his late teens, tall, thin and gangly. He was looking towards Mayorhold, completely ignoring me.

"Stupid question, but did you want to get down?"

There was the slightest shake of his head and I took another step forward. The kid didn't move, so I took another step. I was fifty yards from the parked cars. Another step and he held his hand up.

"Do you want me to stop?"

The kid let his arm drop, so I risked another step. "Shall I ring someone, a friend or your parents or the police?"

There was no response, so I took my phone out and unlocked the keypad. The ping was really loud in the oppressive silence.

"I'll ring the police, they should know how to deal with this kind of thing."

The kid held his arm up again and waved his finger – no – at me. My hand hovered, the line ringing, then "Emergency, which service please?"

"Hold on," I said.

"Don't be clever."

"I'm not trying to be, there's a kid on the parapet of the multi-storey, but I don't think he wants me to ring you."

"I'll put you through," said the voice quickly.

The kid shifted his stance, not swaying at all and as he turned his head towards me, I saw that there was something wrong. The left side, nearest to me, seemed fine but there wasn't much of the right side. A terrible dark gouge appeared to take away his nose and right eye and as his head turned, I could see the bus station where I should have seen the right side of his face. It was as if it'd been cleaved away.

"Police," squawked my phone and that the attention of both of us. The kid raised his hand in a half-hearted wave and then stepped into nothing, disappearing from view.

Sound seemed to flood back into my head, but not what I was expecting. Apart from the operator shouting loud enough for me to hear even though my phone was dropping with every heartbeat, it was normal noise - the rush and horns of traffic, the languid sound of a train coming into the station.

I raced to the wall, expecting the worst but when I leaned over there was nothing to see. Cars were moving and nobody was screaming. Nobody was trying to cross the road to see the jumper and there was no crimson smudge across the tarmac.

I was standing where the kid had been. A sign on the wall said 'wet paint' and streaks of it were now on my jacket sleeve. There were no other marks in the paint, because nobody had been standing on this wall.

Trembling, I retrieved my phone and walked back to the car. So this was what grief did to you.

In late October 1983, a new girl moved into my form. Eva Huntingdon was very pretty, quickly made friends and was a real laugh. I got on well with her and fancied her like mad. As Christmas rolled around, we exchanged cards and she put a little kiss in hers, right after her name. Being an idiot, I read it wrong and thought she was interested in me. I got her a necklace, a beaded thing from Claire's Accessories that probably looked awful, but she liked it.

At the Christmas school disco, two momentous things happened. I took Eva as my date and Neil Dawson had his drink spiked.

I'd last spoken to him the week before, on my way across the market square to buy Eva's necklace. He was coming the other way, his Grifter now looking a bit small for him.

"Hey, mate," he said, "off to buy Christmas presents?"

"Yeah."

"Did you fancy coming down to the bridge?"

"Are you still train chasing?"

He must have caught the unbelieving tone in my voice because, for a moment, he looked genuinely hurt, before he smiled broadly and shook his head. "Course not, I just like to watch them go by and imagine myself on there."

"Do you take the numbers too?"

"No," he said and his hand brushed over his left pocket. "Sometimes."

"I'm alright, mate, you go. I'll see you around."

"Yeah," he said and pushed off, "see you around."

At the disco, some dickheads in the fifth year found his drink and poured in some vodka. It wasn't enough to knock him out, but he lost most of his social skills and at the same time was much more confident with girls. So confident, in fact, that he asked Eva to dance with him and she agreed.

It annoyed the hell out of me, watching them dancing - it should have been me and her, not him and her. Then it happened. Neil seemed to be having some trouble. He was starting to sway and I saw that Eva was trying to hold him up. I was just about to go over when he was violently sick, all over her shoulder and down her back. She wasn't the first to scream, that was Sally Pontin who was standing directly behind and got a nice spray up her legs, but pretty soon the whole of the hall was in uproar and Neil was led away by Mr Clarke, who looked less than happy.

When I got home, I didn't tell Becca about my experiences in the car park. She was aware of the Eva thing and how I felt, if I told her I'd seen a kid jumping off the multi-storey, she'd have thought I was going nuts.

There was a letter for me on the dining table. It was postmarked Kettering but I didn't recognise the handwriting. I opened it slowly and saw the school logo through the cheap photocopier paper.

The twenty-fifth anniversary school reunion. Lynn had said she was going to send out proper invites, to make it 'all official, like'.

My eyes drifted past the printed flannel to the small, handwritten phrase at the bottom.

'I think it's time, I'm coming to see you again'.

It wasn't Lynn's writing and I knew that without checking against the signature.

It was Neil's handwriting.

Eva wouldn't let me take her home after the disco - she got Miss Clough to ring her Mum.

Over the weekend, I debated ringing her but what could I say? On the Monday, Neil was the butt of everybody's jokes but he kept his head down and weathered the storm and once it was discovered how he'd got drunk (the fifth formers were spotted with the vodka bottle), people left him alone. Eva, on the other hand, got the sympathy vote.

I asked Eva out on another date, as we were walking home from youth club and she agreed. She let me kiss her as we stood by her front gate and I tried to cop a feel but she was wise to it.

After a very nice weekend, with a trip to the shops and Wickies and a walk to the Rockingham Road pleasure park, she asked me to help her get some revenge.

I was smitten, I was getting plenty of French kissing and there was the distinct promise, in the not too distant future, that I'd get to feel my first tit too.

I agreed.

Becca & I had an Indian, then watched TV until the news came on and she went for a shower. I watched through to the local news but didn't register anything I saw or heard.

Rationally, I knew the handwritten note wasn't really on the invite because Becca hadn't noticed it. Maybe my grief over Eva was stronger than I thought, or maybe it was because of everything that surrounded my going out with Eva – and after – that was now playing on my mind.

Becca came to give me a kiss, smelling of sandalwood and purity. I reached for her and kissed her again.

"Are you coming to bed?"

"Yeah, give me a minute."

I took longer than a minute – I watched Question Time and then had a long, hot shower as if I was trying to wash the past off me. By the time I got into bed, it was past midnight and Becca was fast asleep.

Sleep didn't come to me, only fitful dozing. It was three

o'clock when I woke with a start. Something was tapping on our bedroom window.

I got out of bed, confused all of a sudden. Had I dreamed the noise? Then it came again and I realised it was pebbles, rattling against the window. As soon as that clicked into place, I knew who was there.

I crept to the window, as if stealth might steal away the vision, but the kid from the multi-storey was under the streetlight. He was wearing a Harrington jacket and blue jeans, his trainers bulky and clumsy, the tongue sticking out over the hem of his trousers. He was wheeling around slowly on a bike that, for a split second, I was convinced was a Grifter but then he moved into shadow. In that darkness, I tried to see the kid's head but it wasn't clear enough. The damage was, unfortunately, and from this angle it seemed as if the head had been sheared diagonally, the skull ending just behind his left ear.

Becca rolled over, snuffling my name and I looked at her briefly. When I looked back into the street, the kid and his bike were gone.

Eva's idea of revenge was simple and, in fact, seemed like it might be a bit of a laugh. How wrong we were.

She didn't want to hurt him because we all knew it wasn't his fault and, anyway, I wouldn't have helped her. But she did want to embarrass him.

I decided the bridge would be the best place. I knew he still went there in the mornings, because I'd seen him a couple of times as I headed to school. I rode down the night before, to make sure the 'Look Behind You!' graffiti was still there and checked the bushes across the way. Everything was set.

Eva called for me the next day at eight and, much to Mum's surprise, we left straight away. I led her down to the bridge and showed her the graffiti and our hiding place. We crouched in the bushes, holding hands, almost giggling at how much fun this was going to be.

Neil came along on his too-small Grifter ten minutes later, put his bike against the wall, got out his notebook and leaned on the metal siding. I'd decided we'd go as we heard a train come - he'd be distracted, hopefully, waving at the driver and I thought a couple of banshees coming out of the bushes as a two-tone blared would scare the crap out of him. Job done.

At the same time I heard the first rumble of the Intercity, I caught a flurry of voices, coming up from the golf course. It was too late to worry about them now, so I squeezed Eva's hand and waited for the horn.

Neil did exactly as I thought he would, waving his hand high in the air. He looked away from the railway, down the hill and something crossed his face, concern and doubt and then it was too late.

Eva and I burst out of the bushes, her with a scream, me with a yell and Neil, his attention already distracted, was taken completely unawares. As the two-tone blasted around us, he fell back against the metalwork, his face a mask of real fear. He slid to the ground, holding his hands out against us, as if afraid we were going to harm him. The crotch of his trousers grew dark.

"Oh shit," I said.

There was loud laughter from the path and I turned to see a gang of lads coming up, Chris Nelson at the front and I felt my balls pull tight against me. Nelson went to our school and he was the hardest person I'd ever known. He wasn't afraid of anyone and some of the beatings he'd carried out – so I'd heard – had actually led to some poor kids being sent to A&E. He was fifteen, going on thirty-five and I just knew he was going to be a worse bully as an adult than he was as a school-kid.

"Fuck me," he said, "if it isn't Neil Fucking Dawson. I wanted to have a word with you, after that backchat you gave me at Tymes the other night. And here you are, on the floor with piss in your pants."

His cronies laughed and Eva and I, to my eternal shame, backed up slowly. We only just managed to make it into the bushes before the bullies arrived.

"And so soon after puking all over that bitch," he said, "Dawson, it's like you know it's my birthday. Your life is going to be hell now, you little baby."

He kicked Neil's foot hard as he went by and my old friend began to cry. That just fed Nelson's anger and they beat him up a little. I don't know how much because I turned away, unable either to watch or to jump out and *try to stop them.*

They finished by picking Neil up and dragging him to school, to maximise his embarrassment. One of Nelson's friends picked up the Grifter and threw it into the bushes, where it narrowly missed us.

Eva and I didn't move for a long time. We didn't say much either. In trying to make Neil look a bit stupid, we'd inadvertently set him up for something much, much worse. And we'd done nothing to help.

I got his bike and wheeled it to school.

I don't dwell on the past much, more for my sanity than anything else. As soon as I was able, I moved out of Kettering and ended up in a house-share in Hunsbury that cost me a fortune. I drank a bit too much, but at least I didn't have to face things every day. Neil was everywhere, I saw people who looked like him on the streets, I saw kids on Grifters, I thought I saw him once at the Headlands bridge, it was awful. Thankfully, Mum moved back to Rothwell in the late eighties, when Dad and his latest piece buggered off to Norwich and so I had no reason to go to Kettering, except to pass through. I was relieved beyond measure when they put the A14 in and bypassed the place.

I was fifteen years old when I should have stepped in and helped Neil Dawson. I am now gliding into my forties and I'm as disgusted with myself today as I was back then.

It's been almost twenty five years since I last went into Kettering. I still have nightmares sometimes.

What we'd seen that morning affected both of us. It almost became a living thing, clinging to us with a foetid stench, but neither of us ever talked about it.

I don't know how Neil managed to cope for the couple of months he did. Nelson let everyone know he'd pissed himself and it was only the intervention of several teachers that stopped Neil being paraded around the playground. People taunted him and sniggered, even the little kids, and whenever he felt it was dying down, Nelson fanned the flames again. I never did find out what the backchat was, but the way Nelson went for it, it must have been the snappiest thing ever.

I wanted to help, I really did and I nodded and smiled and said hello to Neil whenever I got the chance. I even called around his house one night, but his Mum said he was out. She looked very sad. I didn't call again.

I don't think I slept at all after seeing the kid on the bike, but I laid in bed until the alarm went off, clicking it quiet before it woke Becca. I went downstairs in the early morning gloom and made a cup of tea.

I sat in the dining room and fired up the laptop, making a quick check of the Facebook site. I had an Inbox message and clicked it open. It was from Lynn.

Ooh, lovey, so sorry to hear the news. I don't know how this has made you feel, but I'm sick to my stomach. So much luv to you, hope to see you soon.

With a mounting sense of unease, I checked the wall messages, but none of them seemed to be anything that could make Lynn feel sick. I went onto the Evening Telegraph site and found the news there. After I read the article, I went back into the kitchen, to check the reunion letter which was pinned to the corkboard.

Neil's comment was still there - *'I think it's time'.*

I read the Evening Telegraph article one more time. Eva Brampton had committed suicide, leaving a partner and two children. The train driver was in shock but unhurt.

"Fuck," I said.

I was going back to Kettering.

It was early March 1984 and I was on my way to the computer suite, when someone came out of the admin area. I saw him straight away, though his head was down as if he was trying to hide behind his dirty-blond hair.

"Hi Neil."

He looked up and gave me a wan smile. "Hi." Everything about him looked wrong, worse than that first day I met him - his skin was pale, his

93

eyes dark and his mouth was a tight, thin line. He didn't look ill, but he didn't look right.

"Alright?" I said, more for something to say, because I knew what the answer was really.

He made a sound in his throat but didn't say anything. He looked over my shoulder, then back to his feet, then at me again.

"You in trouble?" I said, pointing to the admin area and trying to make light of things.

"You could say that," he said. "I've got to get to geography, I'll see you later."

"Yeah, see you."

As he walked by, I really wanted to pat him on the shoulder, like I'd seen old friends do on TV shows, but I couldn't bring myself to do it.

I watched him push through the doors and go down the stairs and I never saw Neil Dawson again.

The years changed me, as they do everyone, sometimes for the better, sometimes for the worse. School was painful but, like everything, you get by. Everyone knew whose fault it was – as if blame would make everything right – and he was dealt with by the school, though since it was his last year and he wasn't going to make any attempt anyway, no punishment would work for Chris Nelson. As it was, he left school the cock of the walk and hit the real world hard, working in a shitty little garage and growing flabby from drinking faster than I'd have thought possible.

When he rode his scooter into a tree a couple of years later, I don't think many people mourned him.

Eva and I drifted apart. Was it to do with the incident? Before reading about her suicide this morning, I'd have said no but now I have my doubts.

Kettering had changed too. I came off the A43 and over junction 8 into Northampton Road. The housing estate was new, as was the pub and I followed the road round past Bowhill to the lights at the bottom. The two car dealerships that had butted up to the railway bridge were now one - Honda on the left, an empty space on the right. The old Drill Hall, a glorious blue-bricked Victorian monstrosity where I'd sometimes played 5-a-side in the summer was gone now, replaced by Housing Association flats. It wasn't an improvement.

When the lights changed, I turned right into Northfield Avenue. More cheap housing had been put up, already showing signs of neglect and decay. The train station was still in situ, though it appeared to have overhead walkways now. I wondered if they'd got rid of the subways under the tracks, terrific tunnels made of white marble bricks that always reminded me of the Hoth corridors from "The Empire Strikes Back".

I turned into Station Road, then immediately right onto Queensbury Road and followed that to the Headlands. Toller Hales & Colcutt had gone from the corner, the local radio station now in residence. I turned right, driving past dentists, chiropractors and solicitors offices and then Hawthorn Road. The fire station was there, as was Bishops Stotford and where the road curved into Bishops Drive, I saw a load of new houses on the right. I cruised slowly to the new junction and pulled in at the kerb.

The bridge was about two hundred yards away, two black bollards prevented me from driving across it. A metal fence on the left stopped access to the rails themselves and bushes had been allowed to grow unhindered. Metal plating, lighter than what was originally there, had been attached to the sides – perhaps to stop jumpers, though that had obviously failed.

I got out and locked the car and started to walk.

It was April and I was in my room, trying to study for my exams but failing spectacularly. Whatever I read seemed to slide straight out of my ears the moment I'd finished the paragraph.

I heard Mum coming up the stairs. She stopped in my doorway, leaning on the jamb.

"Ad," she said, "I've got some bad news."

It can't be Dad, I thought, she'd never mistake that for bad news.
"What's up, is Gran okay?"
"She's fine, love, it's nothing to do with her. It's your friend, Neil."
"What about him?"
"Well, love, I'm afraid he's dead."

The new executive houses, on Ostlers Way, were built up against the railway line, heading back towards the station. The alley was gone, there was just the road, a bit of verge, then a wooden fence to block access to the tracks. I imagined the fence would be about as much use as a leaky wetsuit for cutting out the sound.

Feeling nervous and nauseous, I crossed the road, fighting the urge to turn and go home. I didn't really want to see where Eva had thrown herself to her death, nor be back on the bridge where Neil had decided to end it all.

But I couldn't leave, I couldn't pretend that nothing was happening. I had to see.

Of the two bollards, the one on the right had been transformed into that modern memorial we're all so familiar with. At least ten bunches of flowers were sellotaped to it, along with a dozen or so laminated sympathy cards and a handful of small cuddly toys. Another laminated card, with Eva's picture, was taped to the top of the bollard. I stood in front of the memorial and stared at the face of an old friend I no longer knew. My feelings of nausea increased.

I heard a bike coming up the hill from the golf course and my already rapidly beating heart seemed to pick up a gear. There was no saliva in my mouth, my scalp felt as tight as a drum and my fingers were tingling from constantly making and unclenching my fists.

A new estate covered the land between the bridge and golf course and with the houses came fences. A metal one hemmed in the bushes from which Eva and I had leapt, all those years ago, starting the whole horrible chain of events. I couldn't see a fence on the right, overgrown bramble covered the abutment almost completely.

The kid rode into view, the one from the car park and outside my bedroom window, the one who twenty six years ago decided life had thrown one too many bricks and the easiest way out was to come into direct contact with the 16.30 to St Pancras.

He made a lazy circle, the chain clicking but made no attempt to speak to me - he didn't seem to realise I was even there.

I swallowed, which was painful and took a step forward, which was even more painful. We had the span of the bridge, approximately 20 feet, between us and I didn't know what to say or what to do. Had this happened to Eva? Had she come here, pre-empting that handwritten addendum, to try to find an answer? Had she seen the kid, seen Neil with his half sheared head?

I took another step and each time the kid ignored me, I took another. I was quickly over half the bridge and the kid was still cycling in lazy circles. I heard the horn of a train, coming from my left, from London.

The kid got off his bike, letting it clatter to the ground. In quick movements, he was at the side of the bridge and up on the brick wall supports. He moved like a cat, finding his feet and balance easily.

I stared at the graffiti on the bridge, as clear now as I remembered it being all those years before – 'Look Behind You'.

The kid, my friend Neil, looked at me, the side of his face that was still there crinkled in a half smile.

"Neil," I said and took another step closer.

He shook his finger at me and leaned forward, as if checking out the drop. I took another step – I was only a pace or so away from him now, if I grabbed him and pulled him to safety, would that count? Would that make better what I hadn't done before?

As if in slow motion, he lifted his right leg and moved forward until it was hanging over empty space. I lunged forward, fingers reaching, grasping. He took his step and fell out of sight.

The train horn sounded again.

I let my momentum carry me forward, bracing my hands on the brickwork so that I could heft myself up. I could see the four sets of tracks, the oil stains and the tufts of grass in amongst the concrete sleepers. There were a couple more bouquets down there too, battered by the trains and elements, looking very sad for themselves.

I leaned forward and heard rustling in the bushes behind the fence, as if two people – supposed friends of mine, perhaps – were about to come out and try to scare me senseless.

I strained to see, heard footsteps and whispered words, then felt pressure on my ankles.

I slid over the support.

The train horn sounded, very loudly.

Arthur the Witch

Donna Scott

The Lent Assizes - A Mummers' Play - Fragment
Herewith, the mummers:
The Mother
The Father
Mistress Kate
Arthur the Witch
Beelzebub and his three sprites, Jack of the Woods, Grissel and Ball
Martha Aspine
Her father, Thomas, a witness.
The Good Doctor – Sir Gilbert Pickering
John, a Ploughjack, good and true

The Father:
Sometimes, when I am in their favour and they will speak to me,
the men will ask me how I could ever love a witch. How I could
ever bed the devil's whore. Had I not wits enough to know I was
fucking a pig – a pig lover? A rider of pigs. *They say as you need to
draw a witch's blood to break a spell,* they say. *Maybe his cock's just not
up to the job.*

There was a time there was an edge to what they said, and
I'd hear the threat in it. But that was when they feared me. They
know I'll not harm them now. John sits in the corner by the fire
and kicks the straw with his feet. He works the plough and has
great square shoulders; beard thick as a wolf pelt. His broad

leathery hands have won him many a wager, but though he often looks at me with challenge in his eyes, he does not honestly speak his will. And so he sits there, in the place where the best of us should sit.

"Strong lad, your boy."

"Ay."

"Took after 'is mother."

"That's the sum of it, ay."

There's no arguing can be done. John means to remind me that my fists are no good to me now. I will heave and carry until I am old and sick, but John has his horses, his boys and his good name. I must work until I drop. My bones ache already. I doubt I'll reach my seventh age.

Still, I do not starve yet. I have heard some of the Raunds women say I am a lonely old soul, but I've known enough folks to know my own company is best. I need no swept floors. I can make my own fire and put a pot on it. I sleep better at night for the quiet, and when I've done my day's labours, there's no more peaceful place to be than a cold, dark room. I would that my grave were like such a room.

John can keep his place by the fire, for heat makes me sick. The woman always had a fire burning; I'd come in to see her face would be red from it, her skin slick, like she'd spent the whole day rutting. "Got to keep Arthur warm," she'd say, for he was a sickly thing when first made, more like a blackbird's young than a human child, all limp in her arms with grey eyes and a slack mouth. We should have put him out that first night, but I only had to speak these thoughts to the woman and she squealed like I'd stuck her. "He'll quicken soon enough," she said, and I said, "Ay." And he breathed and lived, he that was never meant to live, fed by that roasting fire.

And like a fire he took. There was never a boy in all of Raunds who ate so much or so well. It sickens me now to think of all that wasted meat! Many's the time I would come into the house to see the woman sweltering by the fire with a bird in her lap, pulling off its feathers while the boy sat at her feet; the gore dripping on him from the creature's beak – not paying any mind, just idly picking up the stray feathers from the floor and dropping them down again. I see them now; the wife's fingers working at speed over the carcass, as though she were trying to magic some quickness into the food – into Arthur – for the lad had no quickness in his own nature. Not that her efforts helped him much. For what is a bird's life to a boy's? A bird's heart is such a small thing, and such a creature has no soul. No, I thought, as I'd watch her time and time again, that white neck rolling twixt her knees; all that life, all that meat is feeding nothing good. It's all burned up in the fire, like some paltry faggot. Such a waste.

If Arthur had remained a weakling until such a time as God saw fit to take him back, then all might have been well, except I reckon as the babe's soul was given unto the devil in exchange for his life. The times he would not heed me, then would run off and there'd be something happen: a stone fly out the bread oven; a crack through the centre of the table. And never it was Arthur, always, "Jack did it," or Grissil, or the creature, Ball. Jack the mischief, Grissil the temper, Ball who could work quick as lightning and fly invisible to work his wickedness, all bound to the boy. Ay, an innocent babe who has seen nothing of the world could lose his soul; if his parents can lose theirs then all is possible.

That's what must have happened, the more I think on it. Perhaps the deed was done after his baptism, for the lad mewed with a little life when the water crossed his forehead – though that may have been the devil in him complaining at the blessing. Or it may have been that moment soon after he was born, while the caul still wrapped him like some newborn calf. Perhaps the devil entered him before he took a breath. All I know is, it was nothing to do with me. The woman must have done it. Ay, a babe cannot be damned for a sin of the future. It was the woman, then. In her greed, she damned them both. There's nary a woman in Raunds gets to keep her firstborn son, for the Lord takes so

101

many to his side. But the woman turned me from her bed. Her sick looks; her face of protest. She did not trust in God's plan; she did not trust in the power given unto me, her husband. I'm a fool to not have seen it at the time: the parable of the sower. Some seed must fall to shallow ground and the plant withers in the sun. Ay, but a sick plant might still take and then must the sower weed it out. There is no matter to it, for none of us are spared the scythe in the end. A man must have his land.

I sigh and look down at my cup. It runneth empty, as they say. "John, I'm off home." He gives me a hard stare. "If that's all right with you."

"I don't know..."

"John, it's been months. I've scarce any coin for beer."

"All right – but go straight home, mind, lest you leave yourself open to devilment."

"I've hardly drunk enough, John."

"Like you'd need much." He fixes me with the arrow of his finger. "I'm watching you. Remember."

The air outside has a nip to it. The weather is beginning to turn now; there'll be good work in the fields for me to do soon. I can last a while longer. Light grey wisps of cloud flit across the stars like spirits, and I feel a tingle in my bones: I'll see her tonight. I feel the dread of it, and yet I find myself turning a certain way, down the path where John would have led me on the walk home, though not the quickest way home for me. I reach the gate; see the candle burn low in the window. A shadow moves across the light, but the door opens, throwing light onto the path. Her face is still in shadow.

"Where's John?"

"He is still in the ale house."

"Close behind?" I shake my head. She whispers, "Have you brought me something?" I show her my last coin. She nods. "The barn." I follow the sound of her steps, though we both know where we are going, can feel our way in the dark.

Inside, the barn is dung-warm and ripe with animal stink.

Once the door is shut-to, her breath is on my face, her hands pulling at my clothes, at her own: "There's a wily old fox got in here. Why, I had to come and chase him out." Her hand pauses, finding my flesh, my quickening manhood. She laughs in my ear: "I meant in the barn, of course. Where were you thinking of?"

I am too hasty with her, too rough, but I feel her heart flutter in the cage of her bosom as I press down, the short rasps of breath on my neck and it's good. It's been a while since she took her man, I can tell. Too long since she lay with me also, though she feels so familiar: the curve of her hip, the ridge of her bone; those young, silky thighs. Even in the dark, I see her eyes are beautiful, full of a bright smile. I want to kiss her mouth, but she pulls away, eyes screwed up as though in pain. She holds her breath, and I hold mine also, following where she leads. As the waves ebb away, I try to kiss her again.

"Now, now, don't spoil it any more than you have done. And get your cock out of me before it shrivels."

As though I disgust her.

"You play games with me, Kate."

She wriggles from under me. "Your trouble is that I don't." There's a silence before she adds, "You can't win my heart, you know. Whatever prize I might once have offered is long gone."

"Since you married the old ploughman, you mean?"

"Pox, I do not." She smoothes down the front of her skirt and is at the barn door already. "I'm going back in the house now. Try walking home alone again once in a while."

I rise to my feet. "Woman! Is it only my coin you want from me, then?"

"Shh." She comes back to me, and I feel butterflies in my belly once more. "Quiet, John will be back soon." She holds her face close to mine. Her lashes are silvered with the moonlight streaming into the barn between the slats in the wall. "I want what the old ploughman cannot give me, of course."

"And I can?"

"Indeed you do," she giggles. "Better than any boy–"

I push her from me. I have no doubt she has lain with her husband with the dutiful obeisance he deserves, but I have no wish to hear her hint of the others she beds, though I often look at faces in the village, wondering who, who? Is it that man? Is there another? And John's own eldest boy is much a man these days, close to his step-mother in years. And what a teacher she would make, though it is all wickedness to conjure in my mind's eye. Her smile sickens me.

"Go then. Hie, witch. Yes, *witch*. I know what you do with the hearts of men –"

"The cocks of men! Ha – you of all men should know the danger in calling out such a word. Witch, indeed! There's no sorcery in me, and you know it –"

"Like you know a witch when you see one –"

Kate catches her breath to answer, when we both hear the sound of feet approaching, and the crashing sound of someone of burly frame knocking into the hedgerows. The ploughman has returned home.

"Well," Kate whispers, raising her brow. "I must go in now, but think on this. If I were a witch, then you really would be in my power, for now I do believe I have something of yours in my possession."

"Good wife! Where are you?" bellows John.

"I come, husband, by and by."

The flutter of her lash against my cheek, and she is gone.

I must stay still a while, listening to the thud of my heart, while my flesh cools. I can feel a sickness rising in my belly. Why have I risked my life again to come down this path and in the way of temptation? Women do the devil's bidding, whether they heed him or not. Kate knows she is wicked and cares not. Ah but she risks harm to none but herself... I am already damned.

I ease open the barn door and slip out. The night air is like a cool hand on my brow; the night spirits are about, I can feel them. Home then, and let them trouble me not, lest I dream of Kate. I fear still that Jack and his friends cling to the corners of my house now the boy Arthur will be free of them. What if I am weak enough for them to gain possession of me? I have dark thoughts enough, imagining just how I might wrest Kate from the ploughman's shadow. Why did he have to take her to wife, just when I was free of mine?

Arthur the Witch:
Here comes I, who's never been yet, with my great strength and my little wit.
My strength is so great and my wit so small, I come this night to please you all.
I will play my sack till you all dance a jig; my mother rides a spotted pig.
My father fingers his flute of bone, and if you won't dance he'll leave you alone.
  Jack of the Woods: They don't love you, boy. Watch what your mother feeds you: it's full of poison.
  Arthur: Get out of my head.
  Jack: Shitty sausage. That's what's in it. Shit. Shit in your mouth, boy.
  Arthur: I'm not listening.
  Grissel: Let him eat the shit, Jack. Boy's hungry.
  Arthur: ...
  Grissel: That's it, boy, get it down yer. What's it taste like?
  Jack: He knows.
  Ball: Hur, hur, *he* knows. Go on, say it. What's it taste like?
  Arthur: Shut up!
  Jack: Go on, tell her. She's got to know, stupid bitch. She makes a shitty sausage. Tell her!
  Arthur: I'm not saying. Not saying anything.
  Ball: I'm with you, Arthur. We likes the taste of shit, don't we? More in the barn. Shall we go and find it? Nom, nom, nom.
  Arthur: No.
  Ball: Oh – oh! Look Arthur, I just moved your foot, there! I'm going to walk you, see if I don't.

105

Arthur: No, don't. Please...

Jack: Say it then.

Arthur: Shit! Shit! Tastes of shit. Oh! Oh, mother, I meant it not!

Mistress Kate:

Martha Aspine is no friend of mine. She struts and she preens and she thinks she's a queen. The honey in the hive. Look at her. Strolling round the market with her nose in the air. Never had to open her legs in her life, 'xcept to her old man, reckons I.

She'll never know how thoroughly I hate her. She stops my breath when I see her, like as though I'm wearing the sack John the ploughman makes me wear when he pays for a fuck. "Martha," he calls out. He said sorry last night, but only 'cause I was crying. And that was only 'cause he asked her to marry him, imagining her head were mine.

But there she moves, like a swan. Goodly and pure, Martha Aspine. Oh, all the boys want to be the one to pluck that flower.

Oh, but if a man were to lie with her – what a merry thought, the face of the father, hearing of his daughter spoiled! But how to bring such a delight about? She would never lie with a man willingly, not to begin with, though I'm sure she'd get the taste for it.

Let me see what I can conjure.

Arthur the Witch:

I chop the wood. One and two and three and four. Keep the numbers in my head and one and two and three and...

"Hello Arthur."

'Tis Kate, the new wench from the tavern. She's got her hands on her hips as she walks forward, pushing out her milky bosoms at me. That's right, you look at her bubbies, says Jack.

"Oh, hello there, Miss... Mistress Kate." I swallow.

"You're a big, strong lad, aren't you, Arthur?" I nod. Strength is the only grace God gave me, my father says. She's not talking about your strength, lad though is she, says Grissil? She's a dirty-minded whore, and you are a fool... She narrows her eyes at me, smiles, glances from left to right. "And I hear you have certain *talents*. I hear you have the counsel of fairy folk."

Oh, lad, she's touching you, says Ball. We can touch her back. Let us. See, I move your cock.

Shh, says Jack. Didn't you hear her? Fairy folk – that's us!

"I have a job for a big, strong lad like you," says Kate. "And for the clever creatures that whisper to you."

Oh, she knows, says Grissil.

Told you, says Jack.

We need to be more careful, they'll strangle us out, choke us, says Ball. Quiet now.

"I – I don't know what you mean? What Fairies?" Please be quiet. I don't want anyone to hurt me to get to you.

"Never mind that, Arthur. Will you come?"

"And what's in it for me?"

"You shall get a kiss, sweet Arthur."

"Oh... a kiss?" Idiot boy, says Jack. When a whore speaks of an offer of a kiss, she means it not. She means you can make the beast with two backs with her. Oh don't drop your jaw, boy, it's just a fuck she's after. Go – move her barrels or whatever pretence she's conjured to get at your cock.

I can help, says Ball.

Too right you'll help, says Grissil. We'll all help. We'll flip her and poke her and choke her and stick her. Oh we've been too long in the bodies of children and idiots. At least this idiot has a man's body now. Let us go and make the most of it.

I follow Kate down the street. She walks towards the market. I don't normally like it on market day. Too many people – all noise. I have enough noise in my head already. Also, some of the women jeer at me, call me bad things.

They're right to, Jack says.

It just makes me angry. Oh, I hope she takes me to the tavern cellar to shift some barrels or something. It's nice and quiet down there.

Nice and *private*, says Grissil.

"Wait here," says Kate. She goes over to speak to a sweet, young girl. I have never seen her before, but she is beautiful. I'm sure she's never been in the tavern, or I would have remembered her. Her face has none of Kate's slyness, mind. Kate is full of smiles, and the girl blushes at something she says and smiles back. Then Kate beckons me over.

"Here, Martha meet Arthur! Oh, what a sweet rhyme your names make." She giggles, but Martha and I do not. "Arthur, my friend Martha has lingered too long at the market, and still has a good distance to walk home – a long way to carry all these provisions." I look at the basket Martha is carrying. It does not look so heavy, though the girl is so slight, perhaps she is like the runt pig, all weakness.

You think she is a pig, that's nice, says Jack. Want to ride her home?

Hur hur hur, says Ball. I'm sure he does.

The girl nods and I take her basket, the three of us walking together, the girls chatting pleasantly about the weather, what was good at the market. I try not to think about the faces staring at my back as we leave. I feel the sweat on my back, and my neck is hot. Soon, though, the village is far behind us.

"Tell me, Martha," says Kate, "have you ever seen a fairy ring?"

"No, I haven't."

"Ah, well there's a good one just this way, through the woods. Follow me and I will show it to you."

"Do we have time?" It's already quite late. You will be walking back to Raunds by moonlight as it is."

"The time is perfect. Come on."

We walk a little way into the woods. It is growing dark and cold already, and I see my breath misting, curling into the air. Shafts of light pierce the trees; leaves on the floor glow in pools of green. It is most strange.

You know what's coming, don't you, says Jack?

Oh, but this must be the fairy ring. It is marvellous – I hear Martha give a gasp. Pristine little mushroom heads dot through the leaves in a wide circle.

"And the fairies make this?" Martha asks.

"It is where they come to dance," says Kate. "If we wait a while perhaps we can see them arrive. And then we can catch one and make it grant us wishes."

"They do that?"

"Do you know nothing of fairy folk, Martha? I might have thought you'd know a bit more of the world than this idiot boy, here, but perhaps you do not."

We all sit down at the base of an oak and the girls are quiet for a few minutes. Jack whispers to me of all the things he would like to do first to Martha, and then to Kate. The other two stay quiet. I listen to my belly instead, which is telling me it has missed a meal.

Martha sighs. "I think they come not."

Kate says, "I think I know why they do not appear. They look into the clearing and see us, wearing the clothes of humans and dare not approach. If we were to undress, perhaps they would think we are their own kind and would not be afraid." She stands up and begins pulling off her dress. "Come on. You too, Arthur."

I don't really want to, but Ball jumps to life and works my hands and fingers and soon I am naked as an animal. I can't help but stare at Kate: those milk white bubbies with pink rosebud tips; the hollow of her belly; that dark triangle of hair between her thighs. Only Martha still has her clothes on. My stomach rumbles again.

"I – I cannot," says Martha.

"Don't be silly, Martha. There's no one here to see except the fairy folk. What? You are afeared of Arthur? Why he has the mind of a child, hence he does what I say, don't you, Arthur?"

Martha shyly begins to unbutton her dress, and soon Kate is

109

helping her, giggling, though the girl looks cold, she shivers so.

Wait for it, says Ball.

"And now we are all fairy folk," says Kate, and turns in a circle to address the space in the fairy ring.

"Come fairy, come demon, come devil, come sprite,
Come dance with us maidens this hour of moonlight.
Come Jack of the Woods, come Grissil, come Ball,
Come forth and make merry, there's work for you all.
Come taste our sweet kisses and tickle our skin
We welcome you fairies without and within.
From sweet Martha's mind, my name will unstitch
But come do as you will with Arthur the Witch!"

The world is growing small, like to a picture on a pinhead, and it is Jack I hear, his voice in my throat. "Jezebel, I know thee. Now for that *kiss*."

The Good Doctor:

"Will you come?"

The Chief Justice, Galsworthy, stands dripping in my vestibule – *dripping in my vestibule!* Oh, should that imagery have applied to my wife, that would have been bawdy indeed. I almost guffaw, but I banish this unclean thought. I am a Knight of the Realm now, and I do God's work, so I have sworn. This man is keeping me from my pie.

"'Tis but less than a half day's ride to Northampton Castle, where you are most welcome, of course, and we have a number of witches for your examination. Foul creatures they are: hideous crones, as one might expect, one bewitching succubus – ah such a sight she is, so innocent of face - and a boy, Sir Pickering. The evil progeny of his parents, both of whom have been named witches also. 'Tis the strange case of the murder of Martha Aspine, brought to our attention by her father, Thomas Aspine."

"And they are from Northampton?"

"Close by; from Raunds. But the witches are held in the gaol at Northampton castle, awaiting trial. I am quite sure there have never been so many witches brought to trial all at once in the same place – does not that make things very convenient?"

I sense my Good Wife lingering a breath away from the door. She is not best pleased that I have left my pie. I daresay I am due an earful if she learns I am to be stuck in Northampton for the assizes. I must anticipate the machinations of a woman. Perhaps there is some good cloth I can have sent back.

"It is for the sum indicated by my man here, or I come not."

My servant passes Galsworthy the letter, which he unrolls, reads and turns purple at.

"For the sum...! Sir, I thought such a case would be of extreme interest to you, given your predilection for all things physick and supernatural."

Damnation – the sum *is* a good deal more than I charged the assizes at Huntingdon, but I was a mere novice, then, and Northampton is near, but not so near to Titchmarsh as my brother's town, and none of the victims or the perpetrators of these crimes will have any connection to me. Must I reassess the cut of the cloth I should send back to the house? My wife will not. And she will want shoes too, most likely. I rest my hand against my hip, trying to appear as unbothered in my appearance as necessary.

"Galsworthy, you need not doubt my *interest*. My inviting you into my household, and my not turning the hounds loose on you straight as I saw you, is a good indication of *that*. But remember this, my good man. *You* called on *me*. And the gathering of so many witches for trial all at once strikes me as truly *convenient* for you – if you are presuming I should assess a quantity of devils at a discount, like some merchant trading in cow-hides , which I am not.

"No, Galsworthy. There is no other man of my status in the country quite so experienced in these matters, as well you know." I arch my brow. "How are you to tell the difference between a real witch and some poor unfortunate accused by her ungodly neighbour for reason of spite? My man, I will tell you how:

111

through the application of a rational mind, through sound interpretation of scripture, and through *science*. I am equipped with all the latest theorems for the practise of my arts. My own kin have suffered the evils of sorcery – hence I have made it my life's ambition to use the superior mind God gave me and to make the thwarting of witches my life's work."

"Sir Pickering, this is exactly why we thought you would be the ideal gentleman to help us. With the Aspine case, sir, the murdered girl named her attacker before she tragically expired, much as your niece did: a much despised boy, already known for many acts of evil in the village. His parents, being ungodly heathens, knew full well their child was in league with Beelzebub's sprites and sought not to prevent him from doing harm. All three are the subject of much gossip in the village; their unclean living, their extravagance, their frequent use of foul speech. Father and son both spent many a coin in the bawdy house and have never observed the Sabbath."

"And is there talk of their keeping familiars? Doing unnatural things such as flying? Holding magical rites?"

"Indeed, Sir Pickering. The mother has been observed riding pigs, and the victim said the boy danced naked in the woods in an attempt to entrap her soul."

I give my beard a good scratch. If Galsworthy is indeed correct about the sins of these named witches, it will be the easiest case to prove I have ever dealt with. Think of the renown I will have! And the coin to follow...

"Sir Pickering, the people of Northampton would be forever indebted to you." The man bows low before me.

"And the fee I propose?"

Galsworthy glances up. "There must be some bargain can be struck?"

"None whatsoever."

"Then, Sir Pickering. We have no choice. Northampton is in dire need."

"Good, then I shall acquiesce, and return to my pie

forthwith."

My goodly slice of pie.

The Mother:
The man, he takes my face in his hands and says, "You trust in God, do you, woman?"
I wish I could speak. The May dew is turned to frost, biting my feet and the ties of my shift whip across my collarbone like spikes of birch, and yet I feel the cold as though it were a hellish flame licking at me. I must be a wicked woman for the cold to burn like fire. Oh Lord, I pray thee save me from the devil, for even now he whispers that he can take away the pain, and then I swear he makes it so that I cannot feel my feet at all. Yet, if I yield I know they will make me suffer for it. Oh Lord, I am thy servant; please do not let the devil take me! Give me back dominion of my own tongue that I might profess my fear of thee. Have I not shriven enough that I must be made to stand in only my shift, bare where I have been pinched all over with looking for the devil's mark? Oh cover me, Lord, for the shame does not burn more than the cold, I am so wicked.

The ground, it moves, and the devil is lifting me up, up, away from my feet, and he takes my legs and shakes them so fast that all watching here can see I am in his thrall. I do not want to fly... I never could fly before, and yet I feel myself leave the earth – oh Lord, it is the devil taking me! He wishes me to fly before all these witnesses and will lead me to my damnation. There is a stone in my belly and yet I am floating – it is but your man holding me down. Your man, black as a shadow, with his hands that are like a boy's hands, too soft to be pinching my skin so. I can feel the tip of the nail on his thumb – he will mark my cheek with it, but I must not turn, must not pull away.

"Ai!"

He presses his thumb to my jaw, so it opens as though on a hinge. What is he doing with me? He peers at my teeth as though I am a farm beast, looks down my throat. His face is so close, the white hairs blur into his face before me and I glance away, to where I did not want to look, my head tilted back like a birthing cow's. There is my husband. I see him held back by John, but I see he has no fight in him and his eyes ... they've all got the same eyes, all the people. Oh God, let me speak! I have no other Lord, save for my husband as thou gave me. Please, do not let them look so!

"Murderess! Confess it!"

Murderess – they call me thus, for poor Martha that died. And yet it was Jack that did it with Grissil's temper, with his curse, and I only the woman that bore their vessel, from what was said. And yet, I cannot speak.

"This is your last chance to cough the spirits up. I know they move within you, for the devil holds your tongue, does he not?" I try to move my jaw, but the man holds me firm. The devil moves me though – my jaw trembles in spite of my will. I try to move my dry tongue away from the man's fingers and swallow, my throat moving against his palm. A nail scores the soft flesh under my tongue. "Come on, woman. You are a weak vessel to be so ruled by evil. Relinquish the devil now, and I will see that you are granted God's mercy. I will pray with you now..."

So quiet, he says it, like the devil can be coaxed from me like a dog with an old bone – not ranting and beating the back of me like he did with Arthur. My simple Arthur, my monstrous child. Oh, they know it is hard for a mother to stand by and see her child in pain, not without taking the same burden on herself. Oh Arthur – once I could feel where I carried you in my belly, but now I feel nothing but stone. Did you do that to me, my child? Or was it one of your spirits? Wicked is as wicked does, they say... The man is hurting me, but he presses me so slight that none can see what he does.

And his voice is so soft, growing quieter still – too quiet. I hear no words for the devil stops my ears. I see the man's lips close to my face, but I do not hear what he is saying, only a keening whistle and a dull rushing wind as the sky turns black.

Turns black and takes the rest of the world with it.

"–pent! Repent!"

"Witch! She's a witch!"

"Devil's whore!"

"We know you, witch – but not as the devil *knows* you!"

The world blasts back and strikes me with a stabbing pain in my lungs. I am suspended above the earth, my knees bent under me, held up by the back of one arm, my own chin pushing weight down on my neck. Did I fly? Oh God, please do not let my body have flown about while I was in the dark place.

"See how she resists the word of the Lord! How she cannot bear to hear one word of the Lord's Prayer! You give me no choice, woman. We must draw out your confession. We will put you to the test."

The stones slice into my feet, top and bottom, and I am pulled to the ground. I feel the bite of air on my leg – there is blood. "I-I d-don't fly..."

"No, woman, you won't. See – your blood has been drawn, so I have taken all the power the devil gave you. Now he cannot help you fly away any more than he can help you in the test."

He puts my wrists together and binds them before threading the end of the rope around my thumbs, and down and across over my feet, pulling between my toes, though I can scarce feel the skin rub off on the coarse thread. The end of the rope is then fed through the top of a wooden beam; some kind of pulley on which I am suspended like the traitor from the cards. It is such a contraption as I've heard tell is used for scolds – those women who make themselves unloved by having strife with their neighbours. Is that not also my crime? Mayhap the devil made me a wretched sort for other women to name me in this, but I never meant for any to hate me so. Ai – the rope bites wherever it touches.

Up, up I go.

For I was never made to fly...

The sky lies so clear and blue above the outstretched fingers

115

of the trees. All the earth is at prayer... I must pray also. Oh Lord, I have prayed for myself, which is the sin of the bad mother; she is cast so far from the mould of the blessed lady, she can never hope to know thee in the next world unless thou grant her the will to put things right, oh, and I do so will for things to be right. I am not so old as Sarah was when she bore Isaac – and still I am devoted to my husband. I have known none but him. I did not know I had taken the devil's child for his, I swear. I just wanted that boy too much. I'm sorry I loved him, but I will forget. See? I forget him already for myself.

Please, Lord, make me a good wife.

The water reaches my toes and I cannot look. The water covers my ankles and yet I cannot look at him, my husband; my tormentor. I feel the slime of weed brush my skin – and the cold – oh, the air is as Lamas-tide compared with this, and I am afeared – the water looks dark as night, and flows with such force against my thighs, that I feel my body lift already. Down, down I must go, or they'll think me a witch! And the water reaches my bosom and my breath falls short; the river presses the very lungs in me, and I cannot scream. I feel the stone in my belly lift, and I know it is the stone that floats, like the man showed us, that flows as fire from the gates of hell and hardens when it touches God's Earth. I see the women's skirts upside down in the water, and the castle walls, and there is my husband – but I cannot look at him. I am a good wife.

I am a good wife!

The Father:
Oh Lord. We do not practise the confession in our religion, but this morning I feel the need to come here, to St. Peter's. I need to speak with You. I am about to do another wrong, and I want Your help to not make it the worst of wrongs. They speak of the eternal fires that await me, for all the wrong I've done already, but it strikes me as the Lord would not make it so as a sinner would have no discouragement from sinning further in his life. That was

what Sir Pickering meant at the trial, I think, when he said I had done much to atone for the wrongs of my wife and child by speaking against them, and naming them as witches. Hence, I have my freedom. If you can call it that.

I go to sleep in my cold bed every night and I dream of her. Implicated in my sin as she was, John the old ploughman thought he could save Kate by taking her to wife. Only now her sins are greater, for she betrays a husband. He is a good deal older even than I. What must it be like to lie with that grizzled old beast of a man? Like sleeping with a maggoty corpse, so near to death is he.

And I wish him dead.

But then what would the point be? She fucks for the pleasure of fucking and there are younger cocks around than mine. Oh, but to own her, as he does... that would be enough for me, even if she would slip the reign every now and then... though that could be to my profit, if I think on it.

Oh Lord, I am kneeling in a church, and you let me make such prayers? Though I know man built this church, and it was the sin of pride made them build the spire so tall. I know the height of the spire brings the building so much closer to God, but they only built it so tall because they could. And so, even Your house is open to sin.

So, Lord, here I am, about to strike another bargain with You, not the devil, for I know he has me already, and no bargain can be struck.

For the lives of my wife and child – the witch and the devil's creature that made him – you granted me my life. But this is no life, with the word 'witch' following me around like a sore on my back, sneaking a fuck from a married whore when I can, which is not often enough. We are both miserable, Lord, and I think she's far from saved from the likes of me.

So I beg your mercy, for I have murder in mind. Mayhap it is one of the sprites that Arthur had, whispering to me, though he swore they had voice to them, and I do not hear a voice as such. But the temptation is there. I want Kate, I want my life, and I want to be rid of John.

But with Your grace, Lord, I shall commit the lesser sin. I have to leave Raunds. Only to start again in another town would be to beggar myself, and I can't have that. Nor can I leave her behind. There are whores in other towns, but being a beggar I will not have the coin. However, it strikes me that if she were to come with me, willing like, Kate could earn coin for us both, and being the devil's strumpet, I'm sure she would be of a mind to free herself of the shackles of marriage for the liberty I will grant her in my care.

So, my prayer is this. Let us leave, Lord, and let it not be writ where we have gone, and we will leave you in peace, by and by. For as the devil took my woman, I must take one of his, as the Bible says – an eye for an eye, a tooth for a tooth...

Goethe's Wig

Steve Longworth

I stared at them.
They stared back at me.
Any second now.
Any.
Second.
Now…

"Please place all loose items in the overhead locker, stow your tray table, make sure your seat is upright, and fasten your seatbelt as we prepare for our descent to Gatwick."

"That means you," said Lisa with a sharp nudge to my elbow.

I sighed, and bookmarked my page. If I'm honest the flight home is my favourite part of any holiday, not because I'm a miserable git, but because by necessity I have several hours with nothing to do but read. Reluctantly, I closed the latest offering from my favourite writer. While Lisa fussed with her post-flight debris, I sneaked a quick look at the picture on the inside front cover of the book.

Laurel Harding was the unchallenged queen of supernatural gothic-eroto-horror, a literary subgenre with a substantial and passionate following. I had stumbled across her work three or four years before while browsing in my local book shop. Maybe it was the racy mix of Victorian manners, sex, vampires and graphic

119

violence; or maybe it was the photograph of the author in a low cut, skin-tight leather catsuit, black make-up and waist length blonde hair streaked with black, hands and feet shackled together, pouting at the camera over her shoulder; but I was hooked.

"How's your book?" asked Lisa, eyebrows arched, as she paused in her exploration of the Tardis-like interior of her handbag.

My novel had just reached a gripping but complex and rather pornographic climax (so to speak) in the hallowed halls of St. Anselm's College in the shadow of York Minster. Not the sort of thing I really wanted to discuss within earshot of the three elderly nuns in the row opposite.

"Oh, um, yes, er, fine. How's yours?"

"Well, it's about these three friends whose husbands are all having affairs…" and to my relief she prattled on happily about her latest piece of throwaway chick-lit. I glanced over at the nuns. They were hanging on to Lisa's every word. I unbuckled my seat belt, stood, opened the overhead locker, and reluctantly stuffed *Violation of the Virgin Vampires* deep into my hand luggage.

The arrival at Gatwick was memorable only for the fact that we were pulled over by Customs for a bag search. This always happens to me. I try so hard to look nonchalant that I look deeply suspicious. Lisa flirted with the Customs officers while I did my unhelpful best not to look shifty.

"This your bag, sir?" asked a cheerful, uniformed cockney. I nodded. "Packed it yourself?"

Another nod. Of course he found the book and spent an overly long time checking for contraband between the covers. He waved over one of his colleagues and they both leered and grinned at the inside cover photo. I suppressed an unsettling feeling of proprietorial outrage, and tried to look like someone who wasn't trying to look like he had nothing to hide.

"Thank you very much sir, we'll let you get on your way." said the cheeky cockney, handing back the book as I repacked my bag. To my intense annoyance he'd lost my page.

"Enjoy your novel," he added, suggestively.

I was used to this reaction. I'd stopped mentioning my preferred reading material to friends and colleagues some time ago. I certainly never mentioned it to any of my patients; a dentist who admitted a penchant for vampire stories was just asking for trouble.

We arrived back in Hinckley without further incident. There was the usual obstruction behind the front door, comprising a fortnight's mail. While Lisa put the kettle on, I sorted through the circulars, local restaurant flyers, professional publications and occasional postcards. One letter caught my eye. This was from my old university. 'Probably after money', I thought, 'they never write for any other reason'. To my surprise, however, the letter was an invitation to a ten-year class reunion. 'My God, has it been that long?' I muttered. I checked the venue and almost dropped the pile of magazines from under my right arm. The reunion was to be held at the Minster Conference and Banqueting Centre, St. Anselm's College, York. Blimey, that was some coincidence! While Lisa poured the tea and decanted the contents of our suitcases into the laundry I slid off with my book and quietly finished the last chapter. As usual, all the plot elements were neatly tied up with enough issues left open to whet the appetite for the fifth book in the current series.

I wandered back into the kitchen. Lisa was working her way through a pile of fashion, gossip and homecare magazines.

"You'll never guess what happens at the end of this," I said, tapping the cover of *Violation*.

"Hmmm? Oh, look at those, they'd go well with the settee in the conservatory," she replied pointing at one of her magazines.

"Yes, love," I said, and slunk off to the study. I had to tell someone about the amazing coincidence concerning St Anselm's College; someone who might be interested; but whom? I booted up my laptop and selected Laurel Harding's website from the top of my 'favourites' list. There she was, pictured in her trademark black leather catsuit. I re-read an account of her remarkably athletic sex life, and I couldn't help but wonder wistfully what it would be like to be with her. I'll bet she didn't waste any time or energy wondering about which fittings to put up in the conservatory; she was probably too busy swinging from them, like the heroine of her novels, the nymphomaniac vampire slayer, Jezebel Pope.

A mystery currently surrounded Laurel Harding. About two years ago she had suddenly disappeared from view. She continued to publish, but she no longer made public appearances at fan-fests or book signings. There were, of course, the usual crazy conspiracy theories; she'd died, she'd been kidnapped by occultists (or the Jesuits), she'd had plastic surgery and stood as a parliamentary candidate for the Green Party. I suspected that her disappearance was a deliberate ploy to boost her mystique. It certainly hadn't done her sales figures any harm, quite the opposite.

I couldn't find any recent magazine or newspaper interviews on the net and the only personal profile available was the one on her website. I did find a clip on YouTube, showing her at a book signing, but the image quality wasn't great, as it had been recorded on a camera phone. Still, I thought she looked fabulous as she autographed copies of her last but one *Virgin Vampire* novel and laughed and joked with her fans, most of who seemed to be adolescent boys or gothy women of indeterminate age.

What the hell was I doing, thinking she'd be interested in my stupid anecdote about a remarkable coincidence? If she was fed up with all the fuss and had become a recluse she was unlikely to respond if I e-mailed her; but if that was the case, why the 'e-mail Laurel Harding' link on her website? Probably a sop to her fans who simply received a standard 'thank-you' from her agent.

Still, the remarkable coincidence had touched a nerve; I had to tell someone. So I navigated back to her website and pressed the 'e-mail' link. The cursor at the top of the dialogue box winked patiently. 'Sod it', I thought, 'why the hell not?' and I rattled off a rather gushing and, in retrospect, recklessly unguarded missive in which I told her of my undying admiration of her literary talent, how stunningly attractive she was, and how we had been spookily linked via fate and St Anselm's College. Within seconds of pressing 'send' I started to have second thoughts. She'd think I was a complete jerk; if she thought anything at all. I'd probably get a polite one-line reply; if I were lucky. What would the folk at the golf club say? Or the Rotary Club, for that matter? Sheepishly, I returned to Lisa in the kitchen.

"So where are those fittings for the conservatory?" I asked, making a determined effort to reconnect with the dull reality of suburban upper middle class mediocrity.

The next morning, with somewhat mixed feelings, I checked my Hotmail inbox. Nothing. I smiled wryly and shook my head. Really, what had I been expecting? I was just about to close the window when there was a soft 'bong' and a new message arrived. I blinked hard at the content of the message title; *'From Laurel Harding to my Delectable Dentist'.* I could hardly believe it. My hand shook as I opened the message.

'Dear Derrick,
Thank you soooo much for taking the time and trouble to write to me. And you're a dentist! You must have a really busy and interesting life. Gosh, what an amazing coincidence about St Anselm's! Do you believe in fate? I think the universe is full of hidden connections. Stuff like this happens for a reason...'

I was stunned. Instead of a perfunctory 'thanks, and keep buying the novels', she had sent me a long and detailed reply that included tales of strange coincidences that had happened to her. The tone was relaxed and friendly; more than friendly in fact. Was this a 'come on'? She seemed to be deeply impressed by my job. I expect I wasn't one of her usual fans. She'd probably had her fill of priapic teenagers and sexually ambiguous ladies of a certain age. The e-mail mentioned that her new novel, *Victims of the Virgin Vampires*, was nearly finished and that she'd also recently been asked to submit a stand-alone Jezebel Pope short story for an anthology that was being published by a small independent press near her home in Northampton. She finished by saying she hoped I'd stay in touch.

I read and re-read the e-mail. I was thrilled and elated. I wanted to reply immediately; but what the hell was I going to say? How to make a connection and maintain her attention? I was sure that she wouldn't be interested in the subtleties of dental amalgam, or the problems of recruiting a new receptionist, or the agenda for the next Rotary Club meeting. Then it came to me. Fan fiction. Some time ago, for my own amusement, I'd written a short story about Jezebel Pope and a pack of werewolf fetishists called "Lycanthropy in Lycra". I dug this out of a forgotten corner of my hard drive and re-read it; even if I say so myself, it wasn't bad.

I replied with another long and enthusiastic e-mail in which I told her more about myself, apart from the fact that I was married, and attached my story as an homage to her outstanding talent. Once again, no sooner had I pressed 'send' than I started to have cold feet. What was I thinking, asking a famous writer to look at a piece of derivative drivel like my story? Bollocks. I'd probably never hear from her again.

My elation disappeared like pink oral rinse down the plughole of a treatment room basin.

That evening my emotional roller-coaster took another sudden upward swing when I saw a reply to my last e-mail entitled *'Clever You!'* In another long and thrilling message my literary heroine was full of praise for my efforts; but she really knocked my socks off with an absolutely stunning proposal. Suppose she edited my story, added another character, changed the ending slightly and submitted the piece under both our names for the Northampton anthology; would I be interested? I was utterly gobsmacked, which, to be frank, is not a good look for a dentist. If my reply had been animated it would have wept with gratitude. She'd even offered to split the (admittedly modest) fee with me. Interested? I was utterly beguiled. I'd have prised my own teeth out with a screwdriver for a chance like this.

Thus began an intense daily correspondence in which Laurel and I discussed our co-authored story in an increasingly flirty manner. I kept wondering at which point I ought to mention that I was married, but she never asked and somehow I just never got around to this. Despite the now extensive electronic correspondence between us, she actually gave relatively little away about her personal life. In fact, when it was all boiled down, all I really knew about her was that she lived in Northampton. Or near Northampton. Nearish.

Encouraged by her enthusiastic response to my werewolf story I started work on another piece, a story about cross-dressing vampires, "Transylvanian Transvestite Tryst". I hesitated for several days before sending her a draft, then fretted all day at work wondering what she would make of this. That evening the title of her reply made me gasp and feel faint; *'Come to a meeting?'*

'Dear Derrick,
Great story! How would you like to join the Northampton Gothic Eroto Horror Supernatural Story Writers Imagineering Group? We meet on the last Thursday of the month in the Wig and Pen on St Giles street where we 'workshop' a couple of new pieces. It would be lovely to meet you and I think you would find the evening very revealing!'

A writer's group? That wasn't quite the meeting I'd be been hoping for before I opened the message; but there was that comment about the evening being 'very revealing'. Would she be wearing the cat suit? I replied with alacrity, and she duly sent me directions. A quick search on the AA route planner established that the venue was only about an hour from where I lived. Great! Now I only had one problem. What was I going to tell Lisa?

"A vampire writer's group?" asked Lisa. "Will Buffy be there?"

This was a little too close to the mark. Lisa knew the kind of books and TV shows that I liked, and while she was hugely tolerant of what she saw as a mild eccentricity on my part she'd never expressed any interest herself. All my Laurel Hardings, H.P. Lovecrafts and Stephen Kings were restricted to my study; none were allowed out to sully the Ideal Homes patina of Lisa's expensively assembled furniture and fixtures.

"Will you have to dress up like Christopher Lee? Or that killer in 'Saw'?"

"No, this is serious writers' meeting. And it's not just vampires. Anyway, they like the look of my work and they've asked me to come along to the group and contribute to the discussions."

I'd decided that the best way to approach this issue was to keep it as close to the truth as possible. I hadn't mentioned Laurel at all, so the 'Buffy' jibe made me jump.

"Where is it?"

"Northampton. In a pub."

"Hmmm. Well, if you're going there, I could start going to salsa classes again."

"What, with pervy Malcolm the Quantity Surveyor?" I'd clocked him surveying Lisa's quantities when we'd been for a series of introductory classes the previous year.

She giggled. "Well, you'll be having a fun night out, why shouldn't I? You never know, maybe Laurel and Hardy will turn up."

"It's Laurel Harding," I replied, affecting rather too much nonchalance. Bloody hell, what was it with the forensic psychic abilities of wives? I'd have to be very careful.

On the last Thursday of that month I booked a lighter than usual late afternoon surgery and finished in good time. We own a small flat above the clinic and I used this to shower and change. Lisa and I were both going straight on from work to our respective exploits.

I had nipped out that lunchtime and bought some flowers. I'd fretted over whether to do this or not, and then over which ones would be the most appropriate. Eventually I'd settled on a bunch of blood red roses. The next agonising decision was how many? If I was going to say it with flowers there was a fine line between too big a bunch that said 'flash bastard' and one too small that said 'cheapskate'. Eventually, I arrived at what I considered to be the optimum rose to bunch ratio.

What to wear? Cravat and smoking jacket or denims and tee shirt? I compromised on smart casual with a hint of individuality, a bow tie with a dental motif of incisors and canines.

What do you take to a writers' meeting? A large pad of A4 and one of those pens that writes in ten different colours? Or a couple of wild women and a bottle of Jack Daniels? I settled on a nice fountain pen, given to me by a grateful patient whom I'd recently relieved of several troublesome wisdom teeth, and copies of the stories to be workshopped that evening. As well as my effort with Laurel there was a story by someone called Dave Derringer.

With the aid of my car's satnav I arrived in good time and found somewhere to park close to the venue. The Wig and Pen looked very promising from the outside and had, I speculated, undoubtedly been chosen for its inspiring Joycean ambience and excellent selection of author-sustaining fine ales. As I approached the door I felt rather self-conscious about carrying a bunch of roses, and it suddenly occurred to me that I might look like one of those swarthy ladies that come round pubs trying to embarrass men into buying a rose for their 'lovely lady'.

A middle-aged man with a beard and a mature beer gut was standing outside the Wig and Pen enjoying a fag. The stare he gave me quickly raised my discomfort level; not so sure about the flowers now, but too late to do anything about them; unless I gave them to the bloke with the beard. I took a deep breath and strode in.

Whatever I was expecting, this was even better. The ambience was indeed wonderful, the result of a recent refurbishment. The jukebox was pumping out *Don't Fear The Reaper* by The Blue Oyster Cult, the perfect theme tune for a supernatural storywriters' meeting. The beer at the bar consisted of a large and promising selection of hand-pumped real ales. There were, as yet, hardly any customers. I looked around in puzzlement. No Laurel. Perhaps she always arrived fashionably late. Then the doubts started to creep in. Was this the right pub? The right night? I gave a faint smile to the guy behind the bar.

"Hi, ah, is this where the writers' group meets?"

From the way he looked at the bunch of flowers you'd have thought I was carrying a decapitated head.

" Aye," he volunteered, "What would you like to drink?"

"Oh, I'm meeting someone, I'll wait till she arrives."

From the far side of the room came a strange snorting noise. I turned and saw three men huddled over a table of half-empty beer glasses. They all had their backs to me.

I wandered aimlessly up and down the bar, and over to the main window and back. The snorts plus occasional coughing fits continued from the small group who were the pub's only other occupants.

'Any moment now,' I thought, 'she's going to walk through that door and light this whole place up. Any moment now.' I stared over the bar at the interesting selection of bottled beers and spirits on offer. What did she drink? I was mentally polishing my opening line when there was a tap on my shoulder. I wheeled around – and there was the bearded bloke I'd seen outside. He gave me a leery grin.

"Hello," he said, nodding his head at the roses. "Are those for me?"

I was just about to tell him what he could do with them when he pointed at my bow tie.

"You must be Derrick," he said, offering his right hand.

"Eh?"

"Good to meet you at last," he said, his grin enlarging. "I'm Laurel Harding."

The three guys huddled over the table at the back exploded into hoots of laughter.

By the end of the evening the feeling of wishing that the ground would open up and swallow me had started to recede. Slightly.

The group had enlarged to nine members and I was duly introduced to all of them. A few lived locally, but most came quite a distance to attend the meetings. It turned out that each of the three guys who had been there when I had arrived had all joined the group under similar circumstances to mine, and they had duly made a point of being at the Wig and Pen in good time to enjoy my 'initiation'.

"Don't worry about the flowers," said the one sitting next to me, a tall, slim Brummie who turned out to be Dave Derringer, "one daft, besotted prick even turned up on his first night with an engagement ring."

"Who was that?" I asked.

"Well, me actually," replied Dave, ducking his head and taking a big mouthful of beer, as the rest of the group cracked up at the memory.

"Ah, the pulling power of dear Laurel, my most successful literary creation ever," said the bearded man.

"You're a sly, evil bastard Stan, and you'll burn in hell for all eternity. Another pint?" said Dave.

"Of course," replied our chairman, "and get one for the latest member of the Northampton Gothic Eroto-Horror Supernatural Story Writers Imagineering Group. Or as we like to call it for short," he declared, raising his glass in my direction, "'Goethe's Wig'."

Stanley Wain was a colourful character, to say the least. He'd learned the craft of creative writing at the local newspaper, the

Northampton Chronicle & Echo, starting as a teaboy and working his way up to features editor. Along the way he'd written articles and columns for the paper, and under various pseudonyms he also became a regular contributor to numerous other publications, the most lucrative being what he referred to with a wink as those covering 'specialist gentleman's pursuits'. He'd successfully turned his hand to short story writing, and had even had a number of plays performed on BBC radio. For a while he'd been part of a stable of scriptwriters for several highly successful TV dramas, but by this stage in his career Stan was fed up with being a team player, and he'd managed to fall out with an epic number of powerful and well-connected people of influence in various media. The coming of the internet era was Stan's salvation and meant that he could make a comfortable living working on his own projects from home.

He'd had a number of science fiction and fantasy novels and horror story anthologies published under names I immediately recognised, having read a fair few of them; but he'd hit the jackpot with the *Virgin Vampire* series, and the creation of its cult author, riding a lucrative wave in the zeitgeist that had made vampire stories enormously trendy.

"So who's the girl in the pictures?" I asked Stan during the interval between workshopping that evening's stories, "the Laurel Harding who turns up to the book signings and conventions?"

Stan grinned.

"Debbie," he said, reaching into his inside jacket pocket. "She's my niece. Lovely girl, works on the checkout at Tesco in Runcorn."

He took a photo from his wallet and gazed at it with a satisfied nod.

"Lovely girl," he said again, and passed the photo over to me.

Not for the first time that night my expectations exploded into dust. The photo showed a smiling, chubby, plain young woman with short mousey hair, her arms around a couple of infants, one on each knee.

"She's put on quite a bit of weight since she became a mum. Those are my great-nephews, Jason and Cody," said Stan, with a rare display of sentimentality. "This picture was taken about six months ago, on their first birthday."

Suddenly, the mystery of Laurel Harding's disappearance was solved.

"About two years ago she put on the blond wig and the catsuit and there was this pretty obvious bump," said Stan. "The silly cow had forgotten to go for her contraceptive injection. I had to get to work fast, floating those stories about her being dead or kidnapped, or having plastic surgery. Worked out all right in the end. What is it they say, 'If life gives you lemons, make lemonade'? Actually, we managed to turn the whole situation into a plus; Laurel's legend is now even bigger than ever."

"*You* started all those rumours about Laurel's disappearance?"

"Of course," replied Stan, "who else? Best to get your own first-rate conspiracy theories in first, before any rubbishy ones start to evolve."

"I suppose that's where all your newspaper experience comes in handy."

He grunted and smiled. "What's the definition of 'news'? It's what the media say it is. The media don't report the news, they create it."

I looked again at the woman in the picture. I'd certainly fallen for his creation, hook, line and sinker. He saw the look of disappointment on my face as I handed back the photo.

"What you have to remember, Derrick, is that ninety-nine percent of sex is in the imagination. The rest is just badly designed plumbing."

The evening was not a complete disaster. In fact, as I left to drive home I reflected on the warm reception that I and my story had received. Okay, my story as enhanced and edited by Stan. Stan-

Laurel. Lisa's 'Laurel and Hardy' quip had been closer to the mark than either of us had realised.

I may not have copped off with my fantasy woman but I had entered a novel (in both senses) world and suddenly found myself with a new and very supportive peer group. I had survived a potentially ego-demolishing rite of passage and was now treated as an equal by a disparate group of literary talents, some of them very highly regarded.

Stan, it turned out, was always on the lookout for talented writers. He believed passionately that the more people there were writing in the genre, the bigger the potential readership, which would benefit everyone. He'd started the group and, using a variety of ploys, had winkled out and attracted folk with literary potential, as well as a number of very well–established names.

Well, never mind the route, here I was. I decided that I was flattered that an expert felt that I had sufficient potential that it was worth the investment of time and trouble to seduce me; so to speak. This sop to my shattered-self esteem, plus sheer curiosity, made up my mind. I was in.

Over the following months, as my confidence in my own storytelling skills was nurtured and matured, I learned about my fellow writers' achievements, interests and foibles.

The other story that we scrutinised at my first workshop was Brummie Dave's twisted fantasy about gnome, goblin and pixie S&M. This turned out to be something of a recurrent theme in Dave's offerings. Fortunately for him there was a niche on-line magazine than regularly accepted his work.

In fact, there seemed to be on-line markets for every type of tale in which my new colleagues specialised.

The other two members of the trio that were lying in wait on my first evening were Wee Frannie from Northern Ireland and Septic Errol. Francis McGinley's last published story was about orgies with ogres. Errol Dent's was an obscene and highly inventive tale of bestiality with mythical animals in which a legion of pan-dimensional perverts groped griffins, fondled fawns, molested minotaurs and found various ingenious and painful usages for a unicorn's horn. We christened him the king of crazy carnal cryptozoology. I hesitated to ask him how he'd acquired the nickname 'Septic'.

Mark Seddon, a shy and markedly fidgety young man, introduced me to a new word – trolling; apparently this means deliberately abusing or insulting people on the Internet. Mark's latest story was about people who use webcams to randomly expose themselves to on-line voyeurs and get thoroughly trolled – by trolls, obviously.

There was, in fact, a woman in the group, the fabulously named Elspeth de Nantes. She was small and grey and old enough to be my mum, and she specialised in stories about dominatrix witches – witches with switches. She had been published extensively and was a regular on the horror convention circuit. She also managed the independent press that was going to publish my co-authored story. I was really delighted to meet her, and not entirely surprised to discover that her real name was a little more mundane: Marjorie Slack.

Other group members were developing stories about rapist wraiths, hermaphrodite fairies, and (my favourite) the fallating phantom that carried his head underneath his arm. The mind boggled; as did the phantom's head.

Over the next year I became an enthusiastic and productive member of Goethe's Wig. I had several more short stories published and started work on developing an outline for a novel.

Stan was a generous and supportive mentor, and his experience and guidance were given freely and enthusiastically to me, and all the other members of the group. But you never quite knew where you were with Stan. What became apparent fairly early on was that he liked a drink. This wasn't an issue most of the time, but it was an open secret that Stan had a pretty volatile relationship with his long-suffering wife, June, and when their relationship was at one of its many toxic lows he would deal with this by drinking heavily. On a couple of occasions he'd turned up at the meeting already well juiced, and as the evening wore on his wicked, but generally good-natured, playfulness had turned ugly, so that other members of the group found reasons to leave early. These incidents were never mentioned at the subsequent meeting, there being a rather fuzzy unwritten rule, more a tacit understanding, about Stan's talent and the licence this afforded him. This was something with which I was never entirely comfortable but, like everyone else, I blanked it out.

Earlier in the year, Laurel – or rather, Stan – had published *Vengeance of the Virgin Vampires*, the sixth and penultimate book of the best-selling series, and he'd now brought the opening chapter of the final novel in the sequence to Goethe's Wig for our consideration and comment. He always listened intently and took all criticism, positive or negative, respectfully and appreciatively. As usual, there was little or nothing I could suggest to improve upon his submission. As a fan, I was thrilled to be having a privileged sneak preview of the culmination of the series.

I couldn't think of anything particularly insightful to suggest that might improve the story, so I asked, "What will the final 'V' of the *Virgin Vampires* series be?"

So far we'd had *Vault, Vale, Void, Violation, Victims* and *Vengeance*.

Stan thought for a moment.

"*Victory*," he said.

Everyone nodded wisely. Yes, of course, it was obvious really.

"Or *Vanquish*," he added.

Everyone stopped nodding, paused and started nodding again. Yes, yes, we could all see that now, *Vanquish*, of course.

"But probably *Victory*," he said, stroking his beard. "Or *Vanquish*."

"How about *Vacillation*?" asked Brummie Dave.

Stan glowered at him.

134

"Cheeky sod," he said, "you can buy me a pint for that."

That evening Stan was much quieter and less contributory than usual. I stood at the bar with Dave in the break between stories during which Stan and the other smokers nipped outside to restore their flagging serum nicotine levels.

"Dave, do you think Stan's okay? He doesn't seem his usual self tonight."

"Probably had another flaming row with June about his drinking, or money, or something," replied Dave.

I wasn't so sure. In those circumstances Stan usually just got bladdered. This was something else.

That night, after the meeting, I managed to get Stan by himself outside the Gents.

"You all right?" I asked. "You don't seem your usual self."

"Bit tired," he replied, "been working hard against the book deadline."

"Is that all?" I ventured.

He gave me a half-hearted smile.

"Sure," he said.

"Well if there's anything I can do, please let me know. Anything at all."

"Anything?" he asked.

"Yes," I replied firmly, "absolutely anything."

He gave me a strange look.

"I might just hold you to that."

And of course, he did.

"Will you be going to Shakespeare's toupee while I'm away?" asked Lisa.

I sighed.

"It's Goethe's wig. Yes, why wouldn't I be going?" I asked, defensively.

"Well I've given up the salsa lessons. Aren't you bored with it yet?"

"No dear." Given up the salsa? What expensive hobby was

she going to take up next?

"There are enough meals in the freezer to keep you going for two weeks. Hopefully Mum will be in and out without too much bother."

Her mother was going in to hospital for a new hip, and Lisa was going up to Leeds to look after her dad, a man whose domestic skills were even more atrophic than mine.

She left straight after supper that Monday evening. I sat down at my laptop and opened the stories to be workshopped at the next meeting at the Wig.

About nine o'clock there was a ring on the doorbell. I wasn't expecting anyone, so I was pretty startled when I opened the door.

"Anything at all, you said."

It was Stan.

"I'm not there anymore," he said, striding straight in. "Got anything to drink?"

"You and June...?"

"It happened just like that," he said, snapping his fingers, "but it had been coming for a while."

We went through to the kitchen and sat down. I poured him a beer and he downed it in one. I poured him another.

Unusually for Stan he was dressed in a suit and tie. He had no bag with him. He noticed me staring at his clothes.

"Bit of a formal do this afternoon," he said. "I hate bloody dressing up," and he pulled off the tie and jacket and slung them over the back of the chair.

"How did you get here?" I hadn't seen a car outside.

"Never mind that, you wouldn't believe it anyway. Thing is, I need somewhere to crash for a week or two, just while I get sorted out."

Thank God Lisa was away.

"And I need to borrow your computer to finish off the novel."

"Well, so long as you don't smoke in the house..."

"Don't worry," he said, "I've given them up; for good."

For the next two weeks Stan became a fixture in my kitchen. I opened up the guest bedroom (thank God Lisa always had this ready for emergencies) and the following lunchtime I visited Marks and Spencer and topped up on Stan-sized shirts, socks and underwear. He really had left in a hurry, and all he had with him were the clothes that he stood up in. He accepted these essentials from me with a grunt. Apparently he'd left without any cash as well. He never offered to pay me back, and I was too embarrassed, and really too much in his debt in other ways, to ask him for any money.

Stan had stored all his notes and drafts for the last *Virgin Vampire* novel on a remote file server, so he was easily able to take up from where he'd left off. He worked at a furious pace, rising early and going to bed late, pausing only to help me empty the food from the freezer and the booze from the fridge. He was typing when I left for work in the morning, and still going when I arrived back home in the evening. The pace never slackened, not even over the weekend.

I asked him a couple of times if he wanted to use my phone to call June, but he shook his head.

"She's not expecting to hear from me. If I call it's only going to upset her. You can't put the clock back."

As far as I was aware he contacted no one else. He was totally focused on finishing the novel, and nothing was going to keep him from this.

"I have to meet a deadline," he muttered more than once. "I've never ever missed one, and I'm not going to start now."

On the Tuesday of the second week I was becoming anxious. Lisa was due back on the Friday, and Stan was still hard at work with no mention of when, or indeed if, he would be leaving. I'd told Lisa that he was staying but I'd assured her that he would be gone before she came back.

To my relief, when I returned from work on Wednesday

afternoon, Stan was on his feet staring out of the kitchen window.

"Finished," he announced.

"May I read it?"

"Sure," he replied, "but first I want you to e-mail a copy to my publisher."

"Why don't you do it?"

"Because my ISP subscription has been cancelled."

"Oh." June must have been really pissed off with him.

I'd been unable to get to my e-mail for over a week as Stan had been almost welded to my laptop and, annoyingly, the server at work had gone down the previous week and I was still waiting for someone to come and investigate.

"That's odd," I remarked as I opened my Hotmail account, "I've had no e-mails for nearly two weeks; not even spam."

"Happens," said Stan with a shrug. He told me his publisher's e-mail address and I sent them a copy of his finished manuscript.

"I'll be off tomorrow," he said, "get out of your hair."

"Where will you go?"

"Don't worry, all sorted."

"But you'll be at the Wig on Thursday…"

"Actually, no. I have to be somewhere else."

He stood staring out of the window for a long time.

The following day, when I arrived back from work, he'd gone. He'd deleted his manuscript from my laptop. I checked my Hotmail account and it was stuffed with messages, some of them two weeks old. 'What the hell's that all about?' I thought as I checked the more urgent-looking business and personal e-mails. There was a lot of traffic from the other Wig members; most of the message titles seemed to be about Stan, which was not surprising given his recent domestic dramas. There was no time to read them, but I'd catch up with everyone later that evening. Now I had to get ready and leave for Northampton.

There was something bothering me on the drive over. I couldn't place what, but then again I'd just hosted Stan Wain for nearly two weeks and then he'd vanished without even saying goodbye. That was enough to unsettle anyone.

I arrived at the Wig and Pen a little late. Everyone else was already there. They were sitting in our usual corner. The table was full of drinks that no one had touched. Everyone was wearing black. Even wee Frannie, who only ever wore tee shirts, was wearing a plain black one. No one spoke.

"What is this, a wake?" I said as I pulled up a chair.

"Where were you, then?" asked Brummie Dave, his tone accusatory.

"Where was I, what?" I replied.

"Monday last week; why weren't you at Stan's funeral?"

I looked at everyone for a moment then I laughed.

"Great idea guys, you all look pretty funereal too. Nice try, but your timing's all wrong. I've just had Stan staying over at my place since Monday last week. He left today; sends his apologies by the way, he has to be somewhere else."

Errol pulled a paperback out of his jacket pocket and handed this to me.

"What, like this?" he said. The book was one of Stan's, written under his own name, an anthology of stories about unquiet spirits with unfinished business; it was called *Somewhere Else*.

"Nice touch Errol, but the gig's up. He came over to mine after June chucked him out last week. He finished off the last of the *Virgin Vampires*, which I e-mailed to his publisher yesterday."

"June didn't chuck him out, he died suddenly of a heart attack," said Elspeth, coolly. "That's what all the rows were about. He was having chest pains and she was pleading with him to go to the doctor, but he was too stubborn, or too frightened, or something, and he wouldn't go."

"Guys, give it up. He's been at my place since Monday last week."

"This isn't funny," said Dave. "Your stupid joke's in really bad taste, Derrick."

"Come on guys, how long are you going to keep this up? This is one of Stan's wind-ups isn't it? Where is he, hiding in the bogs?"

Elspeth reached into her bag and pulled out a copy of the Northampton Chronicle & Echo. This was dated two weeks previously. At the bottom of the front page was an article entitled 'Acclaimed local writer dies'.

'Acclaimed local writer Stanley Wain has died. He collapsed suddenly at his home last Friday evening and was taken to Northampton General Hospital where he was pronounced dead. 'Stan' Wain (60) started work as a tea boy at The Chronicle aged fifteen and worked his way up to become features editor. His wife June has revealed that he was the author behind the best-selling Virgin Vampire *series of gothic horror novels...'*

"It happened just like that," Dave said, snapping his fingers, "but it had been coming for a while."

"It's the only time I've ever seen Stan in a suit," said Mark Seddon, "laid out in that coffin."

I was stunned. Then it struck me.

"Wait a minute – Stan worked for the Chronicle. He's got one of his old mates in the print room to knock up a bogus front page." I laughed. But none of them joined me.

'Come on!" I urged. Silence

This was a wind-up. It had to be. He'd suckered me good and proper once before and he was trying to do it again. Typical bloody Stan; this was how he paid me back for doing him a huge favour.

Who was going to crack first, the rest of the group or me? I surveyed their faces for a hint – the twitch of a smile at a corner of the mouth, the strangled attempt to suppress a laugh.

Nothing.

Just appalled bafflement on each and every face.

They were good, they were very good, but I knew what was going to happen. Stan would be walking into the bar any second now.

Any second.
Surely.
The rest of the group said nothing.
I stared at them.
They stared back at me.
Any second now.
Any.
Second.
Now...

The Old Man of Northampton and the Sea

Sarah Pinborough

"Why did I come and live here? Someone once told me Northamptonshire was the furthest county from the sea in England. That's why."

"Is that true?"

"I haven't measured it exactly. But it's inland and cheap. That's what I wanted," Mr McBride said, huddled over the small dressing table that served as his desk in the room. His fingers trembled as he carefully glued another piece of grey plastic to the model ship that was starting to take shape. Jimmy watched, as he did on each of his night time visits. His fascination with Mr McBride refused to fade. The old man's fingernails were yellow and dirty brown, and his spine was curved like warped wood that had been soaked and then left out in the sun too long; a bony, brittle thing housed in faded brown wool.

"From all the houses in the paper that were renting rooms, yours was closest to the centre of the town. The most inland of all of them." The old man looked up at Jimmy, watery eyes over lenses. "I had a map for that one."

Jimmy was sitting on the single bed, his knees tucked under his chin as much for warmth as comfort. His dressing gown and pyjamas kept him warm against the night air that crawled in under the door and through the gaps in the old windows. He was confused. A lot of what Mr McBride said confused him.

"Where did you live before?" he asked. "My mum says you should be in an old folks' home where they can look after you properly. She says you never go out. My dad says she should mind her own business." Jimmy had no idea what the old man did in the day. It wasn't something he'd ever really thought about. It was only at night, when they shared their secret inability to sleep, that he even really existed to the boy. This strange friendship they had in the hours between midnight and dawn when generations and age gaps didn't seem to matter and a boy and an old man could sit in comfortable silence or chat idly.

"I go out," the old man muttered. "I get the papers sometimes. The ones that count." He held up the model. It was some kind of military ship, Jimmy thought. It was hard to tell when it was still in skeleton form. "Where did I live?" Mr McBride repeated Jimmy's question. "When I was a boy, about your age I lived in Scotland. Long time ago now."

"You don't sound Scottish. You sound like you're from London."

"Funny thing that. When they pulled me out of the water, I spoke different. Must have banged my head or something. That's what doctors today would say. Back then? Well, I think my mum was just glad to have me back." Mr McBride smiled slightly, but his mouth wavered at the edges where the creases were deepest and where tea sometimes ran if he took too big a sip.

"What do you mean 'when they pulled you out of the water'?" Jimmy wondered if he'd missed something. Mr McBride could talk like that though. Jumping here there and everywhere and as if things that made no sense were really important.

"It was a long time ago. Can still feel the cold of it." The old man looked over to the window. "And that awful taste of oil." The curtains were open – Jimmy had never seen them shut now that he came to think about it – and he could see Mr McBride's reflection. The glass was greasy and it made the old man's face distort. Like looking at him under water, Jimmy thought. Funny that. Mr McBride looked afraid, his baggy eyes wide. Jimmy wondered whether that was just the window too. The old man's expression unsettled him and he looked back to the desk. It was a litter of plastic pieces and botched attempts that would all be cleared away back into the biscuit tin by the time his mum and dad got up.

Mr McBride had been living with them for two months now and they'd been having these middle of the night conversations for about six weeks. The ship building had started about a month ago, the old man taking different parts from different packets of model First World War boat kits. Jimmy didn't know much about either boats or the First World War, but Mr McBride was determined to get it exact, whatever he was building.

"Why are you making the ship?" Jimmy asked, after a long silence.

Mr McBride let out a long sigh and his whole chest rattled, as if maybe some of that oil and water he mentioned was still in his lungs. He held the small structure of wood and plastic up in his gnarled hand. He turned it this way and that in the weak light from the desk lamp.

"Sometimes, Jimmy," he said, so softly the boy only just heard. "You have to know your enemy. You have to understand what it really wants."

Mr McBride wasn't supposed to smoke in the house. His dad did, but somehow his mum thought the old man shouldn't. His dad had said something about shutting the stable door after the horse had bolted, but his mum had hushed him and said that an old man in his condition might fall asleep and set the house on fire. Jimmy had heard all this and kept quiet. He could have reassured his mum. As far as he could tell, Mr McBride never slept. He was always awake when Jimmy couldn't sleep, anyway. He'd figured the old man's routine out now. He'd turn his light off at around ten until Jimmy's parents were safely asleep, and then he'd get up again at around midnight. Maybe he dozed in the early mornings,

145

or napped in the afternoon, but in those traditional sleeping hours, Mr McBride was very much awake.

Tonight, the old man had the window open and was smoking through the gap, trying to blow the fumes out into the damp breeze that was determined to push them back in. His cardigan – blue this time – billowed out around his decrepit frame like an oversized sail. Jimmy thought he'd got thinner. The creases in his cheeks had become crevasses, and the backs of his hands flaked with dryness. He was on his third cigarette.

"Are you all right?" Jimmy asked. The old man hadn't spoken since Jimmy had knocked on the door half an hour ago, when the clock had ticked round past one a.m. and he'd realised that sleep had crept past his door and ignored him for another night. The tin was open on the desk and a few pieces were half-heartedly spread out, but it didn't look as if Mr McBride had been working on his ship.

"I'm the last one now. They'll be coming for me soon." The old man's eyes searched the darkness beyond as if there was something in the night he didn't quite trust. "Three in three months."

"What are you talking about?" Jimmy was too tired for riddles. Something was upsetting the old man and he found that it unsettled him. Somewhere in the dark nights they'd passed quietly together, Jimmy had become fond of him.

Mr McBride turned away from the window and picked up a newspaper lying on his desk chair. The large sheet of paper was folded neatly into a square, the edged pinched and squeezed as if it had been worried at while studied. Jimmy took it.

"There," Mr McBride said, one stained finger pointing to the bottom corner. Jimmy looked. It was an obituary.

William 'Billy' Rogan, 10th January 1900 - 30th June 1980. Survivor of the Fastnet, and much loved husband, father and grandfather. Will be sorely missed.

Jimmy still didn't get it. Mr McBride was really old – he must expect his friends to be dying. He must be used to it, in fact. And eighty was a pretty long time for anyone to have lived. "Was he your friend?" was all he could find to say.

The old man took the paper back and stared at it, holding it close under his glasses. "He was my friend a long time ago." He looked up at Jimmy. "I hadn't seen him for a lifetime. Then he paid me a visit a few months back. Not long before I moved here."

He perched on the end of the bed, carefully making the move from standing to sitting as if his bones might snap. The mattress barely dented. He coughed slightly and flinched as the rattle shifted in his chest.

"He said he'd been having dreams. Said there were only four of us left now. He said the other two were dreaming too. He said they weren't waiting any longer."

"What kind of dreams?" Jimmy pulled his knees closer to his chin. Although they had tipped into July, the weather was ignoring the seasons and the wind that cut through the open window was cool and whispered as it darted around the curtains.

"Dreams of the water," Mr McBride said softly. "The sea air. The taste of black oil on the breaking surf."

"What happened?" Jimmy asked.

"I sent him away." The old man got to his feet, pushing hard on his knees to do so. He went to the desk and peered into the open biscuit tin. "I thought his mind had gone. Old age does that to you." He pulled out the small nearly-completed model ship and held it up. "I didn't start having the dreams myself until a couple of weeks later."

Jimmy looked at the boat in the old man's hands. He'd done a lot more work on it and the mode was finally coming together. This was definitely a naval ship – two high funnels coming out of its middle, and there was space for a third. The plastic sections it was built from were a steely grey, which gave the model a sense of solidity, as if it really could take to the ocean waves.

"Do you believe in ghosts, Jimmy?" Mr McBride asked.

"I don't know," Jimmy answered. "Maybe in the middle of

the night."

"I do," Mr McBride whispered. "And I think Billy was right. I think they're impatient."

When Jimmy went back to bed, he didn't sleep, but lay awake listening to the wind beating against the walls of the small terraced house. It sounded like water slapping the decks.

July came to an end. The month had been hot and for the last three weeks of it Jimmy had been forced to visit his aunt and uncle on their farm in Devon. Every year he was sent under the guise of a 'holiday', but as he'd got older it became more about a spare pair of hands for Uncle Brian and less about lazing around and going to the beach. The more time he spent in hard labour on the farm, the more coming back to Northampton felt like stepping into another world.

"You've got taller," the old man said. Jimmy didn't know how to answer so simply sat on the chair by the desk. Mr McBride was in his bed, the sheets tucked under his arms. Jimmy wasn't used to seeing him there. It was Jimmy's place, not Mr McBride's. The old man looked tired and his skin had turned sickly yellow as if the nicotine stains at the end of his fingers had spread up his arms and washed his face. His teeth were too big for his mouth, if they were the old man's teeth at all, forcing their way out between his thin lips.

The room stank of sickness and Jimmy fought the urge to open the window. The air was muggy and warm, holding the kind of damp that would soak you if you stood in it too long. Jimmy didn't know how to talk about the reasons Mr McBride was holed up in bed at barely midnight, so he looked around for something to dispel the unusual awkwardness that now sat between them.

"You finished it, then." Jimmy picked up the model ship. It could only be six inches or so long but everything was defined. The small windows, the funnels, all perfectly placed.

"Just about in time, too," Mr McBride said. "I still don't sleep but I don't have the energy for that anymore."

"Shouldn't you be in a hospital?" Jimmy asked. He felt odd seeing the old man like this. How could someone change so much in such a short time?

"Don't see the point. Your mum and dad have said I can stay here. I've got some put by, I'll see them all right for it." His milky eyes drifted around the room. "I've come to see this as home. I felt safe here for a while at any rate. Can't really ask for more than that."

"Safe from what?"

"The ghosts, Jimmy. The ghosts. I'm the only one left now. They'll be coming for me. I think they all got tired of waiting." His breath came out of him in a rattle. "It's been an awful long time to be down in the water. It's dark down there. I see it in my dreams."

Jimmy stared at him. "Sometimes I don't understand what you're talking about at all," he said, eventually.

"The *Fastnet*, of course," the old man said, his eyes widening in surprise. "The ship. What do you think I've been talking about all this time?"

Jimmy shrugged.

"I was fourteen when I joined her." The old man was staring at the ceiling, but his eyes drifted to somewhere in the past, out of Jimmy's sight. "Billy was sixteen. We'd both signed up too young. I was still fourteen when she went down. Just off Scotland we were. They say she sank in minutes. Had to, that close to the shore. I don't remember much. I'd been oiling the guns. If I'd been below decks I'd have stood no chance. Two hundred and sixty-eight souls were on board, but they only pulled eighteen out of the water. Me and Billy were among those lucky eighteen. He kept me afloat until the fishing boat got us. Swam us out past the pull of her sinking. He was strong, Billy, in those days." He paused. "I should have listened to him when he came and found me. He saved me once. He was trying to warn me of what was coming."

"Warn you?" Jimmy asked. He put the boat back down on

149

the table. He'd thought it had just been some kind of hobby for the old man to while away the sleepless hours. But it sounded as if the ship had caused the sleepless hours. Jimmy couldn't imagine remembering something from that long ago, let alone it terrifying him so much.

"They've been down there all that time, those men," the old man continued. "In that freezing black water, with the grime of coal and steel and oil on them."

The old man coughed, the sound wet and slick and deadly, and then he shut his eyes. The clock ticked a few minutes out and for a horrible moment Jimmy thought he would never open them again.

"We made a pact."

The old man spoke without opening his eyes and Jimmy almost jumped.

"Those eighteen of us. We went out in a fishing boat at dawn. Silent it was out there. The wind was like ice cutting into us, but I don't think we really noticed. All I could think of was how that mammoth steel ship could be broken in two so far beneath us. Imagine that, a huge ship and no sign of it on the surface. Anyway, we cut our thumbs and dripped our blood in the water and said that when our time came we'd join them. Get our bodies buried at sea to rest with our fallen comrades." He sniffed. "Seemed like a good idea at the time."

"Is that what you want us to do? You know ..." Jimmy didn't know quite how to put it. "After?"

"I don't think we have to worry about that." Mr McBride smiled and opened his eyes, turning his head in the boy's direction. "I think they'll be coming to collect me. I think they gave me this rot in my chest to hurry me along."

"Who'll be coming?" Jimmy's blood felt cold. Ocean-cold.

"The ghosts, Jimmy. The crew. They want us all together back in the pit of the ocean. I think perhaps they're jealous of the years we've had. They want us united again." The old man's expression darkened. "But I remember that water. I remember

150

the cold. I can't stay down there forever. Not fourteen and afraid forever. That won't do. I owe Billy more than that."

It was nearly one a.m. and although the sense that they were the only two people awake in this sleepy market town was normally something that made Jimmy smile, right then it made his bones tremble. Ghosts in the ocean. A terrified old man. These were things that wouldn't help him sleep, even if they were just Mr McBride's sickness rambling. In the middle of the night, they felt real, and if they felt real, then they might as well be for all you could tell your imagination otherwise.

"You should go to bed, Jimmy." The old man smiled at him and there was genuine warmth there. It felt like good-bye.

"I could sit with you all night if you like," Jimmy blurted. "You know, just in case they..." he felt stupid saying it, but didn't want Mr McBride laying in here awake and terrified by dreams of the past, "...come back."

"No, son." Mr McBride, closed his eyes again. "I think I know my enemy now. In this case, my enemy were once my friends. Had to start thinking of it that way to see what had to be done. I think I've come up with a way to make it better for all of us. I think I've mended it." He sighed. "I want the sea air on my face, not her cold in my lungs. I've had enough cold in my lungs of late."

Jimmy sat there a while anyway. Just to be sure. When he left, the old man was asleep and so he put the model ship on the windowsill. It would be visible from the bed there, and Jimmy had a feeling that Mr McBride wouldn't be leaving his bed any time soon.

The old man died two nights later. For once, Jimmy had slept like a log from the moment his head had hit the pillow. Afterwards, when the doctor and ambulance arrived to quietly take away the cooling body, Jimmy felt strange about that. Almost disrespectful. To be sleeping when someone died. The sun was shining brightly and it was a hot day. He hoped that was a sign that God was happy to have Mr McBride in heaven, not that he really believed any of that stuff that his nan always spouted when any of her friends died. She had a reason for God to be happy whether it was raining or shining and so neither really rang true to Jimmy.

He followed his mum into Mr McBride's room and watched as she stripped the sheets.

"At least he died peacefully in his sleep," she said. Jimmy didn't say anything, but waited until she'd left and then stared at the bare mattress. It looked old and tired. His eyes caught on a damp patch glinting on the floorboards by the bed and he took a closer look. It was a footprint. Still wet, soaked into the wood. His heart stilled for a second and he lowered his nose hesitantly towards it. Salt and oil and the ocean filled his nostrils and for a second he could only see an endless darkness behind his eyes and hear the creaking of metal in the tides. He gasped and shifted backwards. The print stayed there though, an echo of a ghostly visitor come to claim the last of the crew.

Jimmy's eyes darted to the windowsill and he scrabbled to his feet. It took a moment for his heart to stop racing and eventually, as the sunlight streamed in through the smeary glass and warmed his face, Jimmy smiled. The ship Mr McBride had made so painstakingly was gone.

The old man had mended it for them.

The Last Economy

Paul Melhuish

Brant rode the transport bus under the vast underside of the emwon, emerging in the independent mini-state that occupied the dead space between North Londonshire and South Birminghamshire. He noted the anachronistic housing of red brick sitting under or adjacent to the more familiar plastisteel dwellings constructed over and among the terraced housing. Beyond the dwellings Brant couldn't fail to notice the stacks of factories and logistics centres glowering down upon the town. Vehicle after vehicle wound around the flyovers from the emwon to collect goods from the factories only to rush back to the emwon to deliver these goods to the rest of Europe or beyond.

Under the motorway the plastisteel dwellings clung to the road's support pillars like limpets. Brant was glad he didn't have to walk through there at night. In fact Brant didn't relish the idea of walking through that area at any time. This was clearly a high-crime area. Finally passing under the motorway and out into daylight under a grey sky, Brant gazed as if mesmerised by the tower. Rising higher than the stacked factories that horseshoed the town, this edifice thrust defiantly into the grey sky, its apex bulging, crowned with colourless lights.

The bus wound through the town and even passed the area where North Londonshire bordered South Birminghamshire. Brant got a good look at the dead space where the zones met. Those unfortunate enough to dwell on the land bordering the

153

zone lived under the scrutiny of the security systems, their unwieldy metal heads - a dual function device serving as both camera and gun - swaying slowly from side to side like a sitting canine with a brain injury.

As this tour of ancient streets came to an end, the bus pulled into a vast cavernous terminal that served the whole district. The plastisteel roof and walls were the colour of nicotine.

Now that Brant had arrived a sudden sick feeling washed over him. He'd come here to work, as had most of the country, and now he faced the daunting task of finding his way around the district. He had to:

Find work.

Find accommodation

Comm his mother to tell her he'd arrived.

The bus driver was a Semioid. Brant found it difficult to tell, as the clone

possessed all the features of a full human including stubble and a penchant for whistling tunelessly as he drove. Only up close did Brant notice that half his torso was absent, the pelvic area amalgamated with his swivel seat. The rushing humans exited the vehicle at speed.

"Excuse me, sir." Brant awkwardly spoke to the driver who in turn gave him a quizzical look as if he was not used to being engaged in conversation, less still to being called sir.

"How can I help you?"

"Where can I find accommodation here? Accommodation and a labour resource centre?"

"You here to work?"

"Yes."

"The best labour resource centre here is Swain's."

"Swain's?"

The driver handed him a card almost surreptitiously.

"He's the man to see about work. I'm not supposed to give out cards but he says he'll get me a full body if I clear three thousand by the end of the week. If you sign on, tell him 378 sent you."

Brant thanked him, disembarked and the driver pulled the steaming vehicle out of the bay. It was well known that some people promised Semioids things that they could never deliver because the clones were too naïve to disbelieve them. Already Brant mistrusted this Swain character.

Blund Swain
Labour Provision
Lower Drapery Street
NH District, N. Londonshire.

It would be dark soon. Brant had nowhere to sleep and no money (the transport into the district was free) so would have to find work fast. He didn't have any choice but to put himself into the care of this Swain character. He studied the card again. How quaint, they still used actual street names here.

The labour distribution centre was a large, carpeted circular hall with a wide circular desk where very pretty Semioids, all wearing matching suits and pelvic areas amalgamated to matching swivel chairs, tapped constantly at keyboards and spoke rapidly into headsets. Hundreds of men and women in dark grey clothing hung around the area. Occasionally a Semioid would give one of them a printout and they would rush away, bolting like rats through one of the many exits. Nervously, young Brant approached a Semioid. He drank in her pale face-flesh, shining teeth and bright blonde hair pulled tight into a pony tail.

"Yes, sir."

"Hello. Er…I'm looking for work."

"Have you registered with us?"

"No."

"You need to see Mr Swain personally to be registered. If you go through exit three slash seven he will see you in good time. Thank you."

Brant padded across the carpet and joined a long queue to a large, ornate arched door. Four hours passed, he counted them

155

on the clock in the main room, before he was granted access to Swain's office.

Swain wasn't a Semioid but he might as well have been. The labour distributor wore a flashy suit of dull silver that wasn't cheap and his pitch-black hair was gelled, almost sculptured, across his head.

Brant did a double take, not quite comprehending what he was seeing. Swain, it appeared, had three mouths. He had a natural, central mouth as well as two extra mouths; one located in his right cheek spoke incessantly. The other barked orders in a similar manner from his left cheek. He also vocalised continually from the central, natural mouth. Brant knew that such cosmetic alterations were possible but had never actually seen a three-mouth person with his own two eyes before.

The three mouths jabbered on, each speaking into a triple microphone device that sat over Swains head like a high tech crown.

"...order one from central...stoppage on five labour units..."
"...contract secured on X77...seven day amalgamation..."
"...stoppage rectified...bac-pace to L.C. Z44...no, Z44...not..."
"...delivery on four hour order...overtime given at half rate..."
"...signified if fitting required...assume delivery required..."
"...any problems replace them with loyal substandards..."
"...but you know what they say ..."
"...list on Semioid nine's desk if you want..."
"...assume arse you and me."
"Yes pal, how can I help?"

Amid the noise of the other two mouths chattering Brant was taken aback when the central, and probably the natural mouth, spoke. His mind had wandered; Brant was wondering if Swain owned three toothbrushes or just one very good one.

"I'm looking for work."

"Good. Twelve hours on R 675 or a nine stretch on Z44?"

"Sorry. I don't understand."

"Where the hell have you been? What shift do you want?"

156

"The nine hours. No, the twelve hours."

"Twelve stretch. Good man! Just give me your credit details."

"My what?"

"Credit details."

"I haven't got any."

"Then get up to the bank and get a debit account." He barked.

Then turned away, signalling the end of the conversation.

"...yes, twelve
Stretch on Q 11...no don't mess me about I've got 50 labour units..."

Brant found out from one of the grey-clothed workers that there was a bank on Abington Street. Blank windows stared out onto the street where long ago shops had been. Here he found a small doorway where a Semioid waited at a desk. He asked about a debit account, as Swain had called it.

"Certainly sir, we can open a debit account. Just let me see your registration in the district. No registration? Then sir, you need to be formerly identified at District Central. It's down the street on Lower Derngate Corner."

District Central was a second floor office where an expressionless Semioid told him he would need a Birth Registration. No Birth Registration? Then you would need to go to District Hall, Far Cotton Road.

District Hall had exactly the same layout as District Central. An identical-looking cloned Semioid told him that he would need to verify his Birth Registration at Central Records on Lady's Way. At Central Records they told him he would need a Central Records Registration Pass and that could be attained from Human Logistics on Gold Street.

"A Central Records Registration Pass? Certainly sir." Now, standing in this cramped office overlooking a mass of Plastisteel dwellings, Brant was finally getting somewhere. "I just need to see your Credit Details."

"I haven't got any."

"But you need to pay for a Central Records Registration Pass. For that you need a Debit Account."

"I need a Central Records Registration Pass to get a debit account, or rather to get a Verification of Birth Registration, to be formally identified by the district to get a Debit Account to get a job."

"I'm afraid I can't process this without your Debit Account details."

"I've just told you…"

"Without your Debit Account details we cannot process a Central Records Registration Pass."

Brant raised his voice. "Bloody hell…how am I supposed to get a bloody job?"

The Semioid appeared to instantly fall asleep as if switched off. A message flashed up on a screen above stating that abusive behaviour would not be tolerated in the Human Logistics office. Outside it was getting dark. Brant had nowhere to live, no money and no work.

At least the lobby of the labour distribution place was warm. Brant sat there as the hours passed and the beautiful Semioids typed. He hardly noticed Swain breeze from his office, humming from his right-sided mouth, stop and regard Brant.

"All right son?" He said from his central mouth. "Got those Credit Details?"

"No." Brant explained the situation.

"This happens all the time. Wait there." He strode over to one of the smiling Semioids, said something and she handed him a printout. "Here. Go to the bank, give them this then get up to Z44. I'm afraid the Twelve hour stretch I promised you is now a five hour. Better than nothing though, eh?"

Brant naively thought he would work a seven or eight hour shift a day in the same factory or warehouse and have money paid into a bank account. That's what his dad told him would happen. Instead he was given a five hour shift in Z44, a three hour stretch in S11, a nine hour stretch in A14 and a 74 hour shift in Logistics Centre 16. He'd done these shifts and slept in between, dozing at the Labour Control centre until the next shift came up and eating from a vending machine using his debit card to purchase near tasteless nutrition bars. Another thing his dad had been wrong about: Brant didn't get paid, he reduced debt when he worked and increased debt when he spent it. Credit did not exist, only debt, despite the name of the account. He had to find somewhere to live and so was directed to the Accommodation and Dwellings Centre.

"I can give you a room in a city centre house on Hester Street." The smiling Semioid woman had said.

"That's great."

"On a sixty hour contract."

"What?" He stood there gob-smacked. "What happens when that contract ends?"

"Come back here and I'll give you another contract for another room."

The room was functional and after he'd got over the novelty of living for the next sixty hours in an antique property his next shift at X77 was due to begin. Over the next week Brant did a seven hour stretch at Z33 whilst on a seven hour contract at a room in Peacock Towers, a nine hour stretch whilst renting a bed at Colwyn Road, a fifty hour stretch while on a 70 hour contract at a house on Connaught Street and a seventy hour stretch with a three hour accommodation on Broadmead Way; accommodation which he never saw.

"We have a contract on a room in Hood Street, next to the Semioid production zone." The smiling clone offered him the printout.

Brant had loaded plastic crates from production line to road transport vehicle on a twenty hour stretch and just needed to sleep.

"Fine. How long for?"

"Strange. There isn't a time limit. The workers go in on various time contracts and all leave in less than an hour." Without thinking, he took the printout and walked through the darkness to Hood Street. Again, he was confronted by streets of red brick terrace houses plus smashed pavements covered in litter and excrement from wild dogs that roamed the area. The dome of the Semioid production zone rose up before him to his right as he entered the street from the old Kettering Road.

The room was functional, lit by a single bare bulb. Magnolia walls boxed the occupant in but a window afforded a view out into a night punctuated with flickering streetlights that strobed into life when a person passed, then took one point three minutes to shut off again. He heard someone shuffling around in the room next door. Ignoring it and, too tired to talk to another worker complaining of shift patterns and the not decreasing enough debit, he slept. When Brant dreamed, he dreamed of wide open fields.

It was dark when he woke. He'd not seen the sun for weeks Under the artificial light of the eating area he encountered his house-sharer. Curiously, this man had long hair. No one had long hair in the workplace. They said it always got caught in machines. If the supervisors thought your hair was too long they'd get a Semioid to shave your head as you worked. The house sharer was eating something unidentifiable on toast, munching obnoxiously into the bread, regarding Brant with mean, blue eyes. The stuff on toast looked like worms or thin noodles.

"Right," the fellow occupant said, holding out the toast. "Take a good look at this then feel free to fuck off."

"What is it?"

"This," and he gestured to the toast, "is synaptic nerves. I prefer the nerves to come from the lower end of the spine, the lumbar area, but this'll do."

"Nerves. Where did you get them?"

"From a body." Munch. "A *human* body."

He waited for Brant to react. Brant didn't.

"All right. A Semioid body. I used to be all conservative about it. Eat a liver or some kidneys. Whatever I could find in the bins out the back. Now it's nerves, or spine in a bap. So, now you know, you can be sick in the bin and fuck off with a look of disgust on your zitty, disease-ridden face. Then I can have the house back to myself."

"You must really be hungry. Even back home we never ate the nerves but we did eat kidneys, even brains of animals." Brant said.

His flatmate stopped eating, his face suddenly pale.

"What did you say?"

"I grew up on a farm and we used to slaughter our own chickens. Decapitate, pluck and gut them…"

His new flat mate threw the toast down and rushed over to the bin to vomit. For once his performance had backfired and the tables had been turned. Brant's indifference to the consumption of cloned body parts instantly won him Grotus' respect.

Grotus had a screen in the living room and a file player. He'd explained that the District had once been called Northampton and had manufactured shoes exclusively for transvestites. He proved this by showing Brant a documentary called *Kinky Boots*, made just over eighty years before. There were places that Brant recognised from his travels throughout the district.

"Now of course this is the main place for production and distribution. The only solvent place in Europe."

"Solvent? I've got a debit account. Swain says I'll never be in credit, no one ever is."

"Ha. That's not what Swain's told the banks that lend debit to this town. The banks give them the credit because of that." He pointed to the sky, though there was a ceiling and night beyond his pointing finger. "The tower. That's where they keep their real solid collateral. Everything from cash to antiques. Jewels and coins. All up there in the tower. Waiting to pay the banks off. They say Northampton will be the only place in Europe in credit."

"So we could be onto a winner staying here."

"Bollocks. I've heard all this before. They're too scared to get the real cash out. They're hiding something, work work, produce produce and we'll all have a penny, a credit one day. I've been listening to this bullshit for the last ten years and nothing's changed. So don't tell me; you came here thinking it would be all credit, quick debit decrease and then live your perfect life on your savings. Hey," and Grotus leapt up from his seat and perched elfin-like on the arm of Brant's own worn sofa chair, studying him like some interesting specimen. "You said you grew up on a farm. What the fuck are you doing in an ugly plastisteel excrement-hole like this?"

Brant explained. "I grew up on my father's farm located in the west, on the coast. Just as this place used to be called Northampton, so our settlement was once called the Gower. Now we're called Reservation Zero Point Four for some reason. We had some cows for milk and chickens for food. There was nothing but miles of fields around and the sea. We were the Micro-Economy."

"What's the Micro Economy?"

"A bunch of people living in wooden houses all trading only with each other. We traded with the Macro Economy sometimes but we generally wore clothes made of our own wool and ate our own reared meat or grown vegetables."

"Fields. Wow, real fields. So why come anywhere near a conurbation?"

"Well, the officials from the Cardiff Conurbation arrived to say they wanted to expand over our land. We would have to register with National Control. Registering costs and we had no account. My father said that I would have to go and work in the conurb to get a debit account and earn some credit. As everyone knows, the district, sorry, Northampton, is one of the most prosperous areas in the country. So here I am."

"And is it everything you expected it to be?"

"No. I hate it. I'm leaving soon. I'm not reducing any debit working this way. In fact, I'm actually increasing my debit. I've got this. I'll give this to my dad to show them." Brant pulled out the printout Swain had given him of his debt status. Grotus snatched it off of him and tore it to pieces.

"Hey!"

"Trash. Worthless. The struggle is all that counts. Besides, how are you gonna get out of the district?"

"The same way as I got in. The transport."

"Oh no. Your mate Swain didn't tell you, did he? The transport is free to enter the district but costs to get out. Costs a lot. More credit than you'll ever accumulate. You're stuck, son."

Brant stared at the floor, remembering the journey here; miles and miles through the plastisteel hell of the dwellings. The journey would take days to walk. Not only was that a problem, but judging by the dilapidation he'd seen on the journey here he would have to pass through high-crime areas – too dangerous to walk through safely

"There's only one way out of here," sneered Grotus, a mischievous gleam in his eye. "That's to destroy the system from the inside."

Time passed. Shifts were completed, debit decreased and increased as he purchased and consumed. He acquired a cycle to move around with increased speed from shift to shift, factory to factory. Brant functioned on automatic. All hope had gone from his heart. The officials would turf his family off their land, would build more plastisteel dwellings on the land and pretty soon the Micro Economy would fall. He cycled along the C24 flyover and caught sight of his facial expression in the glass of the office block opposite. Brant wore the same gaunt expression as everyone else who worked here. A dead, hopeless expression devoid of emotion. He'd joined them.

Brant, the boy who'd grown up on the farm, had not seen a single leaf or blade of green plant life since being here. Grotus said that they put herbicide in the clouds, in the rain water to kill off any plants in the district. As the skies were always grey and it rained a lot here he could believe it. Every night Brant dreamed of fields. Sometimes when waking he closed his eyes and saw the green fields of his home but his memory was fading. He was having trouble remembering the geography of his home area. He had to get out of here but there was no getting out. He'd tried taking a bus but the driver had asked for an unfeasible amount to take him to the edge of the district, just as Grotus predicted.

Today Swain had sent him to Logistics' site Z100. He'd pedalled for ages to get there and arrived at the bulky-looking black plastisteel edifice and got into the multi-lift with fifty other workers to start a seven hour stretch, packing multifunction ovens onto waiting transportation haulers. He'd thought about just sneaking into the back of one of the cavernous load containers but knew that the air was sucked out of them once they were closed. He'd suffocate before they'd even left the loading bay.

At the logistics centre he clocked in and a Semioid foreman, a scowling individual in overalls, gave each worker a printout. This printout contained details of items to be collected and a collection deadline. With a hand-pulled trolley he set off into the high-rise shelves to complete his sheet. At the entrance he'd seen some security Semioids. Mean looking, full-bodied clones that, unlike their functionary counterparts, possessed a lower torso and legs to walk on. Grotus joked that they weren't Semioids but Fulloids. Thankfully, among the shelves of the warehouse they were absent.

Once alone in the maze of plastiboard boxes he sat down. Opposite, Brant could hear the sound of something being smashed. He got up and walked, following the sound. In the semi-gloom of one of the aisles Brant saw a familiar figure taking the multifunction ovens out of the boxes, smashing the screens and then putting them back.

"Grotus, what are you doing?"

"Destroying the system from within."

"You're destroying the stock."

"I know."

"Why?"

"So that when they arrive at the customer's houses the mass of complaints will lose the company business. The company loses business, it closes down."

"I don't understand. We'll be out of work."

"Good. Then we can go home. The conglomerate won't bother putting in measures to keep us here." He smashed another screen and put the bits back into the box. "You wanna see something, go to the canteen and look out of the window. This is Z100. Last factory on the eastern edge of the district."

Overwhelmed by curiosity, Brant left his duties and went to the canteen. He bought a coffee then turned to face the empty area. There was nothing unusual here. He moved closer to the window.

Before him, on the other side of the plastiglass window and the fifty foot security fence with at least twenty nodding camera-gun's swivelling over their target area, stretched a mile of green field. Wild cows, once farmed but now redundant and free thanks to processed plastimilk, munched on the grass. Beyond the hill he could see nothing but miles and miles of more green space. Brant dropped the coffee and slammed himself into the Plastisteel glass. He threw himself at it like a wild animal, seized a chair and smashed it into the impregnable transparent barrier until security Semioids were called and dragged him away. It took five Semioids to pull him away from the window.

"You are kidding me!" Grotus sprang up from his seat, animated, his bowl of coccyx stew in one hand. "You've got a seven stretch in A00!"

"Yeah," Brant said. "Weird, because Swain said that after the

165

incident in Z100 he was going to assign me to heavy labour jobs with a security Semioid present. This is a cleaning job. Nice and easy. Not many cleaning jobs about. Someone at the labour distribution centre said that at A000 there's stairs that the Semioids can't get up, something about them being designed with not enough vertebrae…"

"Well of course there are stairs. Do you know what A000 is?"

"I was going to look it up tomorrow."

"It's only the bloody tower. The safe where they keep all their cash. After your attempt at trying to smash out of Z100 why are they sending you there?" Grotus frowned. "Give me a look at that printout." He snatched the paper from Brant's hand and scrutinised it. "There," Grotus slapped the printout. "They've got your name but someone else's reference number. They've made a bureaucratic balls-up."

"I'd better tell Swain."

"Don't you fucking dare! If they're letting you in there, I'm coming. I've waited for an opportunity like this for ten years. To actually get into the tower, where the realcash is. We'll nick the lot of it, no… wait… we'll just chuck it out of the nearest window. Let the populace have it. That'll put an end to Swain and the labour slavery."

Brant tried to protest, saying he didn't want to get into any more trouble but when Grotus explained that with realcash he could pay a transport driver to drive him back to his Micro Economy, Brant decided this was worth the risk.

They arrived at the base of the tower wearing standard grey worker attire. All around them smart, futuristic offices nestled. Brant had been given a pass card to enter the tower's reception area. When he used it, the automatic doors snapped open and Grotus tailgated Brant into the base of the tower. He was used to functional environments but this was something else. Pale laminated flooring stretched out before them like a white lake. To the left, the staircase wound up, the handrail and step details gleamed with plastichrome. There was even a reception desk, unmanned but for a swivelling camera-gun which scanned them. It stopped and registered the two workers.

"Wait!" barked an automated voice. *"Clearance was given to only one unit of labour. Why are there two of you?"*

"Sorry about that." Grotus pulled a greasy frontal lobe sandwich from his pocket. "I can explain. You see…"

The anarchist lobbed the sandwich at the camera, hitting the lens square on. The machine nodded aimlessly before firing blind into the reception area. From his inside pocket Grotus whipped out a metal bar, leapt over the reception desk and, dodging bullets, smashed the camera to bits. Brant simply stood there, too shocked to move. Grotus wasted no time, examining the security layout of the tower on a screen behind the desk.

"There's more of these things every hundred feet up the stairs. I only had one frontal lobe sandwich to spare so we can't take the stairs."

"Perhaps there's a lift?"

Grotus' eyes widened. "Of course there's a lift!"

He leapt back over the desk and began examining the wall beside it. Without warning he began to hack at the plastiplaster with the metal bar.

"If you know anything about this town." Hack. Smash. "History, I mean." Smack. Smash. "You will know." Crunch. Pull. Hack. "That this used to be a lift testing tower. So…" Hack. Tear. A large section of plastiplaster came away. "…there's a shaft running up this tower." He pulled the last piece of plaster away to reveal an old metal door just behind.

It took seconds for Grotus to prise the door open with the crowbar. Brant looked nervously around. The anarchist pulled him into the lift and insisted that Brant sat on his shoulders then push up a ceiling panel. Locating the panel was easy and the boy pulled himself up into the dark space above. Illuminated by the glow from below he could see ancient metal rungs leading all the

167

way up into the darkness. From the lift itself the cable also snaked up into the dark. Grotus joined him, carrying a mini-torch he'd pinched from the cleaning cupboard just down the hall. While Brant chose to risk using the metal rungs, Grotus pulled himself up using the cable, the torch between his teeth.

Grotus was faster and hours seemed to pass, all the time Brant moaning that they could get in trouble for this. As he ascended Brant registered his muscles aching, his hands felt as if they would give out any second and he'd crash to the bottom of the shaft. Grotus pulled himself up the cable with apparent ease, though sweat beaded his brow and determination creased his face. Eventually the rungs of the ladder ended at a similar door to the one they'd forced open downstairs.

"This is it. Behind that is all the cash, jewellery, whatever." He threw the crowbar over to Brant who reluctantly prized the doors open. Grotus had managed to swing over to catch hold of the rungs. Once the door was open they smashed through the plastiplaster then tumbled into the top rooms of the tower.

"Unbelievable," said Grotus. "Just totally unbelievable."

All around them there was nothing but white space. The circular room was totally bare. Before them an automatic door snapped open and three men stepped through.

"Swain," Grotus grinned like a maniac as the labour controller approached him flanked by two fully mobile black clad security Semioids carrying lethal looking batons. They glared at the two intruders, which Brant found very intimidating. Grotus stared back at them, unafraid, a smile cutting across his face.

"You know, Swain," Grotus said. "I can't decide which mouth to smack you in first."

Swain nodded and the two security personnel moved forward. With lighting speed Grotus swung the crowbar up and smashed it into the nearest clone's jaw then instantly retracted the weapon only to bring it down onto the Fulloid's head. In almost the same instant the second guard received a kick to the throat then a chop to the back of the head, Grotus using a fast martial arts move to disable the opponent. It was over in a couple of seconds. Both semioids lay inert and useless on the white floor. Swain backed off, hands held out before him.

"So, this is your scam, it it?" Grotus faced up to him. "You tell the banks that this district has got all the collateral, all the realcash up here secured against the debit you're stacking up."

"We can get the credit. We just need time."

"Where's it all gone? You spent it?"

"A long time ago. Listen, Grotus, isn't it? Grotus. If you tell the banks about this, Northampton is finished. We're building up to credit status, we're nearly there! The banks only give us leeway because of this," and he gestured to the absence around them. "Or what they think is in here. Look, we can be the first district to be in credit for decades! Think what that will mean to you. Better housing. Shorter hours. Permanent work. We are so close. When I heard you were here I came personally to appeal to you, that's how important this is."

Grotus gestured to the unconscious guards.

"Okay, okay. So I had to have a show of strength. It's just policy. Seriously, Grotus. If they find out they'll cut us off. No more credit, no more work. There'll be anarchy."

Grotus thought for a moment then clicked his fingers. "You know, you've just sold it to me with that one word. Hey, bet I can get to the banks before you can. You take the stairs. I'll take the lift."

With that the anarchist leapt back into the lift shaft and slid down the cable. Swain simply stood there, looking broken, his mouths closed.

The labour controller sat down on the floor. He put his hand to his forehead and shut his eyes. He stayed like that for some time until he broke the silence in the big white room.

"I love this town. Not what it is but what it could have been. We could have made it something to be proud of. I could have given people lives, futures. You know, sometimes I'd walk around the centre of the town and look at the old buildings.

169

Derngate, the All Saints Church, the old bus station and I'd plan how we would make the town look beautiful again once we'd reached credit status. I'd plan my speech to the banks on the day we ascertained credit status. How I would tell their corporate money lenders to get the hell out of our Northampton. Now that won't happen. We're finished. Your friend Grotus will tell our creditors and they'll pull the plug." He looked Brant in the eye. "We were this close to heaven. Now, all we have is hell."

Brant went to say something but the words stuck in his throat.

"Just get out, will you," the former labour controller barked, said quietly from his natural mouth.

Brant stood on a hill as the sun set behind him, the lights of the emwon traffic firing north and south cutting through the valley below. Brant studied the distant features of Northampton. He watched as beyond he saw the lights of the district go out, sector by sector, the power cut, the plug pulled. The last lights to go out were those crowning the tower. The banks had withdrawn, the secret was out and Swain's empire was finished. Had the labour controller been lying about the town nearly being in credit? Brant didn't think so. He'd heard what the controller said; the man had shared his dream with Brant that day in the tower once Grotus had gone. It was over, the city was literally powerless, there were no jobs and the district would become just another high-crime area. He felt sad, guilty even for helping to destroy Swain's false economy. Brant even shed a tear on seeing the darkened tower before him and he had to turn away. Hitching his rucksack over his back, he trudged west towards home.

The threat to the Micro Economy from National Control was now no longer an issue. National Control had its own problems caused by various creditors unexpectedly pulling out due to leaked information. Grotus was really getting into his stride. The anarchist had followers and a strategy of Credit Terrorism. He was to be investigated by National Security but they had money problems of their own. Creditors were pulling out and lawlessness was now overrunning Britain.

One day as Brant was herding the cows into the milking parlour, he saw a single man approaching the farm. There had a been a few raids recently, things being what they were, so he fetched the gun from the cluster of huts, told his ageing father not to worry, and approached the rag-tag stranger.

Brant lowered the gun when he saw that the person was leading an animal, a North Londonshire wild cow. Brant sat on the boundary fence and awaited the stranger's approach. He stopped a few feet from the boundary fence.

"It suits you," Brant said, gesturing to the leader's jaw. "You look better with the one mouth."

Swain also had a beard and his hair had grown. "No use for it any more. The speed of society has slowed down. I only need say things once. Listen. I've come a long way and need help. On your file I read that you were a farmer."

"True."

"Money is dead. The economy has devolved into the exchange of realproduct. Northampton has elected to become a semi-rural farming province. A Micro Economy. I'm here because, well, to successfully implement this pastoral society we need the expertise of an experienced professional versed in animal husbandry…"

"You want me to teach you how to milk a cow?"

"Among other things, yes."

Brant jumped down from the fence. A gentle breeze blew in from the sea across the field causing the leaves of the trees that grew near the settlement to rustle. "Come on, then," the farmer said to the former labour controller. "Let's get you started. Grab a spade. There's a lot of muck to shovel away."

Hanging Around

Neil K. Bond

In many ways the day of my execution was the most beautiful day of my life. The sun had awoken early and was strong for the time of year, beating its heat into the cold cobbled streets. Come midmorning Sarah had been in to give me my last meal. Wrapped up underneath her shawl she had brought me both legs of a chicken and nearly half a loaf of fresh bread. We couldn't afford to waste food as good as that. I hadn't eaten meat in months. Sarah told me the chicken had been one of our best layers, but if I was going to be killed in the prime of my life then so could the ruddy chicken. That's when she started crying.

Sarah never swore and rarely cried. She was such a beautiful woman, my wife; our lives were hard and what I did I had done for her. Before we had our baby, Sarah had always been full of hopes and dreams of better times. It was good to see that some of that keenness for life had started coming back to her, but it wasn't there today. Sarah stayed with me while I ate. She didn't want to share the meal with me but I started feeding her strips like she was a little baby and that made her giggle, so she did take a little food, but insisted that I needed to keep my strength up and that, for just this once, I should think about myself instead of her. We were both scared of what was going to happen but we spent the time hiding our fear, being brave and trying to cheer each other up. We both knew that this was the last time we would be able to be with each other and all we did was share some chicken and a little laugh. But that time together was beautiful.

The clock on All Saints Church started to strike eleven and Sarah palmed me some coins for the hangman. The lock on the heavy iron gate at the end of the corridor thumped open and I made Sarah promise to go home and not go to the heath to watch: she wouldn't be able to claim my body so there was no point. She nodded and left the cell, holding back the tears for as long as she could, pushing past the court clerk as he opened the door and read out that in the name of His Majesty, King George II, I was to be taken from this place blar, blar, blar… and that was it, I was never to see Sarah again.

Four guards walked me through the corridors, two in front and two behind. When we got to the cart four more were waiting. The clerk and the first four guards got on the back, and stayed there even after I was shackled to a strut on the front of the cart. The other four walked alongside. Any thoughts I'd had about doing a runner were over.

All of Northampton was brimming with life; everyone was full of energy but even with the sun warming my face there was no life in me, I just felt hollow and empty. It soon became obvious that the guards wasn't there to stop me from running off, they were there to stop the crowds getting to me. Everyone was jeering; they had no idea what I had been through. Executions only happened once a year, if that, so I was quite a big event. This was like a celebration. Some of the shops had closed for the day so there was quite a turn out. Hundreds of people lining Abington Street as we plodded our way up towards the site of the old east gate.

About two hundred yards outside the old town boundary, the cart pulled up into the courtyard of an inn and stopped. The two guards behind the cart dropped down the back and put in place steps so that we could all dismount. As the shackles were unlocked the court clerk leaned forward and growled a whisper into my ear.

"Let's have no funny business now, John."

I didn't know what was going on and I began to ready myself for a fight. I've never been one to take things lying down and I thought that maybe getting into a scrap might be just what I needed to start feeling something other than empty and helpless. After all, they weren't going to get too hurt with eight of them now were they? I walked to the steps trying to work out who was the biggest so that I could hit him first, when the back door of the inn opened and a wide bloke in his mid-thirties stood in the door frame.

"John Cotton." I didn't recognise the man that called my name. "Welcome to The Bantam Cock. How do you fancy a pint of fine ale before you go off to your next destination?" The guards led me into the tavern, each one beaming like a child with a new puppy. As we went up to the counter I turned to ask the clerk what were going on, but the look on me face must have spoke for me.

"Relax John, this isn't a trick. But keep in mind that it's not a reprieve either. It's a tradition that we let a man settle his nerve with a good strong ale before he faces the gallows."

"Well that's awful kind of you sir, but I only have a few pennies for the hangman and I'm not so sure he will tighten the rope enough as is."

"I wouldn't take your money anyway, John." The man that had stood in the doorway was now behind the bar. He placed a full cup on the counter and slid it towards me. This didn't seem to add up.

"I've never seen you before nor have I ever drunk here. So why are you being so kind?"

"I an't that kind, these other buggers are going to have to pay for theirs." A quiet grumble and moaning came from the guards and despite myself I smiled. Coins changed hands and cups were filled and handed out. We all toasted King George and the inn keeper also toasted me. We all took the heads off our beers and I was holding on to the sharp, malty taste when our host leaned forward and spoke to me.

"You know, it's a funny old game running a tavern. I spend my whole life giving people what they think they need. What most of them need is an ear to talk into. Now I'm no vicar but if you want to talk stuff over without having to say a dozen Hail Marys after…"

"Oh I see, you just want me to tell you why I killed my baby son."

"Only if that's what you want to talk about. People talk about all kinds of stuff. I'm just here to help make the journey easier."

"No, it's all right, you can have what you want. There isn't much to tell. Me and my wife Sarah were truly happy before we had our baby. Though that's not to say that we didn't want children, we did, of course we did, and it may have took a few years but when Sarah became pregnant we were over the moon that our prayers had at last been answered.

"That child ruined our lives. Not one hour of one day went by when he didn't scream and cry. We paid a doctor to examine him but he could do nothing, and we paid a priest to try to banish the demon that had possessed the poor child—and make no mistake, the child was possessed, though because the priest couldn't get the demon out he denied it was ever there.

"This destroyed Sarah, my beautiful Sarah. She couldn't cope; nor could I, having lost so much sleep I couldn't work properly so money got less and less. The demon inside that child was destroying us.

"The priest couldn't get rid of the thing so I did. The baby was screaming with torment as was my Sarah for the baby to be quiet. Enough were enough, so I took the baby into the garden and held it by its ankles and I swung at the wall until the crying stopped and then I swung a few times more. I truly believe that our poor son is now in heaven and the demon that tortured him is back in hell. Not all babies survive, everyone knows that. The proof that I was right is that Sarah has come back to herself. But the law must do what the law must do."

"Don't worry yourself about that now John. God claims his own." I looked up at the inn keeper and his eyes there bright and sparkling as if full of reassurance and sympathy. "Just enjoy your beer."

I did and we talked but about nothing much, he really was a nice man. Not many people had been that nice to me before. He really made the place feel welcoming and homely. All too soon my drink was gone and that clerk was insisting that we would have to go so that we wouldn't be late. I told him that I didn't mind being late but he insisted anyway.

As I left, the inn keeper shook my hand and gave me a friendly grin: "Remember, you're welcome back anytime." He pressed a couple of the guards' coins into my hand. I'd never known such kindness from a stranger and no kindness at all since I did what I'd done. I left the courtyard of that tavern shackled back up but smiling and the tear in me eye was a happy one.

The ride to the gallows on Northampton Heath was less than five minutes but it seemed to take forever. From halfway up the hill on the Kettering Road you could hear the crowd baying for blood. The gallows were tall and new. They had been built only four years before to replace the old Abington gallows further up the road. I'd never been to the Abington gallows but I'd seen all of the previous five executions at Northampton Heath. They were moved there for Mary Fawson; a pretty young thing, only twenty years of age. She had killed her husband with poison so was found guilty of petty treason and had to be burnt to death. They didn't have room for a burning at Abington so they decided to build new gallows on the heath. At the same time they hanged Elizabeth Wilkinson for lifting forty shillings from a farmer's pocket. Burnings hardly ever happened and there was so much fuss made about Mary that poor Elizabeth started swearing at the crowd, damning us all, saying that if she had to die for us we should at least pay attention. That still makes me laugh. Not the burning though, the smell was horrible. Mary had begged the hangman to give her the rope before she was burnt. So he put a noose around her neck and nailed it to the stake. He kicked the stool away before putting the torch to the kindling. I couldn't say if the noose got her before the flames as she wouldn't have been able to scream either way. All I know is it took three hours of burning before the body was gone.

My execution was on Thursday the 22nd of March, 1739, and while all the others had been done in August, I still think that mine was truly the most beautiful day. The gallows themselves were less than a hundred foot from the edge of the Kettering Road on the top of the heath. A couple of years before, Lord Spencer had started using the heath for horse racing and the first bend of the racecourse was just in front of me. But no fancy gentry came out to watch the entertainment that day. As the cart pulled off the road, the noise of the people rose with their excitement. The crowd wasn't allowed to get all that close, no nearer than thirty foot away, but as I were marched over I could see the joy that me death was bringing in the eyes of the people in front of me. Most of these people wouldn't have known me but they all had an opinion of what I had done. They were pointing the finger, judging without really knowing, feeling good about their own goodness and relieved that I wasn't them or theirs.

The gallows themselves were three posts held apart by three crossbeams forming a triangle at the top, some twelve foot up. The cart was drawn to a standstill between the uprights and I was taken to the rear edge of the cart to face the awaiting rope. Between the gallows and the crowd were three men: the executioner, a man of God, and a blacksmith. A guard took the steps from the back of the cart and placed them to my right. The vicar climbed up to me and offered me prayers. I prayed with him but I knew that God knew his own and that in banishing a demon I would be going to a better place whatever the priest had said. After the blessing, the court clerk read out the crime I had been found guilty of and the punishment to be carried out. As the clerk waffled on I looked over the crowd that had gathered. It was easily as large as any of the previous crowds I'd been a part of. All of the jeering and the words of the clerk became distant and a feeling of calm washed over me that I find hard to explain. I just didn't care about what was going to happen. I didn't even notice when I was offered the chance to say my last words, the clerk had to nudge me. I had nothing to say so I just shook my head, turned and paid the hangman, who now stood behind me. After thanking me the hangman repositioned me on the edge of the cart, tied my hands behind my back with leather binding and placed a black bag over my head. I felt the heavy rope flop onto my shoulders and then tighten around my neck until I spluttered, but still I was calm. The beautiful sunshine warmed through the hood. I heard the steps being put back on the cart and the footsteps of the hangman making his way towards the driver's seat. I felt the sun on my face and remembered Sarah and my last meal; the kindness of the inn keeper at The Bantam Cock. This day was truly beautiful. When the footsteps stopped a little panic came into me heart and it started pounding. Then the cart drove on, leaving me in midair, choking to death.

Being hanged is a strange sensation and not one that I would recommend. The heat and juices of your body rush up into your head and you feel as if your skull is going to burst. Pressure builds between your eyes as if your nose is going to bleed and your eyes are going to pop right out of their sockets, then the heat starts burning in your head. It's like a coal fire incinerating all of your thoughts and distorting you. But through all of that I was determined not to give the good folk of the town the show they had come to see. I wasn't going to dance for them. I made sure I pointed my toes to the ground and tried to push my feet down. Then I died, slowly. I felt myself sliding out of my body. But whereas all of my fluids slid up, I slid down, seeping out through my feet. I tried to pull myself back up, I didn't want to go down, hell wasn't for me; I had suffered enough hell while on the earth, why was I sliding down? The fall out of my body seemed to take days and then I realised I hadn't fallen far at all. Through the panic I hadn't felt my feet touch the ground but that's where I was, lying down on the grass underneath my body. I just lay there looking up at myself and I felt, well, great. I sat there in awe of myself hanging up above me.

My gaze was broken when, after the customary hour of hanging had elapsed, the hangman started to back the cart towards me. I scuttled out of the way and stood in front of the dispersing crowd to watch as the rope were cut and two of the guards took me body and laid it in front of the waiting smithy. I was only a few feet away as the blacksmith riveted hoops in place and then bars to link the hoops. I knew they were going to do this with me but I never thought I would be there to watch it. Anger raged through me as they disgraced my lifeless corpse. As the smithy placed the final bar I couldn't stand it anymore, I lunged forward to grab his hammer, I wanted to bury it between his shoulder blades to break his back, but my hand went straight through the heavy oak handle. When the smithy took the hammer up I tried to kick it out of his hand but all I kicked was thin air and I stumbled back getting ever more frustrated.

It took four guards to lift the body back onto the cart. They drove off back to my village, Paulerspury, where they were going to hang it over the village green; a rare thing done to me because they'd said my crime was so horrendous. My corpse was to rot in full view and be picked apart by the crows as a warning to others that the law must be obeyed. In reality they hung it there to torment my poor Sarah. As if she hadn't gone through enough. I was going to follow the cart but the idea of seeing my Sarah wailing at the feet of my body would have destroyed me. And if she had stayed away as she had been advised, somehow that would have hurt me more. Some things are better not known.

I spent the afternoon on the heath lying in the sun. I couldn't feel the heat but its brilliant light shone through my closed eyes and I imagined the warmth. As I lay there I decided never to see Sarah again. Our last time together was such a lovely memory I didn't want to tarnish it by watching her grieve. Besides, it was obvious that I was now a ghost. I couldn't touch anything around me so all I'd be able to do was haunt the only woman to truly love me. Why would I want to do that? I couldn't comfort her and when she eventually got on with her life I would have to watch her in silence as her love for me and the memories of us faded into the past.

Dusk came. I didn't get cold but I didn't want to stay on the heath any longer. I had already decided where to go: The Bantam Cock. After all, the landlord had said come back anytime.

It was night when I had walked back into town and through the soot smudged windows the tallow glow of the candlelight looked as warm and welcoming as the cup of strong ale I'd had earlier. I walked through the open door to find the place busy. The friendly inn keeper stood on the public side of the counter, drinking heartily and making sure that his guests were all having themselves a good time. Then a group of rowdy young men called him over to the table they were drinking at.

"Hey Bill, tell us, was that bastard John Cotton repentant for what he had done before he swung?"

Bill's broad shoulders sank as he strode across to the table and he looked mournfully into his half-empty cup before answering. "I can't rightly say that he was, Thomas, no. But I will say one thing, from what he told me as he had his last taste of ale, he was a very troubled man."

"You're too soft on these condemned men you are, Bill. What he done to his own kid was despicable and there is no defending that." The men around the table all voiced their agreement; this railed old Bill.

"I wasn't defending his act. I said he was a troubled man. And if you think I'm getting soft, Thomas Porter –"

"Now, now, Bill I wasn't saying that. I'm not looking for a quarrel with you. I was at the hanging and to my mind he didn't suffer enough, that's all. He hardly wriggled. But no matter, I'm sure he is suffering now."

All of the men sat at the table roared with laughter at the idea of me being in hell. Bill just walked away. I can't tell you how much I admired this man and I smiled to know that he wasn't being false when I had been brought to his tavern earlier that afternoon. I was also smiling at the idea of people cheering at me being in hell when I was but a few inches away from them. That night, after Bill had given rooms to those that could pay and thrown out all the rest, I sat next to the dying fire and thought the day through. I really liked Bill. I saw something of myself in the way he didn't take any nonsense, though he was more kind and generous. Because of that, he was well liked and respected.

I was never really respected by anyone apart from my Sarah. I looked back on my life and I realised that I had never really helped anyone else. But what could I do about it now? I was dead. I sat there all night wishing that I had been a better person through life. As the sun crept past the pub and into the town I worked out what I would do to put things right.

It was one year, one month and three days before I was able to act on my determination to be a better person dead than I had been alive. For most of that time I had moved into the cellars. There are three cellars underneath The Bantam Cock. The first one was only really used as storage so I made that one my home. I came out some evenings to watch life being lived and enjoyed. Sometimes this filled me with happiness as if I felt life returning to me. Other times the jealousy made me so melancholic that I stayed down in the cellar for weeks after. But on this day, that of Friday the 25th of April 1740, a young man by the name of William Welford was brought into the inn to have his last sup of ale before he tasted the hangman's rope. William had been found guilty of burglary, he had confessed and now he was scared. Bill was very much as kind to this man as he had been to me. He listened and seemed to understand. When it was time for the young man to meet his fate, I went with him.

Now, I knew by this time that people couldn't hear me, I had got used to that over the previous year. But even so I walked alongside the cart between the guards and constantly talked to Welford to reassure him on his way to the gallows. I know it was silly but I just wanted to try and help him in any way that I could. The crowd for William Welford was quite a good one considering that crowds were never as big for non-murders.

We arrived at the gallows and the charges were read, the hangman paid. William was tied, bagged, noosed and the cart driven off as was the custom. William danced. William's legs were kicking and thrashing and I was mightily glad that he couldn't kick me. That was until he did.

I was gobsmacked and in pain. That was the first sensation of touch or discomfort I had felt since I'd died and to be honest it took me back a bit. By the time I composed myself and looked over to where the blow had come from, William was half-hanging out of his lower body. I ran over and grabbed hold of his waist and pulled down. William's body spluttered a little harder and then he fell to the ground.

"What the hell do you think you're doing?" William didn't seem overly pleased with me helping him into the next level of existence. "My brother and my dad said that they would have pulled down on my legs to hurry me along but I told them that I wanted to hold on as long as I possibly could. Now the rope's snapped they're going to have to hang me all over again!" He looked at me as if I were an idiot. I nodded upward and he looked to see his body hanging from the gallows and screamed. I tried to comfort him.

"I'm sorry, I didn't enjoy being hanged too much, so when I realised that I could actually grab you and help pull you out of your body, I just did it."

Then he started to fade, the last of his panicking shadow dispersed with the breeze and William Welford was no more.

The next man to face the gallows was another William— William Porter, the cousin of Thomas Porter, the man who had gloated so eagerly and had wanted me to suffer so much on the day of my hanging. William Porter had been caught up in the Kettering riots. He was about to pay for the murder of Benjamin Meadows. Two weeks and a day later his partner in crime,

William Attleborough, also swung on the heath. I was there to help Attleborough but I enjoyed watching Porter. Oddly, young Thomas didn't come into the Bantam after either of those executions. A pity really, I would have liked to see him suffer.

All in all, thirty-one people followed me to the gallows on Northampton Heath and I was there for all of them. There were never any more burnings on the heath; all the rest were left hanging by the cart. I couldn't help all of them into the next world. There were some I didn't want to help. I sat in the tavern as they had their last drink. I watched and listened and decided how much I wanted to help each one. Once there were just too many for me to help all of them. That was the day they hanged the Culworth gang.

The Culworth gang were highwaymen, thieves and bullies. They terrorised the south of Northamptonshire and the north of Oxfordshire for nearly twenty years. I met them on Friday the 3rd of August 1787. Senior amongst them was one John Smith.

I must say I liked John. He was a clever man who had given up a lot to stop his two sons from having to face the gallows with him. John worked as a farm hand, but he knew a thing including how to read and write. Two of the Culworth gang were among the condemned that I didn't take to. Their names were John Hulbert and Richard Law. The people of Northampton wanted to see six men hang and as two of the gang weren't going to be hanged on that day, two burglars were hung with the Culworth boys—David Coe and William Bowers. Hulbert and Law kept goading Coe and Bowers saying that they didn't deserve the prestige of being on the same gallows as them and that they were cheapening the day.

It had been forty-eight years since my last taste of ale and the Bantam had changed hands a few times since my day but I remembered old Bill and how much his kindness had meant to me on my final day. The fact that Coe and Bowers were not being given it riled me but what angered me more was what Hulbert said next. He claimed that they wouldn't be the first wrongly hanged as part of the gang. Two years earlier a James Tarry had been hanged for robbing a house in Brackley. He'd shouted his innocence all through court and from the gallows and here was John Hulbert confessing that Tarry had been innocent all along and that he was in fact the guilty man. I couldn't have hated Hulbert more if I had wanted to.

The size of the crowd that had gathered for the end of the Culworth gang was staggering. The next day *The Herald* said that it was around five thousand. I've never seen such a crowd of people in all my days dead or alive. The noise was deafening by the time we got to the gallows. The first one out of their body was John Smith. He was such a heavy man that he just fell out of the bottom of his feet. He didn't rightly know what I was doing at first and I think the distraction helped him 'cos when he saw his body hanging there he wasn't much taken aback. By this time I was heaving away on the feet of Coe.

"Give us a hand to pull them through to this side!" I was shouting at Smith, who stepped in without question and helped Coe's friend Bowers. These two were easy to pluck as there was nothing to them while John and me were strong men. We left those two sat on the grass and John went to help his gang. I took it on myself however to hinder the passing of Hulbert.

By the time I got to Hulbert he was half out. His feet were on the ground but his chest was stuck in his waist. He was too far out to push back in so I squared up and kicked him hard between the legs. One of the good things about being a ghost is that you don't get tired, so I kicked him again and again and again. When he did get out I punched him hard in the face and he rolled back dazed. I looked behind me to see John Smith holding back the other two of his gang and laughing. He was going to say something to me but couldn't get the words past his laughter. I watched as he dispersed, still laughing. I turned back to Hulbert but he had vanished. I was left there with five thousand people cheering. I felt like a champion bare knuckle fighter and I was proud of a good fight fought. I bowed to the crowd that couldn't see me and walked back home to my cellar.

I saw less than a dozen people on their way after that. The gaps between executions grew longer and longer. Then on Friday the 27th of March 1818 the very last two came in on the way to the gallows. William Corbett and George Wilkin were hanged on that day, both having been found guilty of Uttering, which was what the law called using a forged document.

I did what I could for those two and then it all stopped. Nobody else came to The Bantam Cock for their last taste of life. They took down the gallows on the heath and built fancy new ones inside the prison court yard. These gallows had something called a 'new drop', which were a section in the floor that dropped a few inches to hang the condemned. There were no need for carts and they could control the numbers of onlookers as they said the huge crowds coming to watch the hangings were getting out of hand.

I didn't want to go back to the prison. It was a horrible place and the last time I was there I was with my Sarah and I'm not going to pollute that memory for nobody. So in the cellar I stayed. I'd spent seventy-nine years helping the condemned to pass over to the other side. That's a lifetime of work by anyone's count. I'm not saying that I regret it, I don't. I'm proud of the good I've done since my death, but a big part of that was being with them and listening as they had their last drink and told their stories, walking with them to the gallows and talking to them, knowing they couldn't hear me but consoling them anyway. That was every part as important to me as using my strength to pull them out of their bodies so that they could move on quicker and suffer less.

So back to the cellar I went and there I mainly stayed. Occasionally I would venture up when the inn was busy. I enjoyed seeing the place full of life and people making merry but I would always be the outsider looking in.

I always thought that the reason I had never faded away like the others was because I had found something good to do after

my death and once my work was done I would move on like all
the others. When I didn't, I thought that maybe I had to go back
to the heath, to the place where I had died; but still nothing
happened. I even tried going back on the same date that I died so
I waited three years until 1821, when 22nd of March next fell on a
Thursday, but still I stayed here on this earth. So I went back to
the Bantam and just hung around.

I lost track of time and of dates. At some point in the late
eighteen-eighties they pulled down the old inn and rebuilt it. I
liked the new Bantam Cock: it seemed less cobbled together and
more homely. They replaced the thatch with a tiled roof and put
extra rooms up there. These rooms were big, unlike the old
lodgings, and that's when The Bantam stopped being an inn. It's
now just a house on top of a pub, not that you could tell how
much room they put up there from looking on the outside. Not
that its splendour would last.

At some point in the mid nineteen-sixties the upper floors
were abandoned as living quarters and started to be used as
storage on account that the roof had leaked and it was too damp.
That's when I gave up my cellar and moved into the rooms
upstairs. It must have been about the time of the last hangings in
Britain

So there I was, sat in the upper floors of The Bantam Cock
with nothing to do and nobody that I could help. I still couldn't
touch people or talk to them – not until they were dead – so I
was of no use. Time went by and the town and the pub carried
on changing; the walls in the pub were knocked through which
made the place vast. I couldn't stand the loud music they took to
playing so I just sat there with the whistling wind running
through the upper floor. Unable to move on and totally useless,
until the fortune of the pub took a turn for the worse.

A couple of years ago there was a new landlord of The
Bantam Cock. He came here having made a reputation for
himself by making improvements to the backstreet pub he had
been running before. He refurbished the place, altered the

opening hours to catch the after-hours trade as other places closed for the night. People flocked in. This was going to be a new start for him and the pub. The Bantam Cock was an old-fashioned name and he thought it was too stuffy. He wanted the place to be fun so he changed the name and filled the place full of monkeys.

There were monkeys everywhere. He had an entire wall covered with a picture of a monkey's head with its chin resting on its hand as if it were thinking. On top of the bar above the optics there was even a real monkey pickled in a jar. I hated that jarred monkey. It had been stuffed into the jar upside down and the pickling fluid was so dirty that you could barely tell what it was, only the ear gave it away. But I didn't like it because it was dead and on display, just as my body had been. The barstards who poked fun at it might as well have been making fun of my corpse. The whole thing sickened me.

The pub seemed to work for the new owner; the bar was always packed after the other pubs were shut, but all too often I would hear him in the flat under mine complaining about not having any money. Still he had good clothes and he always had food, which was more than I had before I was dead, and he was always drinking and doing other things that I don't rightly understand; he always looked as if he'd been picking the wrong kinds of mushrooms if you ask me, and that's how it all started going wrong for him.

He was arrested and the pub closed. The landlord soon became a figure of public hate. That was something that hadn't changed since my day. People who had only heard the story second or third hand started to despise him. He started to go to his old haunts, like the pub he had previously run but he wasn't even that welcome there. One bloke broke his jaw in a pub brawl; he said that it was a dispute over fifty pounds the bloke owed him and maybe it was but I don't think it would have gone that far if he wasn't such a hated figure.

The courts found him guilty of the assault and they took

away his licence so he couldn't be a landlord no more. This meant he would never be able to reopen the pub. Then the bailiff came around half a dozen times but each time was sent away with a flea in his ear. Then the letter came; he was going to be evicted, and that's when I got my chance to be useful again.

During all this I had seen this man's soul wither so that he was just a hollow husk of the flamboyant person he once was. He still put on a show and he still gave as good as he got but if you saw him in his private moments you could see that he wasn't really there. I don't know if it was the history of this pub that gave him the idea or not but he decided to hang himself and I decided that I wasn't going to let him.

The first time that he tried was a Sunday. I looked on, powerless to stop him, biding my time until I could be useful. I stood there and watched as he took a chair and placed it under a light fitting just beyond the end of the bar. He tore out the fitting and the plaster around it to expose the beam and still all I could do was watch and wait. I stood right next to him as he took a blue plastic rope out of his back pocket. He had already tied a noose into one end of the rope and I watched him tie the other end around the newly exposed beam. I waited as he tested the strength of his handiwork using the noose as a handhold and pulling himself clear of the chair and then up and down as if he was doing exercises. He slowly lowered himself back onto the chair and turned to address the empty panelled window.

"Okay you've won! Do you hear me, you've won! This is what you all wanted, this is what you've all been waiting to see. Fuck the lot of you!"

His arms shook through defiant anger rather than fear as he pulled the rope over his head and kicked the chair away. This was the moment that *I* had been waiting for.

I walked over to stand where he was hanging and crouched down into a ball under him, pushing my back under his feet. His soul was going nowhere. He jiggled and danced and then I felt the soles of his soul make contact with my back and his feet

189

dance across me. This was the first time I had felt personal contact in ninety-one years and it felt good to know that I was saving someone instead of helping them die. I became more and more elated with every tap of his feet on my back. Then the feet were gone. I looked up to see that he had managed to hook a foot onto a nearby table. Levering himself up he was able to unhook his chin from the rope and he fell to the floor coughing, wheezing and crying like a small child. After he caught his breath he crawled behind the bar, grabbed a glass and a bottle and drank himself to sleep. That night I stayed downstairs watching him, still feeling good about the rescue I had achieved. I told the sleeping man all the reasons why he shouldn't give up life and of all those that wasn't given the choice. I went back up to the flat above his and settled down with my thoughts. Maybe that was what I should have been doing all along. Not helping people die but stopping them from reaching the other side. Old Bill had given me the lead, shown me how much kindness you can give a man, but I could do more. I could never have done it for those heading off to the gallows but this was a different matter. I could do more for people and, if I did, then maybe that was how I could move on to whatever fate awaits me.

I heard the man downstairs wake up groaning, and setting about his daily routine. I felt proud that I had given him this new day. So I went down to see what he was going to do with the gift. I came down to find him pacing around in an erratic fashion. He was mumbling to himself about what he was going to do and how he was going to show them. I would have preferred to see him with a more positive frame of mind but a fighting attitude isn't that of a defeatist, so I felt that at least he was on his way. He looked quite smart and the last thing he did in this whirlwind of activity was pick up his wallet and leave, locking the door behind him.

That evening he came back drunk, shouting "What was the point?" I heard the commotion from the upper floor and so went down to see what was going on. He had already kicked the chair away and was hanging from the rope, kicking. He was already coming through. I panicked. I wasn't sure he could be pushed back up inside but I had to try. I ran over and caught hold of each of his feet, not easy with all the kicking and thrashing about. I couldn't just push up so I gripped the exposed ankles and pulled them together. This stopped him moving about so much. Once his feet were together I got down on one knee and placed his feet on my chest. Keeping hold of his ankles I pushed up with my legs forcing him back into his body. All the time I was shouting at him. "Don't you even think of dying yet!" and "If this ruddy town hates you so much why don't you just find another to live in, start afresh?" Then he must have fitted back inside himself because I flew across the room like a spawning frog trying to reach a spring pond. By the time I had picked myself up and turned around, my newly saved victim had managed to free himself and was lying on the floorboards.

He stood up and grabbed the table he had used to get out of the noose and threw it across the room, swiftly followed by the chair. He staggered upstairs and started throwing clothes into cases. He was packing to leave. Maybe he heard what I'd said when he was partway out of his body. Maybe he was going to move on. Maybe this time I really had saved his life. He took the telephone gadget thing out of his pocket and called someone. He was in floods of tears so I don't know who he was calling or what was really being said. All I could make out was that he was going to go to the doctor's in the morning and that he was going to get help. On hearing this I left him to it and went up to my rooms.

The next day I came down as the sun came up. There might not have been a cock to crow anymore but I wanted to be there before he got up. I was going to watch him today. I wasn't going to be able to trust him to stay on the right path as I had the day before; that had nearly ended in disaster. True to his word he got up, sorted himself out and made an appointment to see the doctor.

The next morning he was in much better spirits. He popped

191

out for a bit but soon came back, he went up to his rooms and he carried on packing. Before he finished there was a heavy knock on the door. The bailiffs had arrived to evict him.

It's fair to say that their arrival didn't go down well. They were greeted with a barrage of verbal abuse. He clearly didn't want to be turfed out. Instead he was going on his own terms. Before anything else could be done the doors were shut and bolted, a chair was grabbed and his head was back in the noose. This time he tightened the slipknot before he kicked out the chair. Not that it mattered. I wasn't going to go through all this again. There's only so much help you can give someone. If they're determined to end their life, they will find a way.

I damn near pulled his legs off as he started to emerge. He hit the floor like a sack of coal but he was soon up and leathering into me thinking that I was one of the bailiffs. I wasn't gong to take it; though this one could throw a punch, I lashed out, giving as good as I got. We were on the floor, grappling, throwing fists, he was yelling that this was his home and I was yelling that it was mine first and that he could ruddy well piss off. And then his grip lightened and I was left holding nothing.

So I'm not much of a saviour. That was a year ago now. There's a new landlord and he's called the pub The Bantam and he never gets tired of people telling him he's left his cock out. As for old John Cotton, I'm left up here in the upper rooms, waiting to help someone else pass over or to try to stop them dying. I keep hoping that I'll fade, evaporate and pass on. Nobody knows that I'm here and you're the first person that I've really been able to talk to in two hundred and sixty years.

I recognised you as soon as you walked in. I thought that you had faded like all the others so it was a bit of a shock to see your face again. You wouldn't be my chosen company but you can stay in the cellar if you have nowhere else to go and we can see how we get on, maybe work out why we're still here. Now you've heard my story, John Hulbert, tell me what's been going on with my least favourite member of the Culworth gang?

I Won the Earth Evacuation Lottery

Tim C. Taylor

April 2nd. The aliens arrive.
I was arguing with Sally the night the Engineers came.

"Why can't you trust me?" she shouted.

"Trust you?" I countered. "Have you forgotten I caught you mooning all over that guy in that Chinese restaurant off Horseshoe Street? *But he was only a friend.* You don't do that with *just a friend.* "

I think the world first heard its time was up when I was saying those words.

We were in the Moon on the Square. You know, the Wetherspoon's pub by the market in Northampton. Oh, but of course you don't know. Well, it was a big place where people came for a chat and a beer. Used to be a big shop or bank or something, I don't know. So anyway, me and Sally were upstairs on this carpeted landing that led to the toilets because she has this daft notion that we must appear the perfect couple in public. We'd left our mates in the bar downstairs.

I ignored Sally explaining why she'd blown me out again last night (I bet she regrets messing me around now), I even stopped my pacing because something told me to listen downstairs. I knew something had changed. Like that moment in old horror films when the hero is running from the monster and stumbles into the remote country pub. Everyone stops talking and turns to look.

There was a scatter of screams. Not many, though. I mean all this stuff with the 'Understudies of God' as they call themselves was so weird you could hardly take it in.

A pair of sobbing girls thundered up the stairs and fled past us seeking refuge in the ladies. Sally and I exchanged one of those quick looks that packs a world of meaning into an instant. We pushed down the stairs against the rising flood of refugees and joined the crowd staring at the big TV screens opposite the bar. You could tell the Sky News presenters were as scared as the rest of us, but they had probably fantasised for years about reporting on a big event 'as the story unfolds'. Planes were being shot down, nukes launched, orders and helicopters and soldiers running around. That was our side (humanity, I mean). The Engineers (the name that stuck a week later when we learned what they were up to) just hung about in the upper atmosphere in those interstellar spacecraft that look like old-fashioned bobby's helmets. No one knows, or is telling, the weapons the aliens deployed but whatever they were killed tens of thousands of soldiers and smeared out all our nuclear capability.

The science correspondent for BBC News (the bar manager had started switching channels just to check this wasn't a hoax from Sky) speculated the Engineers had gone after our nukes, not because they were scared of being attacked, but because they didn't want an irradiated cinder for a planet. With all I've learned since that night, I think he was right.

Getting a drink from the bar was a more immediate horror what with the crowd centred on the main screen. We persevered though (they had a special on Grainstore Brewery — funny what you remember) and sunk quite a few rounds until the news ran out about an hour later. I don't mean they turned off the telly, but the news began feeding on itself. You know, they started interviewing people to tell the story of how they'd heard the news.

Anyway, the aliens told the news channels straight away what was happening as it happened. They got an official story from the government too, of course, but by that time I think we all believed the aliens, especially when the Earth governments all started using the term 'unconditional surrender' at the same time. The story so far was pretty simple, really. The Engineers had come in their police helmet ships and conquered the Earth. The question was what would happen next.

Actually, the Engineers had already told us what would happen next. They would make an announcement on April 10th.

We couldn't see our enemy. Knew nothing about who, what or why. I mean with Hitler just across the Channel in the war, or even now with Al-Qaeda, you have someone real to fight. We only had those grainy pictures of silly spaceships. So when Freddie saw a table come free, my little group (Pascal and his mate Joe were with us) sat down and eventually got to talking about the five-a-side match the day before. As for me, I still wasn't sure who I was most pissed off at. Sally or the aliens.

April 10th. End of the World Party.

The Engineers explained the fate of the world to each little section of humanity in a manner (so the aliens said) best suited to that Earthly culture. For most of Western Europe and North America, the information was placed on the internet and distributed by BitTorrent fileshare. Not Scotland, though. They got it on the Telly. BBC One Scotland and STV special programmes. Danes had the key facts (words and diagrams) hammered into silver sheets that materialised out of nowhere. Not just the people living in Denmark but anyone born there, no matter where they were on the 10th. I think the aliens were taking the piss.

For the Arab nations, the aliens gave their instructions to the muezzins who did their best to relay the message from their minarets while keeping dignity and faith. Many people listened obediently at the mosques but within the hour the richer people had picked it all up from the internet.

We learned all this crowded around the computer in Freddie and Farrah's study. (They live next door to me on Somerset Street. We get on pretty well.)

The aliens have come to mine the metallic core of our planet. Not for the metal as such but for its magnetism. The entire Solar System is to be strip-mined and we've just been served with a compulsory purchase order. Tethers are to be buried deep under the Earth's crust to float on the liquid mantle underneath. They will support tiaras that encircle the planet at an average of a kilometre above sea level. Hundreds of millions of superconducting cables will spin along these rails, flailing high up into the magnetosphere to induct a stupid amount of power. The Engineers can push that energy through an array of quantum wires in Earth orbit that tunnel directly to the Engineers' home system without having to travel the long way round. In other words, the aliens will suck all the energy out of the Earth's magnetic field and plug it straight into the Engineers' equivalent of the National Grid.

Would that be bad? Well, yes. Those who survived the building work would find that, when the aliens switched on their new power station, they would be unprotected from the radiation blasting in from the Solar Wind. Year by year, the atmosphere would be ripped away. And if any humans had the audacity to live through that, the idea was to shatter the crust like the ice layer on top of a frozen water butt so that the induction contraption could float freely on the mantle.

As we crowded round the screen, we absorbed the news in silence, except for an occasional round of "Oh, shit!" or "Fuck me!"

Freddie broke the mood. "Might as well break open the single malts," he said. The little beauty had got some classy Scotch in just for the event. We'd drunk The Balvenie and were advancing on a bottle of Talisker when we realised there was a second message from the aliens. The Universe designed the gift of sapience, said scrolling text, so that the Universe could know itself. Wiping out humanity would make a tiny but still real reduction in the Universe's ability to observe itself and that, it turns out, would be blasphemy. I'm certainly not about to disagree because the upshot is that humanity would not be wiped out, merely relocated to start again on a new planet.

How we cheered, clinked our glasses and toasted our good fortune. Freddie and his girlfriend Farrah kissed and fondled like teenagers. Me and Phil had a think about a manly hug but played safe with a whooping high five.

My Ozzie mate, Aiden, once taught me the term 'shit sandwich' — squeeze a slice of bad news between two slabs of good and everyone's happy. The Engineers resolutely went for an anti-shit sandwich because some more files had downloaded and started to play themselves. "Oh, yes," they said, "your species is not doomed but we only have room to transport a few thousand of you. Now let us explain who the lucky ones are going to be."

Graphics launched at that point. Not the whizzy 3-D shiny balls I expected. Instead, the kind of jerky 2-D stop-motion animation you'd see in a wartime public information film. *Housewives! Defeat Hitler by recycling everyday kitchen waste.* That sort of thing.

So they had this stick man surrounded by a dozen or so ladies. (You knew they were women because they were the A-line icon sported by roughly half of all public toilet entrances).

A narrator started explaining in Received Pronunciation what we were seeing. "We have studied your species, your history, and your mating rituals. Interesting. Male breeding success is dependent upon aggression and yet that same aggression can destroy small sub-tribal groups not sufficiently large to survive warfare. Better to have smaller groups less susceptible to wasteful infighting."

The graphics wiggled a little bit and out popped lots of smaller boy and girl icons. We zoomed out and saw this breeding

197

cycle taking place all over the planet. All in grainy black-and-white.

"Morality and reason align, compelling us to alter your physiology, to replace the failings of sexual reproduction with parthenogenesis. Nonetheless, our religion insists we retain your flawed design because those flaws are part of the Universe's Great Design, indeed evidence of that design as our science can find no plausible explanation for the prevalence of sexual species on your planet. Instead, we shall minimise the cost of males as follows. Your colony will consist of one thousand independent groups each of one man and fourteen women. We shall disperse these tribes and restrict them so that several generations shall pass before we permit them to interact. We will limit the generations of isolation so that genetic drift will not cause mutational meltdown."

"Wow!" Freddie was the first to speak in about five minutes. Everyone else's jaw was still on the floor. "Imagine life as a sex machine. Barry would be a natural. He's already made babies with three women."

I chipped in. "And he's marrying a fourth. Barry must already be on the shortlist."

Back then, a lot of people still acted as if a joke and a drink laced with stoicism would see us through this spot of bother. The aching sadness at the loss of everything, even the loss of the future: that started kicking in the following day.

If the Engineers were interested in Barry or our quips, the narrator neglected to mention either. "Tomorrow we shall explain how the selection of male colonists will be carried out consistently with your local cultural parameters."

"Drinking contest," said Freddie. "Only way that makes sense."

"Once chosen," the Engineers continued, "the males will use their evolved selection criteria to identify their mates. Your reproductive strategies are so alien to us that we trust your genetic programming to be superior at mate selection to anything we can devise."

"What a way to go," said Freddie.

"Freddie!"

"Sorry, Farrah."

I wondered how it would feel to pick fourteen ideal mates. The notion sounded perversely exciting, though my head argued that the reality would prove not nearly as much fun as the idea sounded.

As if to confirm my thoughts the Engineers spoke one last time.

"All humans are required to support the colony selection programme. Failure to comply will not be tolerated."

April 16th. Who will be the lucky ones?

On the night the lottery was drawn, my dad came over. His idea. He talked the language of father-son bonding and, without Sally, I'd no better option, so he came over to my house on Somerset Street.

They're big old houses and were probably posh back in Victorian times. Street's gone a bit shabby since but that suits me 'cos that means I can rent a big three-bed terrace. Wanted to impress someone – not sure who – certainly not Sally, who never quite moved in and is gone now.

"I came prepared," said Dad. He had 'n' all, with a couple of them 'save the planet' jute bags from Sainsbury's, full of chinking bottles.

"Jesus, Dad. How're you getting home?"

"Driving."

I huffed a little but was already resigned to this. (I'd agreed for Dad to come over the day before they announced the 10:15 pm curfew.) Dad snores so loudly the aliens can probably hear him from orbit.

"Dad, why don't you stay the night?"

"Well... if you're sure, son."

By the time I'd cleared the crap off the spare bed, Dad had

done us proud with four bottles of single malt and a sea of beer bottles. That's what fathers are for.

"Broke the habit of a lifetime," said Dad. "Went all Fred Goodwin. Cashed in my savings and put it into shares of booze companies. Reckoned no one cares much about their livers anymore."

"Good for you, Dad." I poured another bottle of Thornbridge Jaipur.

The Big Event was due at 9:30pm. We watched BBC1, which showed a special programme of pointless studio interviews interleaved with news stories. Twin anchors were Jeremy Paxman and Dale Winton. I guess if anyone had been in doubt the end of the world was coming, that line-up would force the last bastion of denial.

"It's like this, son." (Dad spent much of the night in the verbal style of explaining birds and bees.) "Civilisation is based on a simple calculation. Don't do anything really bad because the punishment will be terrible. Thing is, punishment doesn't seem so bad anymore and so the dynamic equilibrium shifts decisively in favour of viciously uncivilised behaviour."

Did I mention my dad used to be a professor of inorganic chemistry? He's the only person I know who can work 'dynamic equilibrium' into most conversations.

"Just getting the fear out of people's systems," I said. "Things will settle down. I mean right now we're living through the Phony Apocalypse because no one knows if we'll be wiped out within months or whether we can cling on for centuries."

I wasn't so sure when the news items moved from rioting, arson, and looting to the defence correspondent who was explaining the Chinese would probably invade Taiwan because they calculated the U.S. would not bother to intervene. For that matter, the Taiwanese wouldn't either. We talked death row nonsense until the Big Event came.

The Scottish clans lucky enough to be given the chance had already picked winners. Did I mention that? The aliens lumped the Scots with Pashtuns and Berbers, delegating the choice of colony seedlings to the clan leaders. At 9:30 we saw a little box at the bottom of the screen naming them. For England and Wales – National Lottery Special.

They'd set up a CGI version of the National Lottery balls. From a pool of swirling spheres, a red ball shot up through a tube, corkscrewing and bouncing around like an 80s platform game until finally coming to rest. The 'camera' zoomed in on the number... Actually an 'N'. Up close I could see the ball wasn't a uniformly red ping pong. I saw the shapes of continents under cloud cover and the terminator between night and day.

Thanks for reminding us what's at stake, guys.

The next ball escaped. Dark orange this one. An 'S'.

"I won't tell you it's going to be all right, son." Dad put his arm around me. Not a comfortable feeling but I appreciated the gesture all the same. "I'm proud of you," he said. "A father can't ask for more."

"We're not dead yet," I said.

An orange '4' then a dark yellow zero.

I swivelled round and stared at Dad for a while. The attention didn't bother him. "You know," I said. "I've just realised all this alien invasion crap is worse for you than for me."

He shook his head without conviction.

I pressed my point, a bit cruel in retrospect. "You've had your pass-on-to-future-generations meme buzzing for decades. I was never old enough. I'll lose my life but you feel the loss of your potential grandchildren don't you?"

Dad sniffed took a sip of Speyside and shrugged. "I've narrowed my aspirations as the years have passed. I'm proud of you. That has to be enough."

A sunny '2' ball dropped into the winners' enclosure.

Dad started saying something as if it were meaningful and I couldn't hide under the TV pictures because they paused the lottery for a ten minute advert break. At first I was angry with the BBC throwing us adverts but Dad made me laugh with the daftness of LV and Direct Line trying to sell us insurance in the middle of a programme that confirmed the end of the world.

The first ball after the ad break was...

Oh, bollocks. You already know I won.

When the balls finally dropped, they spelled out my National Insurance number. Meant nothing to me but then they posted my name and date of birth onto the screen and Dad and me were bouncing up and down for joy (after a scramble for a payslip to check my NI number).

That's enough of my dad, bless him. Move forward to 9:58 when the press got hold of me. Phone calls at first but that was easily solved by a little unplugging. Soon, though, they were knocking on the door and shouting my name from the street.

Dad and I turned up the telly to drown out the interruption. From up the road I heard angry shouting. I poked my head out my window, got a face full of camera flashes, and saw angry residents unable to get a precious parking space due to the journos' cars. Finding a parking space in our maze of streets has always been simple and no one was sure how seriously the authorities would apply the curfew penalties. Curfew was in two minutes.

I gave up and walked downstairs to meet the press.

The level of noise surprised me. Individual shouts, clicks, and scuffles blended into an aggressive hum of noise.

Residents seeped into the gaps between the fishbone parking bays, pointing and joking. The reporters formed a disorderly scrum around me on the pavement outside my house, each straining to lift his or her recording equipment higher than the others', shouting their questions louder.

"How're you going to choose your girls?"

"Is there any truth to the rumour you're gay?"

"Terry Dudley, *The Sun*. Let us help you pick your companions. We can team you up with the girls from Hollyoaks."

Call me shallow but I might take *The Sun* up on that, though not through Terry Dudley. At the time, I didn't feel like I was about to enjoy a personal FHM photoshoot with a bevy of TV babes. Oh no, I was far too busy being scared.

Sounds wimpy, I know, but this was a mob and its entire purpose was to get at me. Nothing could reason with the mob. No one person had control. The pack pushed at me. I retreated back to my doorway where Dad stood beside me.

I shouted at the mob to go away but I had no human channel through which I could reason with them.

A burly man in a tweed jacket and safety shoes had one foot on my doorstep. Perhaps that was the line they should not cross because I suddenly got this weird whiff of liquorice and the unnerving sense that the journalists were all looking over my shoulder. They were. An alien had appeared in my hallway.

The Engineer had an indefinite form rather like a snail, oozing the vaguely man-sized body to create the shape it wanted. The creature exuded limbs as it desired, bifurcating repeatedly and then reabsorbing the limbs or digits when no longer required. I found the most fascinating aspect of the Engineer was the blue paper overalls it wore. That's what the clothing looked like except whenever the limbs bifurcated; the clothing grew to accommodate the change of form. I was amazed.

"Hello," I said to the alien. Sorry, I know that sounds daft but just think about what you would do. Being polite felt a good start. I didn't know where to look. I think the dark patches on the tips of some limbs might have been eyes. I couldn't see a mouth or head.

Mobiles rang. Simultaneously. Everyone's except mine. I turned in time to see the press all sheepishly drawing out their phones.

"We need this male to use evolved selection criteria to form a colony team." I could hear the mouthless alien speak behind me and a tinny version from the mobiles pressed against the ears of the journos. "Your presence jeopardises his success. Withdraw and come no closer to this male than fifteen metres."

Some ran, many stepped back but were too intent on

recording the alien to comply with its request.

"Excuse me," said the alien. I think it meant the words for me. The base of the creature rippled and limbs shot out toward me like vine creepers in a cheap horror movie.

I got out the way and watched the beastie move through the door. The vines grew tiny limbs that scattered on my hall carpet, hauling the bulk of the body toward the threshold like fingers dragging the rest of a disembodied hand. Above its scurrying bottom layer, the Engineer glided over my doorstep and out onto the pavement. It almost tottered over the kerbstone but righted itself by thrusting a good portion of its base over onto the deeply cambered road surface. I hoped the alien was all right because a river of broken glass runs along that kerbside.

Most people were standing well away by this point. The alien exuded a metal device from its body and pointed this thing that looked like a ray gun at one of the journalists who remained too close. Everyone tensed in horror but nothing obvious happened. Then the alien waved his gun at the other journalists, including Terry with his offer of Hollyoaks girls. Terry laughed.

Then he vanished. Without a crack of thunder or swirly blue outline, the people the alien had pointed at vanished. A moment later, cameras and mobiles clattered to the tarmac or came to rest among the discarded clothes because wherever Terry and his friends had gone, their clothes and equipment had stayed behind.

I'm sure those people are dead. The way they died was so weird and bloodless that the horror and anger took a long time to visit me.

A couple of seconds after they died, I heard the sound of the TARDIS dematerialising – my ringtone. Someone had sent me a text. Hardly got my attention but then my friend, the Engineer, unmoved from its kerbside position, waved some of its eyestalk bits at me and oozed a new limb right at me. I did not move. Face it! I could hardly run from these guys. As it neared me, the limb divided and divided again before snaking a dozen narrow digits into the pocket of my jeans and drew out my mobile. The creature held my phone in front of my face. Except held is not the right word because it never quite touched my phone, its fingers never got closer than half a centimetre.

The text message was clear enough.

Expect a parcel from us tomorrow.
Open it.
Rgds,
Engineers x

April 17th. Press the button and run.

The morning after I won the Earth Evacuation Lottery, head still alcohol-blurred, I went to work.

Surprised? I've credit card bills, a mortgage and beer to pay for. The Engineers haven't mentioned a BACS transfer in their dealings with me. Basically, I'm broke.

As I walked from the half-empty car park, everyone stood and stared. Karen on reception said, "Congratulations." Don't think she meant it.

Got formal 'Good morning's from the fellow denizens of my pod of desks. Even this was chipped and nuanced.

Pascal was the first to be full-on about my new status. Ushered me to the office kitchen and gave me a long two-handed handshake while the coffee machine did its thing.

He said, "We were so excited for you when we heard."

"Thanks," I said, tentatively at first but then I decided Pascal's good wishes were genuine.

"How will you pick your women?"

I gave a Gallic shrug – sorry, in-joke. "Don't know mate," I said. "I didn't want to think of details. Just for one night, I've enjoyed the idea of taking my pick of hot babes without killing the fantasy with all the ugly practicalities and... context."

"What about girls from work?" Pascal shrugged. "We've spent enough pints talking through their merits."

"I can't do that!" I sounded all vehement. Didn't mean to.

The ensuing silence told me those figures dimly perceived at the periphery of the kitchen, pouring milk on their cornflakes or cleaning their mugs – they all listened intently.

We sat at one of the little round tables. "Why not?" asked Pascal and about this point he began to make sense.

My turn to shrug. "Dunno. Just doesn't sound right."

Pascal leant over the table and gave that look over the top of his glasses (except he hadn't got glasses) and squeezed my shoulders. I'd seen him do that before. This was French for 'Please pay attention.'

"My friend," he said. "Sooner or later you must leave the safe realm of fantasy and intersect your new obligation with the lives of real women."

Pascal's advice reverberated through my thoughts when, back at my desk, I tried to review the website mockup we were making for a new government initiative: Understand Your Benefit Entitlements.

I put on my big red cans that say 'don't disturb me' and made the mistake of starting up a playlist of Fado singers. Mariza and Christina Branco had such soulful and deeply sexy voices – didn't exactly help considering what was at the back of my mind.

I cycled through Miles Davis, Black Sabbath and a Grieg piano concerto but none of them could stop me thinking about choosing a team of women and the idea that some of the girls sitting in this room could be a part of that team.

Cans off for a pee. Everyone stared at me. Every step. When I got back I gave up any pretence of working and sat back listening to Jeff Wayne's *War of the Worlds*. Finally the music fitted my mood.

Just when the Martians gave their first "Ulla!" the MD tapped me in the shoulder, scaring the bejesus out of me.

"We wish you no ill will," she said. "But you are too disruptive. You have to go."

I guess that's what makes her a director: no messing – decision made, decision delivered. Me? I sort of grumbled incoherently.

"We will continue to pay you indefinitely," she said.

Sweet, I thought, though I kept my frown and said, "Can you give me ten minutes to clear my stuff?"

"Of course," said the MD. Off she trotted.

Pascal was right. Time to get real. I composed an email, setting the distribution to 'All at Northampton, Riverside' and 'All at Bedford', the head office where I used to work.

"Regarding the Engineers' offer," I typed. "If anyone would like to apply/audition for a place, please be at 125 Somerset Street, Northampton at 8pm on April 19th."

I deleted 'audition' because it sounded much too tacky. Without and the text sounded far too dry. I wasn't exactly sure what I was going to do at 8pm on the 19th but I didn't want anyone to come unprepared.

I thought back to Pascal's words and said to myself, *"There has to come a point where I accept one person over another because I find her more attractive."*

My mumbling got such a dirty look from Penny across the desk that I... Well, I got a little cross. Penny fawned over the male directors and hadn't time for someone as poor as me. "Oh, I could never be seen out with anyone who earned less than 70k," she once told me. I undeleted 'audition', hit the send button and waited until the message reported itself sent.

Then I bolted for the exit, pursued by a wave of pings as my email arrived at every workstation in the office. I kept looking forwards and didn't (quite) run, distracting myself with back-of-a-beer-mat calculations. The two offices had about 1,800 people. That's about 1,000 women, probably half of them under thirty. So, I mumbled to myself as people began shouting at me (mostly helpful advice from the younger men), let's say 97% of them would prefer to die within the time that remained to us rather than take a chance with me. Still leaves about 15 turning up.

That would be a good start.

April 18th. Sign here please.

The UPS delivery guy had no idea of the significance to the package he delivered to my door. 'Sign here' and 'Cheers, mate' and off he rushed, more bothered by the impatient car drivers he had blocked with his brown van than any threat from alien death rays.

Inside the cardboard box was a device looking suspiciously like an iPhone. An enclosed letter explained my task was to use this Dictaphone-cum-camcorder to record the events between the arrival of the Understudies of God and my departure to the colony planet. (Note to aliens: next time, don't translate your species name into something guaranteed to annoy the hell out of every religious group).

The letter was typed but – get this! – at the bottom was hand written:

> *Yours sincerely,*
> *The Engineers.*
> *P.S. Please activate your recorder by calling this number -*
> *69909 371 4885*

"Hello," said a female human voice when I called the number. "Congratulations on your new role. Do you have any questions?"

"How long do I have? I mean, when do we leave for the new planet?"

"Answering that would spark mass panic. Do you have any further questions?"

I got a few details cleared up then packaged them all together as a question with a binary answer. "If I do what you ask, you will transport me and fourteen women to another planet. We will emerge from deep sleep and will have sufficient equipment and shelter to make colonisation viable. Before we become terminally inbred, you will let us mingle with neighbouring communities. The planet's atmosphere will be breathable by humans, we will not be zapped by toxins or radiation, nor will we be killed off by the local equivalent of the

Solar Wind. Is that right?"

"Yes."

I couldn't think of anything else to ask and the voice took that as cessation.

"Good luck," it said, sounding like a particularly cheery careers officer. "We look forward to seeing you at embarkation."

April 19ᵗʰ. Deep breath. Here we go…

At 8pm last night, I began choosing my fellow colonists. 'Breeding Picks' – that's what the *Telegraph* calls them. My 'harem' says *The Sun*.

Picking who to sleep with from a room full of girls sounds as good as it gets, doesn't it? Well, last night wasn't so simple. Maybe I'm not as used to this as your everyday sultan. Next time I'll do better.

Anyway, last night at eight I peeped out the upstairs curtains and saw a small crowd of women dressed in their going-out finest. They milled in silence out on the pavement, trying to ignore the lads whistling at them from the other side of the street (but not daring to come closer). One of the girls spotted me and pointed. Half the girls started waving and calling my name. The other half shrugged into themselves as if a chill wind had just blown through Somerset Street.

Time to stop ignoring the doorbell, I decided. A couple of minutes later, eleven women squeezed into my lounge finding perches on sofa arms, crowding in front of the fireplace or flowing out into the dining room. Everyone fidgeted; no one spoke (I forgot to mention, I had asked them to be quiet before inviting them in). Mobiles were fiddled with, floors and ceiling stared at, and yet I could feel everyone's attention stuck as firmly on me as the journalists' had been.

While I steeled myself for what I must do next, I looked for familiar faces.

Tina and Laurel from Telesales were there. They did everything together. In fact, I had sometimes fantasised about having both of them... Sorry.

Oh, who am I kidding? I don't know who is listening to this. I might be discussing your mothers. I can't say everything so you'll have to use a little imagination. Let's just say that in the moment before I told myself I was a very bad person for even thinking of taking such liberties with Tina and Laurel, my stomach lurched when I realised anything, or at least many more things, had become possible.

"Record your experience with maximum fidelity. We will know if you do not." That's what the note from the Engineers had informed me. "You must tell us how you feel because we cannot record that any other way."

I don't want to disappear like Terry Dudley, so I'd better say something. I've always liked Tina. She has that slightly uncertain but genuine smile that gets me more than a mouthful of perfect white pegs. That time when I walked her home from Dave's leaving-do we had such a good chat that I felt sure we would have ended up together if I weren't going out with Sally. I don't know Laurel very well but she seems nice and she's certainly very pretty. Perhaps if they made the effort to come tonight, I might ask them back. Just the two of them. And me. No, not for three-in-a-bed but because just two of them would be easier to manage.

Sorry for the tangent. Big changes. Still figuring them out.

Back to my lounge. Most of the girls were from the Northampton office. A few came from Head Office in Bedford. Some had brought friends, and Amy McLachlan had brought her younger sister. No one looked comfortable.

Of the eleven, I could name about half of them and had spoken more than a few pleasantries only to Nadia, Tina and Snita.

When I saw Snita Karia step through my door I got a serious jolt down my spine and straight into... I became aroused. Snita is one of those girls that gets a lot of mentions in a lads' night at the pub. She possesses that captivating sensuality that stays clear of being aggressive, sluttish, or arrogant. Snita spins the illusion that she makes no effort at all to capture the heart of every man who meets her.

Now those kohl-enhanced eyes were in my lounge flashing their divinity. I mean, after they began to strip off, all the other girls looked so awkward, hands grown to the size of melons, feet velcroed to the floor and suddenly conscious of their facial expressions. Not Snita. Her movements were so fluid she didn't move so much as morph.

Oh, boy! Back up. Missed a bit out of my narrative, didn't I?

"Thank you for coming," I said to the gathering as soon as I'd got up my courage. "I have to pick fourteen fellow colonists. You've read the papers. Either we have no children or we have as many as possible to make the generation after us as viable as we can. Before we get to whether you can skin rabbits and tie knots, I need to know you are for having children. And that's going to be a lot more practical if I find you attractive. We'll face perils and disasters. We will catch diseases, get exhausted, and sometimes we will hate each other. Despite all that we will still need to reproduce."

"Does that justification mean you're going to shag us all?" shouted out Amy's sister. "If you can really do all eleven of us tonight then I'd do anything to be your sex bunny, sweetie."

That won a titter. Didn't do anything for my mood. I mean, I didn't choose for any of this to happen to me. The women quickly clammed up. I think they were too frightened to queer their pitch by saying the wrong thing.

"All eleven?" I replied to Amy's sister. "No. Only those of you who get through the first round."

I know. I know! That was mean. Truthfully I had no idea how I was going to work this. How would you have chosen your companions?

"Would you please...?" My courage failed me. Not for long, though, because I'd practised all afternoon. I ignored the knowing glances between the women and pressed ahead. "Would you kindly undress to your underwear. I know this is uncomfortable..." Too right it was. "Even so, I think we all know this needs to be part of the selection."

No words were spoken in reply and none were needed to express the mountains of resentment I saw behind their eyes. Only Snita had the grace to look quietly excited.

While I watched Snita, a tall girl, her hair a bouncy black bob streaked with blue (I vaguely recognised her from the Bedford office) grabbed her skirt from the floor where she'd just dropped it and raced for the dining room. Joanne from the Helpdesk followed.

I looked at the women and they looked at me. The crowd parted to let me peer through the doorway to the dining room where Joanne had her arms around the black-bobbed girl who was clutching her skirt to her chest.

That was hard. Something about a pretty girl in her undies, clearly distraught, pierced my resolve and left me feeling the most disgusting pig. I couldn't imagine anything worse at that moment.

I wanted to give the poor girl a cuddle but I didn't even know her name and I felt a bit responsible and the weight of the women watching what I would do... The weight crushed me.

So I offered to make some tea.

"Oi! Have you forgotten about us?" Amy's sister had popped her head round the door.

"No, of course not," I said.

"I heard what you said," said Amy, emerging from behind her sister. "You make the tea for crying-girl while we're getting all teed up ready for your porno epic."

Her sister gave Amy a sharp nudge with her elbow. "Shut up," she shouted in a whisper. "Don't piss him off."

"*I'll* make the bloody tea," said Joanne from somewhere behind me.

Now, I'm not as stupid as my prattling into this recorder makes me sound. Not quite. I know these girls weren't parading in their undies because I'd used an extra dose of Lynx in the shower that morning. Even so, I was hurt that Amy's sister was so frightened that she might annoy me. Upshot was, I finally took charge.

I shooed Amy and sister back into the lounge. This time the crowd did not entirely part. Tracy Stone pressed her breasts up against me in passing. An ambush, definitely not a liberty taken by me. When I turned to look at her, Tracy's hips were sort of tilted and her hands rested on them. Certainly her breasts in a lacy black thing were pointed deliberately at me. I think she meant the effect to be seductive but her face was too full of meaning. Her eyes (a tint of green, most captivating) did that emotional TV drama thing where her gaze wiggled from side to side as if my face was a metre wide and covered in writing.

I suffered another silent pause. Tracy's expression carried volumes of meaning. Unfortunately, I had not the foggiest idea what she was trying to tell me.

"Where do you want us to put our clothes?" rescued Snita.

"Err..." Like a plonker I surveyed my lounge as if I'd never seen the sodding place before. I waved at the dead space behind the flatscreen, and then dived for the cover of my sofa.

You know those hairs at the back of your neck that are supposed to prickle, tickle, stand up, or do some sort of dance when you get all pumped up. Well, they were doing all those things because, other than Snita, no one said a word. That freaked me out. I was sitting on my sofa before a crowd of (admittedly comely) zombies whose disconnected jaws and atrophied larynxes meant they could not manage more than a "hrrrrr." And they were too embarrassed to say even that.

"I know this isn't easy for you," I said in my best impression of someone in charge. "But we need to do this. Anyone joining me on the colony ship needs to do their part to make the next generation and what turns me on is a part of that. Awkwardness all round. We'd all better get used to the idea. If the prospect is unspeakably awful, you'd better join them in the dining room. If you're quick, they're just putting a brew on."

Everyone looked at everyone else, but no one else bailed.

213

"You can't get rid of us that easily," said Louisa Peretti. "What happens next?"

That little slither of control I'd just won – I almost lost it at that point. I'd never rated Louisa. At work, she's something to do with Events Management. Knew some of her mates but she never had the time of day for me. Kind of pretty but her face a little too bony and her nose a little too pokey and her attitude too superior. Now she was standing in front of me with her dark mane swirling down her delicate neck. Wearing just cream-and-chocolate silky things, Louisa was a revelation, not nearly as skinny as I'd thought, lots of smooth flesh, with a bit of give to it, and a certain poise to the way she stood and moved that few of the others possessed. Louisa Peretti was beautiful. I mentally updated her form card, and then couldn't help thinking about having just me and her in the room...

Shards of silence slashed at my fantasy, the pointy bits all aimed very much at me.

"Line up please," I said while grabbing for the remote to start some music playing. Swirly piano (Debussy or Satie, can't remember which) soothed away at my tension. And for the first time I stopped glancing out the corner of my eye and had a good look at the people in front of me and allowed myself to imagine what we should do next.

Oh, I'm so buggered! Now I know I've gone too far. I'd erase what I just said but I don't know how and I would be too scared if I did. If I'm your ancestor and I disappoint then I am truly sorry.

On the other hand, I should stop stressing about being a dirty perv because I mean it when I say I feel a duty to help prevent the extinction of my species. If you are a straight guy, would you do any better? You must have had private thoughts, imaginings about what you could do with a room full of girls eager to do whatever you want. No need to admit to me what you would do, I can't hear you, but you know I'm right. For me, the brick wall that kept these ideas conveniently private just got twatted with a fifteen pound sledgehammer.

I thought back to the aliens' letter telling me to record everything. They had finished cheerfully: "We will know if you leave anything out." Problem is, I've committed so much to resist these insane events threatening to overwhelm me that I've nothing left in reserve to film them as they unfold.

At this point in the proceedings, I *did* do some filming. Don't know what you get to see but I can replay the film by pressing on a red squiggle. See for yourself as each candidate in turn gave their name and telephone number. Hear me order decent people to turn around in ninety degree chunks like prisoners on parade. And yes, laugh as I swear under my breath when, with their backs to me, Louisa decides to strip naked. Then hear the catch in my voice when I ask the girls to turn again, the camera trained on Louisa.

So I am not going into any more details about what the girls looked like or their effect on me. Except to say that if you hearing this are blokes, then imagine yourself watching all this going on right in front of you because your imagination can do better than my words. Despite years of talking about girls with my mates, I haven't the vocabulary to describe this without sounding as cold as a medical text or as cheap as a porno novel (I know, I had a go earlier).

If you are imagining yourself behind my eyes, remember that I'd fancied some of these girls for ages. Then confuse the lust with the awkward truth that these women were only here because a lot of people, including many in this room, were going to die. Even the comfort that life could get better for future generations had been squashed.

Line up nicely. Wait your turn and be polite. We English are supposed to be good at countering the most terrible adversities through a mix of politeness and queuing and tea. Even if this were so, my attempts to civilise the moment snapped. A sort of sexual arms race escalated rapidly. More girls starting stripping further; others dropped out and put their clothes on. A girl I

215

didn't know called Lisa Kettle ran out of clothes to take off and started touching herself. Some of the girls were shouting at her, others at Louisa who shouted back. Plenty were shouting at me and many of them looked daggers at Snita who was keeping aloof from the scuffle (no idea why they had it in for Snita). All this while a tacit demilitarised zone still held between me on the sofa and the girls. We reached DefCon1 when Louisa penetrated the DMZ and grabbed me for a sloppy snog.

"That's enough," I shouted. I shoved Louisa back across the DMZ, which raised a brief bubble of dumbness around us. The French piano music made the moment surreal, and its pauses let us all hear the weeping coming from my dining room.

"Thank you for coming. Everyone go home now."

I would say I threw them out except that isn't entirely true. Egged on by her sister, Amy spent a good five minutes telling me exactly how little she thought of me and then ten minutes sobbing her apologies and making me promise that her 'being honest' hadn't blown her chances.

By that time I had a secret reserve of strength. In the general retreat I had whispered in Snita's ear that I wanted her to stay behind. All the while that Amy was laying into me, Snita was waiting for me upstairs.

I hope Snita hasn't gone to sleep, or shimmied down the drainpipe to escape, because it's over an hour since the girls left. I've recorded these notes so they're fresh. And I've reviewed the film I took because… Never mind that. It's been a long night and if Snita's still awake, it's not over yet.

April 19*th*. I thought it was all over.

We winners of the Evacuation Lottery have not exactly been popular with those who will be left behind. The Engineers made it very clear that they expected human governments to afford protection and assistance to us. Or else. Now we have a taste of *or else.*

Indonesia saw the first deaths. While I was interviewing girls in my lounge last night, my Indonesian counterparts were all lynched. A couple of the victims hadn't wasted time fannying around like I have and were surrounded by a harem of girls. The crowds strung them up too.

The Engineers weren't best pleased. Every senior member of the government disappeared. Like those journos in Somerset Street. Now, not everyone is too fond of politicians. So to make the point clear, the Engineers killed everyone in East Java. That's a province or state or something. Everyone inside the line on the map dropped dead. Anyone crossing that line since has died too. The Engineers released a new list of winners on Indonesian TV and told the populace to stop messing around. I pity these new winners.

So that was pretty scary. There's more, too. I left my last recording when I was about to pay Snita a visit. Well, yes, we had lots of sex and that went brilliantly and Snita had the grace not to leave me feeling guilty about why she was letting me do all this. I guess she's my first definite vacancy filled.

There was more to the story last night. Between the girls going home and me finishing my recording even more complication came my way. I had just sat down with a glass of Glenfarclas whisky to calm my nerves when I heard a rap on my front door. I turned up the music.

The rap turned to hollering through my letterbox, not from one of the girls but from my mate Pascal. Well he is a good pal so I couldn't ignore him. We had an awkward conversation on my doorstep.

"You're my friend," he said. "I don't expect that to mean you do whatever I ask, but I do expect you to listen carefully to what I say." I had a premonition that this wasn't the last time I'd hear a line like that.

He went all Gallic with an arms-outstretched shoulder-squeezing thing that probably works better on the Continent. "My wife and I have been trying for a child for three years. The fault is mine. Low sperm count."

"Look mate, I'm really sorry…" But Pascal wasn't done yet.

"Soon the world will end and this little tragedy of mine and Bernice's seems so small. But you, you could give Bernice what we've both desired."

"No. No. No!"

"My friend, I love my wife. If you could at least consider including her in your group, this would give me great comfort."

I remember shaking my head for ages before I could think of anything to say.

"Pascal. Mate. Bernice is your wife, for Christ's sake. She's a wonderful and beautiful woman but I can't. I just can't. It's not right."

I'd said the wrong thing because Continental shoulder squeeze was withdrawn and Pascal got heated. "I shall tell you what is *not right*. I have been next door at Freddie's all night. We've just seen a collection of women leave your house. They are not your friends. Bernice is your friend. I am your friend. Would you offer salvation to people who care nothing for you and condemn to death those who love you?"

No wonder we're supposed to hate the French. I couldn't argue with a word he said.

I must have mumbled 'okay' because the next thing I remember, Pascal had been replaced by Bernice and once more I was back in my lounge with an attractive woman. Except this time the woman in question was my friend's wife and I couldn't hide because there were just the two of us.

Actually, I could hide. Bernice read the situation perfectly and gave me just what I needed so she could make her pitch. It still doesn't feel right. I mean she's my friend's *wife*! But my head is already telling me that we are going to need some strong and sensitive people at the emotional core of our little group. I'm certainly not qualified to do that.

Here's what she did…

First she topped up my whisky. Then we chatted and laughed about things we'd done and people we knew. Finally, she slid her dress down and kicked off her shoes.

I backed away. "No, Bernice. I'm not comfortable with this."

Bernice fought back with a loving smile. She put her finger to my lips and moved in for a hug. I felt comfortable being held, even though Bernice wasn't wearing a stitch other than this sexy cream camisole thing.

"This is not comfortable for you. I understand that," she said. "However, I talked to the girls as they left. They wore very little and so it is only right that you permit me to present myself in a similar fashion."

She laid me down on the sofa. Keeping her back to me, off came the camisole. Then she reversed into me until she was sitting on my hips, at which point she took a couple of deep breaths and began to unzip my jeans. I knew I'd gone too far and tried to get Bernice to stop. She wouldn't. Not until I swore I would include her in the colony and no I didn't film any of this.

Bernice was in. I didn't like the idea but she would be good. The French buggers were right. If I had to pick companions, my friends should have first shot, however bastard awkward that made me squirm.

April 22nd. I can't take you all.

Listen to this phone call. I get this all day every day. Here goes…

"Sorry, I'm back. Tell me again what you want."

"Come on. I'm your cousin. We used to build sandcastles together every summer at Weston-Super-Mare."

"I know, Lucy. But I've met a lot of people in my life and I've not seen you since you emigrated to Oz."

"I'm family for Chrissakes. Your dad is my Uncle Larry."

"I'm so sorry. But, Lucy, you have to admit that splashing each other on the beach is hardly the same as making love on the sands of an alien planet."

"Making love? I'm not talking about me, you cretin. I want you to take Hermione."

"Oh."

"Yes, *oh*. Give my daughter a chance to have some kind of future. It's not much to ask of family."

"Isn't she a bit...? How old is Hermione?"

"Twelve."

"That's... young."

"No, that's perfect because if your little tribe starts having babies then that will mean a big age gap between you and your children that my Hermione can help fill. She's strong and intelligent."

"I suppose that makes sense."

"Damn right and I want your word you'll never touch my girl. No mucky stuff not now and not when she's older. You're going to have plenty of other girls you *can* touch. Save one space for your family."

"I hear you, Lucy... Let me get back to you. Bye for now."

You see my problem. There are so many people I have to leave behind that my capacity to feel guilt has burnt out. I've nothing against Hermione. I've never even seen the poor girl. I'm not certain who I will pick but I do know that if I leave Hermione to die on Earth then she will not be my responsibility.

April 23rd. Fishmarket, Roadmender, and Guildhall.

Can you hear this ruckus? I reckon there's over four hundred people here. Soon as I came through the main door the shouting and pointing started. Like being a rock star except I've all the attention but none of the adulation. Good job Bernice found me four security guards from God knows where to act as a protective cage.

We're in the Fishmarket, not far from the pub on Market Square where this all started for me. Used to come here for a quick coffee...

Oh, this is hopeless. I can barely hear myself speak. This place is chaos. Thank goodness, here comes Bernice.

"Get yourself into the office and wait there. I'll get the

crowd sorted out."

That was the lovely Bernice. She's a wonder. "Hey! Please stay back. Keep calm and wait your turn."

Me again.

Bernice is organising this interviewing event at the Fishmarket. 'The SEX-Factor' some wag in the local news called it and they aren't far wrong except I appreciate how much organisation must go into a real talent show. All I've got is Bernice on the inside and about a hundred grumpy policemen and women outside trying to keep me alive and preventing public disorder. They wouldn't stand a chance if not for the column of purring Warrior armoured cars waiting alongside in Silver Street, looking cosmopolitan in their rain-drenched desert camouflage.

I ought to explain a bit more 'cos you probably don't know what I'm talking about. The Fishmarket doesn't have buckets of ice and smelly haddock (it once did, and is smelly again today from the hundreds of warm bodies wet from the rain). Instead, a spacious L-shape of white walls and complicated black ceiling rigging houses funky gallery displays, arty shops, and the Nook Café. If Sally and I we were shopping on a Saturday, we'd have a quiet coffee in the Nook indulging in a little people-watching.

Today we have a lot of excitable and steaming people from whom I am bravely hiding in the office, sitting on a frayed chair at a desk where a keyboard is wedged amongst piles of paperwork, hammers, and bundles of cabling.

I'm supposed to do three of these gigs today. Snita and Louisa are over at the Roadmender, a nightclub and concert venue. Tina and Laurel are the Guildhall. Both places used to be five minutes' walk away. Today I think I'll have to travel through Northampton by Warrior.

I've already tried Snita's mobile but she wasn't answering. Let's try Tina at the Guildhall. Ah, good. Her phone's ringing.

"Tina, how's it going?"

"Madness."

"Same here. Look, this could go wrong very quickly. I want you to start picking candidates for me."

"Me? How? What am I looking for?"

"Pretty but not vain. Don't put too much value on survival skills. Sure we'll need them but they'll fill you full of lies and we don't know what we're facing anyway. Better to look for clever people who show a bit of gumption."

"Don't want much, do you?"

"And I want them to be team players. Got to fit with the rest of you girls."

"What, like Snita?"

"Excuse me?"

"Nothing. I'm beginning to see what being you must be like. Laurel and me can't just interview people. We'll get mobbed."

"I've thought of that. You've given out the cloakroom tickets to everyone?"

"Yes. And written their contact details on the stub."

"Excellent. Have a quiet chat with likely ones. And make a mark in the stub if you like them. If you get too frightened before I can get to you, just do a runner."

"Name please."

"Sarah Dinethorpe."

"This is like a camcorder the aliens gave me. Should help me keep track of everyone. Does it bother you?"

"A little."

"Me too. Now, Sarah, just to ensure no misunderstandings. If I include you in my team, part of the undertaking will involve having children."

"I get that. We will also need survival skills and a strong constitution. I'm a serious swimmer and, don't laugh, I was in the Girl Guides for years. But, yeah, you need to know I'm willing to have sex with you. Let me show you."

"Wooah! Stop that! Do your buttons back up. I'm not going to ask you to undress."

"Will it help my chances if I do?"

"No."

"Then what? Multiple choice exam?"

"We'll talk about what you could bring to the colony. But first, I need to know if there could be a spark between us. Just a kiss and a cuddle. Except my hands might —"

"Your hands will want to feel the goods. I get it. Here we go... There, that wasn't too bad. And now a... Kiss. Good so far?"

"Uhuhh. Very... good. Oh!"

"Mister, I never promised *my* hands wouldn't roam too. Looks like you've got your spark."

"True."

"So, am I in?"

"Sarah. You're the first person I've seen today. Look... I didn't mean. Hey! No need to trash the place."

"I'm sorry. I'm sorry. I'm sorry. I don't normally kick things. Please believe me."

"Hey, it's all right. Anyway, I'm the one who'll have to apologise to the Fishmarket people. Given the way your boot went through that speaker grill, they're going to be listening through headphones for a while."

"Being filmed doesn't help. Can you turn the recorder off please?"

"Sure. The bloody thing's creeping me out too. Now, tell me what you learned with the Girl Guides."

"Hi, I'm Laura Mendoza from the Fox show *Last Men*."

"Sorry, she barged in."

"Really not a problem, Bernice. *Last Men* is that cult SF show I keep telling... Pascal about. The best telly out of the US since *Buffy*."

"I know you like our show. I read your blog already. There's an entry that seems most apposite. The one where you describe me as the *hottest babe on the box*. Thanks so much for the

223

compliment. Would you like me to join your troop?"

"Well... Bernice...? Something wrong?"

"Can I have a quick word?"

"Sure."

"In *private*."

"This French lady. Is she in charge?"

"No. Well, yes. Of today's madhouse in the Fishmarket. Sorry, Laura, would you mind stepping outside please."

"Okay. You're the boss."

"Come and sit down, Bernice. I think I know what you're going to say. I still need to hear the words."

"Very well. I happen to think you are a good man. Strong, intelligent, and also warm. Laurel doesn't. She says you imagine our colony world will be the planet of the sex bunnies. Those girls outside that door – including your actress – do you think they will crawl at your feet, rubbing themselves against your leg and kissing every part of your body in gratitude for saving them?"

"I'm not that stupid, Bernice. You're not being fair."

"Fair? That's a luxury that ran out the moment the aliens arrived. Let me tell you of one *morceau* of unfairness you need to consider while your actress waits outside. All we women will resent you. Myself included. There is an angry cancer in my heart that will always hate you for taking me from Pascal. We will need to create a sense of community that can overcome this resentment. This Laura... She will never be a part of that community."

"I know. You're right of course. As always. But, hey, one of my greatest fantasies just walked through my door. Do you really blame me for being distracted, Bernice?"

"So long as you have now recovered your wits. No."

"Good. Your turn. You have a sister."

"Yes. I do. Nathalie lives near Amiens."

"Invite her. She can join our group."

"She will not want to."

"Why not? Have you asked her? Is she married?"

"My sister is rootless and uncommitted."

"Unreliable?"

"Not at all. More dismissive of easy choices. Nath still seeks for her life's challenges. Also, she is a lesbian."

"So?"

"Ahh… You shame me. I have told Nathalie nothing of you. Of us. For her to make love with you… this is a big ask and I am sure Nath would say no and still I have not spoken of the main problem. My sister has no interest in motherhood. Still, I should ask, not assume."

"Do ask. The Engineers must have factored redundancy into their plans. Nathalie might be more useful as a balance for our team. Perhaps some relief for that resentment. Oh, I didn't mean that in a sexual way… About time I took this seriously and looked for more than pretty girls. Bernice, why the tears?"

"Why not? A few more will make no difference. I am thinking of your cousin, Hermione. If Nath agrees, will you pick my sister over your cousin? Will you pick her over your sexy American starlet?"

"I resign myself to being hated. Yes, your sister over my cousin and starlet."

"Then, perhaps, I can dare to dream this might work."

Let's recap on a monster of a day. I'm back home. Snita's upstairs in tears thinking everyone hates her because she flunked and ran from the Roadmender leaving Louisa who soon ran too. I'm not sure I'd have done any better.

The army have put roadblocks either end of the street, which means I am a figure of hate for all my neighbours.

Glasgow is still ablaze with the rioting and over in the Caucasus everyone is playing shell-thy-neighbour. Amazingly no one was hurt badly in Northampton, but next time… Well, there won't be a next time.

Tina gave me the names of four women I've never met because I never got to the Guildhall. We picked Sarah and three more from the Fishmarket and abandoned the Roadmender crowd. I've slots for Snita, Louisa, Bernice and her sister, if she wants it. With Tina, Laurel that makes fourteen and I'm done. Northampton's grown too threatening. Time to go to ground.

May 12th. The North Londonshires

For the past three days, our tribe has been holed up at Rushden Hall in the northern wilds of Northamptonshire. I'd asked to take over Rushton Hall fifteen miles up the road toward Kettering (a much fancier pile) but I think the nice Captain Grady deliberately misheard me. I expect he was keen to install new residents here after they disbanded Rushden Town Council, which was based in the hall before martial law.

Not first choice, perhaps, but Rushden Hall is a lovely place. I'm lounging in the sun-drenched gardens after a group fitness session, far enough away from the main road to feel safe. The house behind me is a limestone architectural hodgepodge after centuries of tinkering. That suits our tribe's heterogeneity.

Talking of which, Bernice's sister, Nathalie, has flowered since arriving. She cracks jokes and behaves in an absurdly French fashion to amuse colonists and soldiers alike.

After those horrible days with the entire tribe stuffed into my house in Northampton, the extra space is giving us a chance to think and plan and... play. Snita and I have claimed a room for our own and made long use of the opportunity. She's still the only person in the group I've been intimate with, except that one time with Laurel who was desperately needy. So much so that I was far too worried about her to enjoy the experience.

Snita wasn't jealous, quite encouraging really. Still, creating the Planet of the Sex Bunnies has somehow wandered off the agenda for the moment.

Talking of agendas I've got us thinking about the practicalities of colony settlement. Tomorrow we'll meet in the most formal room of the hall – all fiddly 15th century wood panelling – for our first council meeting where we'll start to draw up plans for the colony. Tina came up with the name of our new tribe. The North Londonshires. Comes from a marketing name someone dreamt up for this part of Northamptonshire a while back. Guess the name will last longer than anyone thought.

We need to focus on what happens next because the Earth's doom advances. The footprints of the first induction rail are going down. They started in the depths of Russia and are advancing west like a Mongol horde, spreading mass panic before them. The footprints are 300 foot diameter circular holes that appear in the ground every half mile. The holes deepen until the magma starts welling up. The line spreads due west like a border being drawn on a treaty map with no deviation for mountains, lakes or cities. Kiev has evacuated. Even in the US, people are calculating where the line will fall and are packing their bags.

May 13th. North Londonshire Council – pass the conch shell

We are in the Panelled Room of Rushden Hall, Earth, for the first meeting of the North Londonshire Council. We've arranged a circle of fifteen chairs facing inward and I am placing this recorder in the centre before calling the meeting to order.

"Ahem. I declare the inaugural meeting of the North Londonshire Council open. First thing. We need a council leader. Any nominations?"

"I nominate Sarah Dinethorpe."

"Thanks, Bernice. That's most gratifying. Anyone second my nomination? Thank you, Louisa. Are there any other nominations?"

"I want –"

"Him. Yes, we thought you'd back your man, Snita. Anyone second Snita...? No. Too bad. Let's go through this properly. Who will vote for me? O-kay that's thirteen... fourteen votes. Everyone except Snita. That's very... accommodating of our man. As leader, I have one item of business this morning. I want to change the membership of our tribe."

"Hey! You can't do that. I picked you. Picked you all."

"Yes, and we've moved beyond that."

"But... The aliens —"

"Might zap us for being naughty. Yes, that is a risk, but we'll take it."

"I don't want you to."

"Noted."

"I won't let you."

"How exactly do you intend to stop us? Laurel, bring in our new member, please. Snita, I'm sorry. I get absolutely no pleasure from saying this, but you're staying behind. You never acted as a functioning part of this team and so now you're out."

"This is evil. I didn't ask to pick you all. That obligation was placed upon me and I did the best I could. Who would you replace Snita with? Your best mate? Your sister? I have family and friends I could have saved and did not. Instead... Sally?"

"Meet the final member of the tribe. I figured we need an expert on the North Londonshire man. So please welcome Sally Foster, his former girlfriend."

May 20th. Colony Ho!

To begin with, sitting outside the mint green enormity of the Cardington airship shed had something of a Scout camp feel after being cooped indoors for so long. Maybe the army uniforms made me think of Scouts, or perhaps sitting on the sandbags touched youthful memories of gathering upon straw bales in the open air.

Laurel pointed excitedly when we saw a heron fly overhead toward the lake at Priory Park, the bird's implausibly long legs rigid behind.

Even though we (mostly) think this is our embarkation point for a new world, the wait soured as it lengthened.

My fault. My weakness. Another colony group had arrived before us. Their bloke is called Damien. Comes from Cardiff, though I don't think my mate Geraint would describe Damien as properly Welsh. He comes across as sheepish but is basically okay. The women of both groups mingled briefly but quickly returned to the safety of our own groupings. No animosity but frankly I don't care how Damien found the experience. I wish him well but we want to get on the ship and away.

Then the idiot men arrived. God help the human race. A couple of guys from Scotland, one is called Danny, can't remember the other one, keep going on about founding New Scotland. The women of the Scottish groups got on as soon as they met, mostly ignoring us foreigners and definitely giving their men the cold shoulder. Last came Tristan from Macclesfield. God's gift to women wasted no time boasting of the number of pop and soap stars in his group, but I mellowed to him when we realised I used to drink in the same pub as him when I lived in Macc. Then he called me a twat for bothering to use this recorder. Says he never bothered. Right now he's talking with Danny and pointing at me. Laughing.

Finally, we have the spectators outside the wire fence. Some with crossed arms and scowls making no secret of what they think of us, and what they might do without the fence and the machine gun nests. Recently the press had downgraded us from undeserving lucky bastards into full-on alien collaborators.

Louisa is struggling to keep her fear under control. We're all being very protective after her parents' house was petrol-bombed. (They got out safely). I keep trying to cheer her up by reminding us we have only a few hours left on the Earth.

And I mean *hours*. We've been here two hours already. We've already turned a patch of grass into a toilet because we're far too scared to stray far from the soldiers.

Wait! Something's up. Soldiers are running from the side doors of the shed.

There! The sheds are made up of thousands of metal panels and they all just shimmied. The windows and vents rattled. That's Shed #1 that we sat outside. Shed #2 alongside is standing serenely ignorant of whatever transpired.

A grinding whirr of great engines has started up. Starship

engines? No, the door to Shed #1 is opening.

Did I mention the doors were big? I often used to see them from the Bedford Bypass when I was driving to the A1. I'm sure my brain can calculate the size of the sheds by comparing with the sprinkling of farm buildings and houses nearby. The cogs and gears inside my mind can work this out but then refuse to supply the answer because the sheds are just too big to be real. Now each 500 ton door (I Googled the stats when the Army told us they would escort us here), is edging sideways along the rail tracks at the front of the shed.

The doors have slowed to a halt, leaving a gap in the middle of about six feet. Squaddies are herding sheep, goats and a honking gaggle of geese through the gap. Makes me think of Noah's Ark except only a few animals are being fed to whatever is waiting inside. I suppose there must be more ships elsewhere taking on other beasts.

I can still hear the geese inside. More soldiers are wheeling in a large glass container filled with buzzing insects. The geese have suddenly been silenced. What does that mean? I look to my fellow colonists but no one has noticed. We've all turned inward now, each colony group ignoring the others and the crowd of civilians who wait at the perimeter fence, growing ever more numerous and uglier. Can you hear them?

Who do we hate? The alien lovers.
How do we want them? Dead!

Classy lyrics. I hope this really is departure time. If we have to go back to Rushden Hall, we're so buggered.

Me again. An hour since my last recording and a couple of soldiers are waving us through. Looks like we're to be the first group of human colonists to pass through into the shed.

Blimey! The place looks bigger on the inside. The spaceship is sitting dead centre, a little lost in the vastness of the shed. We're trooping towards it. No aliens in sight.

The building's interior is dark but the three rows of windows in the side of the shed throw bands of illumination onto the 150 foot high spaceship. Looks like an old bobby's helmet with windows where the police badge would be. Can't see landing struts – the ship is sitting directly on the painted concrete floor.

The outer skin of the ship consists of panels that are frayed and ill-fitting, mottled grey, green, and brown. I mean I don't know how spaceships work but I wouldn't buy a used car with panel work like this.

Getting closer now. I can see open circular hatches leaking diffuse light high overhead and a gentle hum. The colouration on the hull panels looks like mould. Perhaps that's –

Jesus! Is everyone all right? Are we all here?

Everything's okay. Just a few bruises and vertigo when we look down from the hatch. We were walking down there and then... suddenly we were up here.

"Why are you still talking into that thing?"

That's Sarah. "Because it might be an important record."

"Leave him alone."

That's Bernice. She's looked after me since they kicked out Snita.

We're sprawled in a circular tunnel. The walls are made from proper spaceship material – a smooth and luminescent – but plugging into the walls is a lattice dirty and sticky to the touch and sprouting a variety of plugged-in devices that might be lights, sensors, or disintegrator ray guns for all I know.

Freddie is a bit of a closet Gardener's World addict. If he were here, he'd be explaining this isn't lattice but trellis and think what he could do with laburnum.

The outer hatch is sliding shut. The interior doors are opening, are being opened, by an alien. Like the one in Somerset Street except this doesn't give any impression of having an up or down. Scores of fingers grab onto the lattice from every direction. One fatter limb extends towards us and transforms into a slug's idea of a human arm and hand which beckons us in with a finger. I get that whiff of liquorice again.

We humans look at each other and shrug. Sarah and Bernice exchange a few words but we're hardly going back now, so we follow the Engineer along the rattling lattice as it backs into a wider chamber, beckoning all the while.

Laurel's slipped. Sally's swaying and I'm feeling groggy.

They've gassed us!

I'm back in the empty shed. All alone except for the partially dissected corpses of the animals led into the ship and my head that's twenty-pints groggy. The ship has gone and something has changed about the shed itself. Same cavernous size. Same three bands of light but from cracked or missing windows. The sheets of metal on the wall are streaked with rust. I think they've transported me into the future. Maybe I'm here to witness the final days of the Earth.

You know, with this alien iPhone gadget I honestly thought I was leaving a message to my children. I can't believe I'm still talking into this thing.

Doing so gives you comfort.

What?

Repetition of familiar behaviour protects you from the stresses of reality.

I meant "what?" as in "you're a talking box". Hello?

Oh, I see. You ascribe sentience to this device. Not so. In addition to saving selected passages to local storage, this device has transmitted an unbroken record of your past few weeks. You are now experiencing the capability to receive transmissions.

But… You told me this sodding thing is only a recorder.

No, we only told you this sodding thing is a recorder. You should pay attention to word order.

Why? After all this, I expect to be transported to a colony planet. Not back in the shed, transported into my future.

Not accurate. We have translated you only fifty metres. Temporal leap is an illusion caused by interruption to consciousness.

My head's so fuzzy, it's playing tricks. Time travel, my stupid arse. This is Shed#2, isn't it?

A naked man has appeared. Hold on, that's Damien. Why am I naked? My balls hurt. Oh my God. They've cut open my... Sally's here!

I think she's all right, just unconscious. I'm worried about the livid wounds in her lower belly, though there's a tough transparent layer that I presume means a decent wound dressing. Sally popped out the air, naked, and flat on her back – six feet in the air. I ran to grab her before she split her head in the fall but she wafted down like an autumn leaf, followed by our thirteen other women.

Can you still hear me?

Yes. What's going on?

I am thanking you. Observing your life has been worthwhile. Good fortune to you.

Wait! You promised I would stand on the soil of another planet. You would take me to the colony planet. Me. My body. Personally. All of us.

Yes. We lied.

I'm alone again. The women, from all the groups, are still here but not awake. Nathalie and Bernice are showing some signs of waking. Tristan, Danny, and the other Scot have done a runner, making for Shortstown, keeping the sheds between them and the crowd. Damien is doing a recce of Shed#1.

I'm not leaving the girls. We've been through so much that we're a team now, even if everything that brought us together was false. Damien feels exactly the same way. Please don't judge us harshly. The women are here because they wanted to live. So did I. Would you have done differently?

Here comes Damien, racing through the side door. Shit! Two guys in England football shirts are... They've got him! Damien's down getting seven shades kicked out of him.

We're so buggered.

The Tower

Nigel Edwards

Right in the heart of a housing estate might not be where you'd expect to find an industrial needle standing over four hundred feet tall, but follow the lane known as The Approach to Tower Square in Northampton town and there it stands: the National Lift Tower. It'd had other 'official' names as well, but locals knew it well as the Cobbler's Needle, or the Northampton Lighthouse. Those were jokes, of course, particularly the latter; Northampton was pretty close to being as far away from coastal waters as you could get in mainland Britain.

Sol Keeble moved with the knot of people towards the entrance to the listed building – certified as being of natural architectural importance. The midwinter air was crisp enough to warrant rubbing his hands to keep the circulation flowing as he looked towards the summit. He recalled how his da' had once taken him to the top, many years ago, pointing out some of the sights that marked Northampton town: Victoria Park, St. Matthew's Church, St. Giles, All Saints, the Telephone Exchange, the Fire Station.

Built in the 1980's, with conifers round its base, the edifice had been a testing platform for elevators until market forces took the industry elsewhere in the late 1990's. The tower languished for a while as the trees disappeared and homes were built in the hope of a brighter tomorrow. Towards the end of that decade things began to look up as the building was preserved for the

235

nation and rejuvenated. The following twenty years saw visitor facilities built around the base and university student engineers reinventing the tower's original purpose, researching technology to improve lift performance and safety.

For a time the 'Lighthouse' was an attraction for visitors to the county town but eventually the view from the top ceased to entice, and the shrinkage of the university's research budget took the tower once more into disuse and disrepair – much like the homes that now surrounded it, Sol thought. Fifty years on and the district was run down and largely decrepit. Even the famous Saints rugby stadium had relocated away from Weedon Road. The site was now just wasteland where young kids came to explore and kick cans in the early evening, and older kids came even later so they could do the things they did beyond the view of a careless society.

The narrow arched doorway to the tower was kept barred and locked now, decorated with notices admonishing any who thought to enter without the necessary permissions. At least, usually it was locked; today, of course, the gate was wide open. The small crowd passed within, one by one.

The interior was a mess of dust, strewn papers, tin cans, bits of masonry and other items too unwholesome to mention. There was no light except that which followed them in.

"What a mess," a man standing close by muttered. Sol nodded.

"I came here near sixty years ago with my da'," Sol told him. "It were good then. Got to the top and saw the view. There were a lift but it weren't working day we went up. I 'ope we haven't got to do that climb again today. Legs aren't what they were! But it were great when we *did* get to the top. You could see everywhere. I remember that Saints were playing at home. All them burly lads looking no bigger than your thumbnail. Couldn't get to the *very* top, though. You weren't allowed to climb the final ladder. Not safe, y'see. Too much wind."

"My dad remembered this place being built," the stranger

replied. "In fact he worked in lifts. He used to fit out the interiors. Carpets, mirrors, that sort of thing. Not the one here, though."

"My da' were in shoes. Started with the Michel family 'till they were took over by United Leather. Stayed with them a good long while 'till he was laid off."

"Dad always wanted me to follow him in the trade and I did. I worked in the welding section putting the cages together. I remember the burns I got from the hot metal, and the cuts where I got caught on raw edges. Of course, that was during my apprenticeship. I got a lot better at it."

"I followed my 'da into the business, too. Set up our own shop, we did. Always found crafting with my hands to be mighty satisfying, and leather work were something I guess I had a particular knack for."

Sol looked around in the gloom.

"So where do we go now?" he asked.

From somewhere came the hum of a powerful winching engine. In the back end of the room a door, to that point unnoticed by any of them, slid open. Diffused light shone through.

"I suppose that's the lift that wasn't working when I came with my da'," Sol considered. "Guess it's fixed now."

Someone appeared at the edge of the lift door, a dark silhouette to the people staring.

"Hello there." The voice was rich and calm and carried with it a sense of wellbeing. "I'm Otis. If you'd all like to step this way we'll get started."

Sol looked at the man he'd been talking to.

"How about that?" he said. "Same name as this tower once had. Might as well go in. It's what we've come for. I'm Sol Keeble, by the way."

"James Walton," the man responded. "Most people call me Jamie."

"After you, Jamie."

Sol followed his new acquaintance through the door, the others close behind.

"That's it," Otis beamed. "Plenty of room inside." He had a white moustache that looked as though it would grin all by itself, even if Otis wasn't smiling.

There was a four-legged stool in a corner near the door. Otis sat himself down proprietarily.

"I'm your elevator operator," he said. "It's my job to see you folks get where you're going."

"How long will it take?" asked one of the two women in the group. "Only I've got to get back before school's out. My granddaughter's coming to visit and I want to make sure tea's ready for when she arrives."

"No need to worry about your granddaughter, Martha," Otis assured her. "She'll do just fine. Besides, the canteen here needs someone who knows how to make food that's good for the belly of a working man."

"How'd he know her name?" Sol whispered to Jamie, who shrugged.

"He probably knows all our names. He's probably got a list."

"Certainly I've got a list," Otis told him, picking up the quiet words. "I've been expecting you."

The wrinkles around Martha's eyes increased a little as she frowned.

"Feeding grown men's all very well, but there's the church to think about. I like to help out when I can but won't this new job's make it difficult?"

Otis shook his head.

"Martha Bradstreet," he said to everyone, "has devoted a great deal of her life to good works at All Saint's. Ah-ah, don't deny it, Martha. You've helped out in the Tony Ansell coffee shop for years, as well as taking in the occasional laundry for the choir. Do you want to tell them about the choirboys at the Christmas nativity? No? Then I will. The angelic faces of the children were looking to the heavens while singing a popular and

238

well loved carol. Only the words got kind of mixed up, didn't they Martha? I believe even the Bishop smiled when he heard: While Martha washed our socks by night..."

Otis gave a big grin while Martha brought up a hand to cover her own smile.

"Don't fret about the church, Martha. You'll have plenty of opportunity to help others. Okay folks," Otis said. "We'd better be on our way."

He reached up and pressed a button and the door slid shut. "Everyone just hold onto the grab rail until we get underway. This here box is older than I am, which is saying something. She judders a mite while the strain's being taken, but after that she's as smooth as can be."

Otis pressed the button again. The sound of the lifting gear increased a little. There was a jolt that lasted for just a moment before Sol felt the downward press of gravity as the lift began its ascent.

Jamie was puzzled. He was staring at the wall just above where Otis was sitting.

"There's only one button," he said at last.

"How many would you want?" Otis asked affably.

"You can't have a lift with just one button. How can you get it to stop at the right floor? How can you tell it to go down instead of up?"

Otis smiled. His moustache smiled even more.

"Only really need one button, Jamie. If you want to get out you press it and the elevator will stop. When you're ready to restart you press it again. If you're going up but need to go down you just press the button. It's really pretty simple."

"But... but that doesn't make any sense." He scanned the walls. "How can you tell what floor you're at? There's no counter. How d'you get the door to open and shut with just one button?"

"By pressing the button," Otis replied enigmatically.

"No. No, that can't be right. Lifts can't work like that. All my life I've been working with them, making them, fixing them;

and I've never seen a lift that you can work with only a single button."

Otis gave a gentle laugh.

"Don't worry about it. You'll soon be building them again, maybe ones that are just like this one. That's the job you've applied for, isn't it?"

"Building lifts?" It was Sol's turn to sound uncertain. "But I thought the job were in shoes…"

"Well of course it is," Otis reassured. "For you. There'd be no point putting you to work somewhere you wouldn't be happy, would there? No point in wasting all those skills you've built up over the years."

"Then… there's jobs for all of us, guaranteed? I mean, jobs that we're good at?"

Otis turned to the man who had just spoken. He was wearing the uniform of a security guard and stood straight-backed in spite of his evident age. In fact, Sol observed, every one of them had long since left their salad days behind.

"Sure there are, William. Got to patrol the premises, don't we? Keep things in order. It's what you're good at and that's why you've come, isn't it? To get back to work doing the things you love best. To be useful again. Appreciated. Not just being left to feel like discards from a stacked deck. That's what you're here for, right? Sure it is. Don't worry. It's all going to be fine.

"You know, William Howell here is an old soldier, a sergeant. Saw action in some pretty dangerous places and saved more than one life through his bravery. Yet when he retired he found his service discounted, almost ignored. Nobody seemed to care until he was taken on as a security guard by the council. It's sad to think so little is thought of men like William. But this corporation recognises the good that he's done. That's why you're wanted, William. That's why the job's there for you.

"And speaking of wanting, this is your floor. Just report to the desk at the end of the corridor. They'll take good care of you."

William nodded as the lift slowed to a halt.

"Very good, sir, and thank you."

"It's no more than you deserve. Look after yourself, now. I'm sure we'll meet up again when you're making your rounds."

The lift resumed its journey.

"So all of us have offers of work here?" Sol asked.

"Not just offers, my friend. Jobs."

"But," Sol worried, "we haven't even had the interviews yet."

"Of course you have," Otis soothed. "Don't you remember? And you did splendidly. That's why you got the invitations to start here today. You surely wouldn't have received those unless everything had gone well."

That must be so. How odd it had slipped his mind. True, he didn't actually recall the detail but he knew the meeting had taken place, and that he had been warmly congratulated afterwards. He was exactly the fellow they'd been looking for, someone with years of experience in the trade. A craftsman. The job would fit him like a glove – or perhaps boot. All he had to do was turn up on the day and begin work. And today was the day.

"You see?" Otis chuckled. "Nothing to worry about."

The pitch of the winch motor changed subtly as Otis stabbed at the button. The lift doors slid apart.

"Your floor, Martha."

"But… where do I go? What happens next?" That wasn't concern in her voice, more curiosity.

"Just follow the corridor, my dear, and go through the door at the end. It's all there waiting for you. I hear the kitchens have been modernised, right up-to-date, all shiny steel counters and ceramic floor tiles."

"More mess to have to keep clean, I suppose," Martha answered, though she didn't sound that upset.

"It's an important job, Martha. Besides, there's a couple of juniors to help you with the heavy stuff. They'll need training up, I expect, but you'll soon set them right."

"Oh, well. If there's assistants that'll makes things a lot easier. Right, I'd better get off then. Bye-bye, Otis."

"Bye, Martha."

"I still don't understand how the controls work," Jamie said after Martha had gone and the lift was under way once more.

"Neither do I," Otis replied warmly. "I've always been the guy who pushes the button. What goes on behind the panel with all those little wires and bits of solder is just a mystery to me. But I don't think it matters; I don't really *need* to know. If I did, it wouldn't make me any happier than I am right now, and when you get down to it being happy's the most important thing, right? And that's what I am."

A thought snuck up on Sol. Otis had a definite transatlantic accent.

"So," he said slowly, "how long have you been doing this job?"

Otis settled onto his stool.

"Just as long as you've been doing yours. For nearly always, I reckon. I started out in the back streets of downtown New York…"

"New York?" Sol asked. "You're a bit out of your neighbourhood aren't you? How did you end up in Northamptonshire?"

"The work's the thing. Corporation sees me right and one elevator's much like another so I go where the corporation needs me to be. I've got no complaints.

"As I was saying, I didn't have any parents of my own and I lived in the alleys and the dumpsters. Those were tough days back then. You took what you could find and were grateful when you didn't get caught. But I wanted more. I didn't want to turn out like some of the others in my neighbourhood. I got myself a job shining shoes for the rich folk that passed by. There was this one guy that was a regular. He was rich and white and dressed in the most expensive suits I ever did see. So one day he says to me, Otis, do you want to shine shoes forever? No sir, I told him.

242

Come with me, he said. He took me to this tall building in the heart of the city and he said Otis, this is my building. I own it. It has three elevators inside that ride shafts from the basement to the penthouse. Two of those elevators got operators already but the third is open for the right man. Do you think you could be him?

"Well, I looked him in the eye and said sure I was the right man, though needless to say I'd never even *seen* an elevator up close. He took me in and showed me a place I could stay, a small room in the basement. It wasn't much I guess but it was better than anything I could recall. What do I have to do to be an operator? I asked him and he asked me right back, can you read? Can you count? Or do you need some teaching? Sure I can read, I said. And I could, too. Not enough to read a whole book, maybe, but I had enough letters to read the headlines and numbers enough to reach a hundred if I had to. He introduced me to Willis, the senior lift operator. He'd come through life just like me and we hit it off fine. He gave me a cast-off uniform to wear, and taught me how to speak to the folk that rode my elevator. He taught me how to press all the buttons – and there was an awful lot of them! Buttons for opening the doors, going up, going down, floor numbers and flashing arrows to say which direction you were headed." Otis smiled in contented recollection.

"And that was me set up for life. I had a place to sleep and a job to do, and a wage to buy food and clothes and treats for myself now and then. I was never better than when those elevator doors hushed themselves open or closed and the important folk got in or out with their concerned looks and worried frowns. I reckon they all had so much they were forever scared they were going to lose it. But me, I just rode the shaft from sun up to sun down and knew I had the best of it."

He pressed the button again.

"And now here we are at your floor, Jamie. Just go down the corridor and find your dreams. They're waiting for you."

Jamie looked at Sol.

"What do you think?" he asked.

"It's what you're here for, Jamie." Sol extended his hand which the other man took hold of. "It's been nice meeting you. Hope to see you again."

"Yeah. Martha's canteen, maybe. See you."

The lift moved on.

Sol looked at the remaining passengers, a neatly dressed man with a walking stick, and a woman with blond hair and dark eyes.

"You're next, Phoebe," he heard Otis saying. "I hear the bar at this place is pretty classy. You're going to meet some real nice people, I reckon. Good tips too, I shouldn't wonder."

"Money's always useful," she answered., "just as long as the customers behave themselves. I've met some right ones in my time."

"You sure have, Phoebe. Didn't I read once you were involved with some crazy guy that pulled a knife on the landlord of the place you worked at?"

"What? That was *years* ago. Fancy you knowing about that."

"Sounds pretty scary to me," Sol volunteered.

"Well yes, afterwards, when I had time to think about it, it gave me a proper turn. But at the time it all seemed to happen so quickly. Anyway, the poor lad was just down on his luck and I'm sure he wouldn't have hurt anyone really."

"Even so," Otis said, "it was a mighty brave thing you did. Should have got a reward too, I reckon."

Phoebe shook her head.

"I only did what anyone would do. And the landlord saw me right with a bit extra in my wage packet for the rest of my time at Shipman's. But I'll tell you something," she added, conspiratorially, "I'd rather face that knife again than meet up with Harry Franklin's ghost. I've heard him often enough, an innkeeper that did for himself a long time ago, but I never did see him I'm glad to say! You gentlemen come and visit me behind the bar here and I'll tell you a story or two I've heard about old Harry!"

"You know, I reckon we might all just do that." Otis beamed. "Now don't you be late on your first day, Phoebe. Your new landlord's waiting."

The woman nodded, smiled and waved and was soon gone down her own corridor. Now there were just Sol, Otis, and the man with the stick. The latter looked a little uncomfortable.

"What's the matter, Tom?" Otis asked.

"I don't want to appear to be putting myself above the others," Tom answered, his voice describing a good school somewhere in his past, "but, well, I don't seem to fit in. I'm a manager. The others are, well, they have trades. They make things or protect things or care for others. I'm not like them. I just move paper around."

"And you don't think there's going to be paperwork here? There's a lot of people employed by this corporation, Tom. Someone has to manage them, make sure their leave applications are filled out correctly, check their records are properly filed, write out the reports for the directors. That's you, Tom. It'll be your job to organise things. It's what you do best."

Tom nodded but still looked uncertain.

"I suppose that's so, but..."

"But nothing, Tom. You're a good administrator – in fact you're *more* than a good administrator. We've done some checking up on you – don't be surprised at that; the corporation doesn't take on just *anybody*. We know all about your good works." He turned to Sol.

"Mr. Tilly here gave up a chunk of his own time to help out the local YMCA in their Outreach programme. It takes a big heart to do that, Tom. Mind you, you've got the heritage for it. Wasn't your ancestor the first appointed mayor of this town? Sure he was, one William Tilly, way, way back in the 13th century. He was a good man, Tom, and a great organiser. It's no surprise to me to find out you're his descendant."

Tom smiled modestly.

"Thank you for those words, Otis. They make me feel a lot

happier. Is this my floor?"

"You know it is, Tom. Bye now."

And at last there were just Otis and Sol.

"Just how big is the corporation, Otis?"

"As big as it needs to be, Sol. And it's a good employer. You won't find anyone working here that wants to leave. They're all happy, you see. Content."

"But what's its business? I've never worked with lifts and I'm definitely no administrator. I just know shoes."

"Which is why you're needed, Sol. Everyone needs shoes. From the directors down through Tom in his office, William patrolling the corridors, Martha in the canteen, Jamie fixing the elevators and Phoebe serving refreshments after the day's work is done, right down to me in my elevator. We all got to have shoes."

"My da' always used to say that. He'd say the world needed shoes. He'd say there weren't anyone that had to go anywhere that didn't have to have something on their feet." He sighed in easy reminisce. "We had our own shop. Said he'd always dreamt of having his own business so he invested his redundancy. St. Crispin's, he called it. For luck. It was something he could hand on to me, he said. A proper trade. He learned me the how of it, working the leather, cutting the templates, everything. We weren't just cobblers you see, we were proper cordwainers, took a pride in our work. I learned to make them all, you know: boots and shoes; sandals and clogs; lace-ups, pull-ups, brogues and hob-nails. Made them with my hands, the old way, like my da' taught. He didn't have any time for those machine-made things. They got no soul, he'd say. That was his joke. They got no sole."

"But *you've* got soul," Otis grinned. "It's in your eyes." He reached out to take one of Sol's hands. "And it shows in these. The creases. The calluses. There's honest toil, here."

"It were hard work, you're right. My da'd buy in only the best materials. Full-grain leather for the finest boots and dress shoes; good top-grain, properly sanded and finished for everyday wear; split leather for comfortable suede; and rawhide for the

246

laces. We had a shed out back where we'd finish off the raw stuff ourselves, get it to just the colour and texture wanted." He laughed, "The dyes never come off your fingers for as long as you're working at it! And the smell of the chemicals was no better once it got into your clothes.

"Of course, we couldn't compete against the big players in the industry, with their big budgets and advertising campaigns. But we had quality, and craftsmanship. You bought shoes from us and you knew they'd last you a lifetime." He sighed.

"Then when my da' passed away I kept the shop going and kept on making shoes. Even after he were gone I always felt that he were watching over me, nodding his approval while I worked at the last, or pattern-stitched the uppers and fixed them to their soles. I clicked and made, cut, closed and finished, with the smell of the leather, and the tallow and oil dubbin, and the dyes in my nostrils. I sometimes wished I could go on making shoes forever." He sighed again.

"But age catches up. My eyes don't see like they used to. And the arthritis in my hands makes it hard to hold a needle or a knife. I had to retire and leave the shop. I'd got no son of my own. Never got round to marrying, you see. I tried to find a buyer but nobody wanted to take it on. No one knows – or *wants* to know – how to make shoes anymore."

"But *you* do, Sol. And your skills are exactly what the corporation needs. There's suede shoes and soft leather boots to be made in all sorts of sizes. Black ones, brown ones, with laces and without."

"What about the materials? To create a quality shoe you got to have the best. My da' taught me that and he were right. And then there's the tools. I'll need hammers and awls, edge trimmers and glazing irons, not to mention a set of lasts for the feet I have to fit."

Otis smiled at him.

"I have no doubt that everything you need is provided, Sol. Why don't you go look for yourself? This is your stop."

For the final time the lift doors slid apart. Sol looked down a corridor that turned left a dozen metres on.

"I guess it is," he replied, stepping out. At the turn he looked back. "It could be," he said, "that I'm the only one left who knows how to make shoes."

"And that is why the corporation needs you," Otis answered with his joyful smile. "You'll find you're most welcome here. Your skills will not be wasted. Complete your journey, cordwainer. Make your shoes. Your last is waiting."

Sol looked at the lift operator.

"Are you happy here, Otis?"

Otis smiled.

"Never been happier, Sol. And you will be, too."

Sol raised his arm. It was a gesture, not just of friendship, but of kinship.

"I know it," he said before turning the corner. And he meant it, too.

About the Authors

Having done little in the first thirty years of his life he'd admit to in public, **Neil K Bond** decided to become a writer. Neil believes that a good story should be like a good chocolate: dark, easy to consume, and melting – relaxing you into its world but leaving you with a slightly bitter aftertaste.

Neil joined the Northampton Science Fiction Writers Group in 2003. He is extremely grateful to the group for helping him to develop his writing skills and giving him the opportunity to help organise the Newcon conventions. Neil lives in Northampton and, when he isn't writing short stories or radio plays, he enjoys socializing and debating. He can often be found around the stand-up comedy circuit performing under the name *Ewan* Ker*shaw*.

Nigel Edwards claims he was born far too many years ago. He currently lives in Milton Keynes, middle England, with his good lady wife. Every month he attends the Northampton SF Writers Group, where members tear each other's work to pieces (just kidding – there's a lot of writing experience in the group and everyone really is very, very constructive... honest). His ambition is to win the lottery and retire to the romantic coastline of Cornwall, there to remain until he becomes a part of the scenery in the fullness of time.

Nigel has a motorbike that's rusting nicely, and a car that serves as target practice for any passing birds. Sometimes he and his wife go for a cycle ride. Sort of. They pedal for about 200 yards then pause whilst pretending to adjust the chain or something. One day they hope to reach the end of the road.

In the fantasy world of the day Nigel works in IT, but in *real* life he's an undiscovered world-famous author, with several short stories plus a novel already written, and a children's book that's fast approaching completion.

Steve Longworth became a long term SF junkie in 1975 after reading a novel called *The Jonah Kit* by a certain Mr. Ian Watson. Thirty-odd years later, under Ian's expert tutelage and with the invaluable support and encouragement of the Northampton SF Writers Group, Steve had his first story published by *Nature* in their 'Futures' section, a feat repeated in April this year. Another of Steve's stories appeared in the NewCon Press anthology *Subterfuge*. He has also co-authored an international bestseller, but as this is a specialist medical textbook you are unlikely to have read it. He works as a full-time GP and part-time hospital specialist in Leicester, where for the last 25 years he has been battling the alien occult conspiracy that has been trying to re-organise the NHS to death.

Paul Melhuish is an occupational therapist. He is far too bored by his job to explain the exact details of what an occupational therapist does but he thinks it's something to do with old people. By night he writes short stories and novels. His hobbies include sitting on his arse, watching telly, and drinking beer. His first publishing success was a short story in the British Fantasy Society's *Dark Horizons* magazine about a farm that bred humans for meat. More recently a story of his featured in issue 13 of the magazine *Murky Depths*. This joyful piece was a satire on euthanasia entitled "Do Not Resuscitate".

He has been a member of the Northampton SF Writers Group since 2003 and they still let him turn up to monthly meetings. He has also written several novels, all unpublished, though he's working hard to change that.

Sarah Pinborough is the author of six published horror novels and her first thriller, *A Matter of Blood*, was released by Gollancz in March 2010. This is the first of The Dog-Faced Gods trilogy, now under option for television development. Her first YA novel, *The Double-Edged Sword*, was released under the name Sarah Silverwood from Gollancz in September 2010 and is the first of The Nowhere Chronicles. Her short stories have appeared in several anthologies including *Hellbound Hearts* (ed Paul Kane and Marie O'Regan), *Zombie Apocalypse* (ed. Stephen Jones) and *The Mammoth book of Best New Horror 2009* (ed. Stephen Jones).

Sarah was the 2009 winner of the British Fantasy Award for Best Short Story with "Do You See", from the NewCon Press anthology *Myth-Understandings*, and has three times been short-listed for Best Novel. She has also been short-listed for a World Fantasy Award. Her novella *The Language of Dying* (PS Publishing) was short-listed for the Shirley Jackson Award and is currently short-listed for a British Fantasy Award.

Donna Scott originally hails from the Black Country, but had only been living in Northampton for eight months when the town made her their first official Bard. Besides performing her poetry, she also writes short fiction and won a place at the inaugural MAC Short Cuts competition event, judged by novelist Helen Cross, in 2005. Since then, she has gone on to have work published in several magazines and anthologies including *Under the Rose* (Norilana Press), *The Bitten Word* (NewCon Press) and *Bloodlust-UK*. Donna is also a professional editor, which means she gets to read lots of brilliant SF, fantasy, horror and noir novels... and correct the spelling. Along with Jamie Spracklen, she produces the cultish magazine, *Visionary Tongue*, full of 'dark' fiction and poetry from up-and-coming writers. Into this *already very full biog*, she must also squeeze in that she is the administrator for the BSFA Awards *and* that she is a stand-up comedian, with the accolade of having reached the semi-finals of Jongleurs Comedy Callback in 2009, and having 'very nearly' made Sarah

251

Millican piss herself.

Susan Sinclair is an Essex girl living in Northamptonshire, with an imagination that reaches beyond that quiet shire. An SF fan since she was a kid, Susan loved Dr Who. They say your Doctor gives away your age, and her favourite has always been Patrick Troughton. A single mum, currently self-employed as a gardener for want of more concrete work in these tough times, she started writing in her youth and has completed several novels. There are a million excuses for why these have never been published, or even submitted anywhere, most of which boil down to a fear of rejection. Susan heard about the Northampton SF Writers Group in 2003 and knew it was exactly what she needed: honest, constructive criticism being as good as hair smoothing encouragement in her view.

With his wife, son, and extensive Lego constructs, **Tim Taylor** inhabits a house heavily promoted in the local non-human media as a home for disadvantaged spiders, while his garden is a hospice for terminally ill herbs.

Once, almost a decade ago, Tim won a CD in a BSFA short-fiction competition. Such early success threatened to overshadow his literary career but, fostered by the Northampton SF Writers Group, and a thing called 'OWWW', his writing is now invigorated.

He is currently writing a four novel fantasy allegory of the Great War's origins. This features sneaky technologies such as time travel, and he may have need of such devices to be finished in time for the centenary of 1914.

The story here was inspired by a (theoretical) interest in alternative reproductive strategies. The *Engineers* in this piece employ asexual reproduction complemented by genetic recombination through artificial means. They do not pay the cost of males. This theme was explored by the author in an earlier story, published on HardSF.net, called "Red Queen" (which you can still find if you Google hard enough).

Andy West has a passion for evolution and his stories tend to have an underpinning of evolutionary mechanisms, from the 'big engines of history' to the tricksy workings of individual memes. Andy's novella "Meme" was serialised across four issues of the webzine *Bewildering Stories* and also featured in the 'editor's choice' edition of April 07. His other published SF short stories include: "Impasse" in the anthology *Dislocations* (NewCon Press, August 07), "Rescue Stories" in a special edition of the BSFA magazine *Focus* (March 09), and "Empirical Purple", due soon in the *Matters Most Extraordinary* online anthology. Andy recently completed a techno-thriller novel, *The Waters of Destiny*, co-written with Ian Watson. Andy and Ian are actively seeking publication for this, as is Andy for his three novel SF series *The Clonir Flower*.

Mark West was born in Northamptonshire and now lives in Rothwell, with his wife Alison and son Matthew (who is five and directly inspired the tale in this book by saying "Dad, can you write a story about train chasing?"). Writing since the age of eight, he discovered the small press in 1999 and, since then, he's published almost 60 stories in various publications around the world.

His collection *Strange Tales* appeared from Rainfall Books in 2003 and was followed in 2005 by the novel *In the Rain with the Dead* from Pendragon Press. His novelette, "The Mill", was part of the critically acclaimed five author collection *We Fade to Grey* (2008) and Rainfall Books published his short novel, *Conjure* in 2009.

He is currently working on a novella and a zombie novel.

Mark can be contacted at www.markwest.org.uk

Ian Watson's most recent book, from NewCon Press, is the first appearance in English of his erotic SF satire *Orgasmachine* begun 40 years ago, almost published by Olympia Press till it collapsed, then almost published by Playboy Paperbacks until Playboy lost its casino licence in London; but a best-seller in Japanese.

No, it isn't: his most recent volume is *Space Marine* finally unbanned by its own publishers, Games Workshop's Black Library, for heresy and bum-branding, and now permitted to be ordered as print on demand from their website, although not to appear in shops.

Also recent from NewCon Press is *The Beloved of My Beloved*, transgressive tales written in collaboration with Italian surrealist Roberto Quaglia. "The Beloved Time of Their Lives" from this book won the BSFA Award for best short fiction, Easter 2010. Two other tales were reprinted in Mammoth books of *Best New Erotica*. Speaking of which, along with Ian Whates, Ian recently edited *The Mammoth Book of Alternate Histories*.

Ian also wrote the Screen Story for Steven Spielberg's *A.I. Artificial Intelligence*, based on almost a year's work eyeball to eyeball with Stanley Kubrick. He has written much SF, fantasy, horror, and poetry over the years, and is translated into quite a few languages, including Latvian, Hebrew, and Catalan. He has lived in a little village in South Northants for rather a long time and presided over the Northampton SF Writers Group since its beginning in the early Naughties.

Ian Whates represented his school at football, squash, table tennis, and Eton fives, whilst swimming saw him perform for both school *and* the county of Hertfordshire! Such athletic feats are now ancient history. These days he exercises only his mind and his imagination (and, occasionally, a cocker spaniel called Honey).

Ian is the author of some 40-odd published short stories, two of which have been shortlisted for BSFA Awards and many of the best of which are gathered in the collection *The Gift of Joy* (2009). He is responsible for two ongoing novel series: a space opera, which began with *The Noise Within* (Solaris, May 2010), and an urban fantasy with steampunk and SF overtones, which started with *City of Dreams and Nightmare* (Angry Robot, March 2010). The second volume of each is due early in 2011.

In 2004, determined to resurrect a nascent writing career abandoned some sixteen years previously, Ian joined the Northampton SF Writers Group, and immediately became embroiled in helping to organise a convention, Newcon 3. This led to his founding independent publisher NewCon Press without even realising he was doing so. Stories, covers and anthologies produced by the Press have won a number of awards and accolades and, in 2010, NewCon Press itself won the prestigious 'Best Publisher' Award from the European Science Fiction Association. The rest, as they say, is history.